12-93

| DATE DUE | | |
|---|---|---|
| MAY 0 2 1994 | | |
| SEP 2 2 2009 | | |
| DISCARDED BY | | |
| URBANA FREE LIBRARY | | |
| | | |
| | | |
| | | |
| | | |

# MISUNDERSTANDINGS

Novels by the same Author

The Foreign Husband
Sachiko's Wedding

# CLIVE COLLINS
# MISUNDERSTANDINGS

## Short Stories

Marion Boyars
London · New York

First published in Great Britain and in the United States in
1993 by Marion Boyars Publishers.

24 Lacy Road, London SW15 1NL
237 East 39th Street, New York, NY 10016

British Library Cataloguing in Publication Data
Collins, Clive
 Misunderstandings
 I. Title
 823.914 [FS]

Library of Congress Cataloging in Publication Data
Collins, Clive, 1948–
 Misunderstandings : short stories / by Clive Collins.
 I. Title.
 PR6053.042486M57      1993
 823'.914--dc20                          92–42604

ISBN 0–7145–2968–0 Hardcover

Typeset in 11/13pt Baskerville and Optima by Ann Buchan
(Typesetters), Shepperton
Printed and bound in Great Britain by
Biddles Ltd

# CONTENTS

# Acknowledgement

The author wishes to thank Faber & Faber, London,
and Vintage Books, Random House, New York, for permission
to use three lines from Wallace Stevens' poem 'The Snow Man'
from *Collected Poems* in the story 'The Snowman'.

This book is dedicated to William Gater, who,
over the past ten years, has entertained me
with wonderful meals, terrible advice and
some of the best stories I have ever heard.

*Hunting* was written for Walter Allen,
whose memories of teaching in the United States
during the 1950s gave me the idea
from which the story eventually grew.

*A Floating World* was written for
my friend Mitsuru Kamachi, who was blown down an English
hillside by a freak gust of wind and broke her shoulder,
was subsequently bitten by a cat in Paris,
choked on a fish-bone in Venice . . .
and on each occasion lived to tell the tale.

# THE SNOWMAN

The canyon must have been closed with the first snows, which came early this year. I thought about Spalding all alone up there, and I worried; although I knew he would despise me for doing so. He understood about the snow and the isolation. They told him the place got closed off every winter when I went with him to look things over. It was why he bought it. It was what he wanted. He wanted that loneliness; he wanted that isolation. As we drove back down into the valley after he had closed the deal, I remember I asked him if he really understood what Jack Nathan had said to him about how, if a big snow caught him when he was in the cabin, there was no way out; he would pretty much be alone for the whole of the winter. He said he did. I told him I would not want that kind of aloneness: the weeks of snow, the wind, and being in a place where a man, Jack Nathan's father, had died just the winter before. He asked me if I thought the old man's ghost might come back to haunt him and when I said, well, maybe that *was* just what I thought, he laughed. He told me not to worry, that he planned on taking his own particular ghost along with him when he moved into the cabin. I knew he was talking about Irene.

He'd gotten this idea into his head about Colorado, and so we went up there together one week in July. We looked at a couple of houses in the Springs, and then at some more over in Aspen, but they were not what he wanted. What he wanted was a place where he could be alone, he said. Now I understand that what he wanted was a place where he could die. Somebody suggested we might drive over to Alamosa. The realtors there would know of cabins in the Sangre de Cristo and the San Juan mountains. Spalding liked the idea. We got seats on a flight out of Aspen and arranged the hire of a 4 × 4.

Alamosa is the kind of town where the stores sell tee-shirts with 'Where the hell is Alamosa' screen-printed on the chest. There's a Mexican restaurant that closes around eight o'clock in the evening and a pub called the Purple Pig that doesn't, where most of the drinkers look underage. The Adams State College has its campus there; there's a triplex cinema and a summer drive-in. Pitch in a K-mart, a rod and gun store, and a couple of other businesses and that is Alamosa. Its single claim to any sort of fame is that a local character calling himself Alamosa Bill one time rode down into New Mexico looking for Billy the Kid. He did not ride back. The only people that remember Bill are in Alamosa, and there are not many of them. But Spalding found what he went to look for. He found his place to die.

The realtor showed us a couple of other things before he took us up to the Nathan spread. I doubt he used words like 'spread' ordinarily, but he had us two city people and wanted to act authentically, I guess. It did not really deserve the appellation. Jack Nathan called it a cabin, but that was not exactly accurate either. What it was was a decent-sized house, put together out of timber and adobe, with two or three outbuildings and a corral. It was all at the bottom end of a small canyon, with a stream running through, a stand of trees and then the canyon walls, not steep the way I thought they would be when I heard the word 'canyon' the first time, but sloping up towards the mountains. They were steep enough, though, steep enough.

Jack Nathan's father had built the place back in the

Fifties. He worked in the dry goods business then, but eventually became manager of the K-mart. He would take the family up to the cabin for weekends in the spring and summer. Then, after he retired, he and Mrs Nathan would go up there for most of July and August. It got too much in the end and the place was put on the market. It was at a time when a lot of Texans were starting to come into that part of Colorado, buying up anything with a roof on it, and the Nathan place seemed likely not to be on offer very long, but then old Mr Nathan was up in the house and died there, of a heart attack or stroke, I don't remember exactly which, and it seemed no one wanted it any more.

Looking at what Spalding paid for the place from a certain point of view, you could say he got a bargain. It needed a lot of fixing, of course, and Jack Nathan was particular to ask Spalding if he was used to working with his hands. He said he was. Nathan didn't know it then, he didn't know it until after the newspapers got the story, but he was talking to a man many people in the art world considered one of the coming sculptors of this half of the century, somebody who would rank one day right along with Giacommetti and Moore, with Calder and Smith and Caro. Alan Spalding was used to working with his hands.

He came to me in 1970. He was a kid, just out of school, just out of England. He was in New York on his way to work as an assistant with Peter Labin — he had a scholarship of some kind — but his tutor in England, a woman whose work I had handled for a number of years, had given him an introduction to me. He called from his hotel, about an hour after he got there.

I wondered why he had been sent to me. I was more or less retired by then, already an old man, and as my people left me I did not look to take anyone else on. Still, I said I would see him and he spent two hours or so with me, showing me slides of the work he had done as a student, drawings, talking about himself. He was twenty-two years old.

When he left I had agreed to act for him, and I wondered why. There was no contract, of course. I have never tied people to me with contracts, no matter who they were, just my word that I would represent him, and his word that he would pay me my commission. I remember after he had gone, sitting back in my chair and thinking, I am too old for this and that kid is too young.

I was not even so very impressed with his work. The slides showed me why he was going out to be with Labin. I was already too old, too New York old, for all that California light and space bull, especially coming from some English kid whose skin said he had never seen light or space. But there was something. In the drawings there was something. A lot of his drawing was representational: figures, the same figure, a black girl, always the same black girl. I asked about her. He said she was his friend, not his girlfriend, his friend. I asked him where she was now and he said she was in England, waiting for him. He wouldn't see her again for a year. I said a year must look like an awfully long time when it was only just beginning and he said yes, yes, it did, it looked like an awfully long time for both of them.

I thought, when I was on my own in the office, that I probably would not see the boy again. I was wrong. A month later he was back. He had decided to go home, go back to England. He told me his girl, the girl in the drawings, was more important than the scholarship. I remember I asked him if she was more important than his work, than his career. He looked at me very directly, not hard, not like a tough guy in the movies, just a completely direct look, an honest look, and he said, 'She is my work.' I wished him luck, and this time I knew I would not see him again because he had just taken what I thought to be a very stupid decision. I was wrong for the second time.

He wrote to me from England. Long letters, long, long letters, not always making sense, but bouncing ideas around, trying to find which way he should go. He had a day-time job

in an architect's office in London, and with the money he
was making he had got an apartment and a studio. He
worked, he did his real work, at night and on the weekend.
His girl, Irene, was with him. He said the month in
California had been the best thing that could have happened
to him because it had shown him how wrong the road he had
followed was. He was looking in another direction, he said.
He said he thought he knew what he had to do, and he
thought it could be very good.

I had to be in London myself later in the year, winding up
some things there. Spalding called me at my hotel. He had
some work for me to see. I went over to his studio, it was in
Hammersmith. There were a lot of drawings, and one piece
of sculpture in the making. It was the girl. He had been
looking at a lot of figurative work, the Italians Marini and
Greco, Manzu, and Butler, Meadows, Chadwick, and back
beyond them to people as diverse as Gill and Brancusi, and
out of all that he had found something of his own to say in
the most difficult of arenas. I took him and his girl out to
dinner a couple of days later and told him that if the piece
was as good when he was finished with it as it looked like it
could be now, then I could sell it for him. I gave him $1200
as a personal advance.

I sold that piece to the Japanese. I had intended to from
the moment I saw it, unfinished, in the studio. I knew it
would be difficult in England, and impossible here, but the
Japanese were just beginning to enter the market, not as
private collectors, that came later, but the municipal author-
ities had started to build and wanted pieces that looked like
most people think sculpture should look like for their town
squares and public offices. I remember my first visit to
Tokyo, and the amount of absolute junk standing around by
fountains and in the public parks both sickened and
intrigued me. But I sold Spalding's piece to a public gallery.
It was followed by a lot more.

It was always Irene. She was at the dead centre of his

talent. It worried me, I have to say that it worried me. I thought he would burn out, or go stale and begin to repeat himself, or else the market would get tired. But none of that happened. Each piece seemed to show a new part of him, a new side to her. He had a reputation in Tokyo before he had one in London or New York, but then he had a reputation in London and New York. He used to spend part of the year with me then. I say he: I mean they. He and Irene were always together. If she left him for anything, any reason, he would worry; more than that, he would get scared, like a kid in a department store in those few seconds when he begins to think he may have lost his mommy.

We used to go to the house in Maine then. He liked the sea. My daughter would be there with her kids at weekends and it was wonderful for me because I felt that Spalding and the girl were her brother and sister, and there I was with all my children and my grandchildren together under the roof of my house. And on those days it did not seem to matter any more that I was an old man because I had my children and my grandchildren under the roof of my house, and in that I had completeness. They were the good times.

I had a question I always used to ask him then, 'Why don't you marry that girl?' It was always an honest question even though, with time and repetition it came to sound like, it came to seem like, the punchline to a very bad joke. He would laugh, and if Irene was there she would laugh, and my daughter would raise her eyes to heaven and we would all laugh. But it was an honest question, and I felt, even then, that he never gave me the honest answer it deserved; the honest answer he would have given me when he was still a kid with no name and no money. I asked Irene about it once, when we were alone together. She said that she did not want marriage with him if he did not want marriage with her. She did not want him to feel that he was trapped by her, tied to her, and she did not want to marry unless it was going to be a marriage until death broke the bond. She said that she knew she could deal with it if he told her now, or tomorrow, or the day after, that he did not love her, that he wanted her to go. She said she would go. But if he married her and then said she must go, she thought it might kill her.

Fame accrued, but it was of a very glittery sort. In the public mind he was a celebrity before he was an artist. When he went to Tokyo for his first retrospective he was mobbed; it was like The Beatles. Well, maybe not quite like The Beatles but it had all the trappings of the rock circus. I told him I was too old for all of that, and he turned to me and said, 'No. I'm too old.' He frightened me. It came out like a joke, but it frightened me because I could hear that there was bitterness in what he said.

1983 was a very big year for him. There was a camera team from the British Broadcasting Corporation with us in Japan; they were compiling material for a television special to coincide with the opening of the retrospective in London in 1984. They were with him, on and off, for three or four months. I did not like the presence of the cameras, and I know that Irene found it a strain as well. They came into the studio to film Spalding at work; and, of course, Irene was there, and a lot of the time she was naked. She didn't want them showing her like that on television. It was a difficulty between them. I know because she talked to me about it. I think they even quarrelled. The television people were very keen to use the footage of her. Of course they were, she was a beautiful woman and she was naked. The television people were thinking of all the men who would watch their pro-gramme, who could watch this beautiful woman naked and justify what they were doing by the fact that it was art. It was the best kind of cake: the kind you can have and eat at the same time. In the end Spalding got her to agree that the studio shots could be used, but she was unhappy and I felt something had gone from what was between them.

I think what hurt Irene was that the studio scenes were a load of baloney, a set-up, because Spalding was not working that year. He had come to the end of a series of six pieces, a three-year project. A Japanese distilling company had bought all six, the only offer we received which met his stipulation that the pieces be kept together. They had been taken to Japan and immediately loaned to the National Museum of Contemporary Art for the retrospective. After that they were going to the company's own art museum, as a curious little afterthought to what was becoming the best collection of Post-Impressionism anywhere. They were not to be in London for the Tate show.

Part of the deal was that Spalding and Irene make a series of commercials for the company's premium brand of whisky. Spalding replaced Paul Newman. The commercials showed only in Japan, but I was given a cassette of the series when I signed the final agreement. It was for Spalding, but he didn't want it. He looked at the contract and said that he felt he had finally arrived. When I asked him why he should say that, he told me it was because he had just been paid more for an hour of his time pretending to drink this piss-awful Japanese scotch than for anything else he had ever done.

They went to Africa at the end of the year. Irene's mother was Scottish, but her father was African, from Sierra Leone. He was a rich man, a trader. At the house he still kept in London was a fine collection of artefacts: soapstone carvings of hunched little figures, like homunculi, and masks of the secret societies, the Bundu and the Poro. Spalding had an idea in his head for a series of pieces, busts of Irene, but stylized, like the masks of the women's society, the Bundu. He wanted to see the carvers at work. He said he wanted to see them cut the wood, shape the figure that they saw inside of it for, unlike him, these men did not work from a model, they looked and looked into the wood until they saw the face inside and it called them to release it from the tree. Only that way could the mask have a spirit. Only that way could the spirit be freed to inhabit the body of the dancer who, one day, would wear the mask.

So they went to Africa and it all fell apart. I don't know precisely what happened. I heard a little of it from Irene when she called me, that last desperate message on my answering machine. I was away, you see, and when I got back to New York she was already dead. She said she had been trying to get me at all of my numbers. She said she really needed me because Spalding was gone and she didn't know what she was going to do. She asked me to come to her, 'Please, please come', and then she put the telephone down. It took me three days to get a visa from the embassy in Washington and have all the shots; then I had to fly this assed-backwards route to Freetown and she was dead. She must have left the telephone office and, there and then, driven out to one of the beaches along the peninsula and parked her car under a tree in the village. When the sun turned the sky and the land the same glowing shade of pink, and the first stars claimed the sky as their own, she walked out into the sea and let it take her. Fishermen found her body a little way down the coast.

I saw where she went into the water. Her father took me there. It was sunset. I looked around me at the sky and the sand and the water, the smoke rising through the trees from the fires in the village as the women started to make the food for the evening. I knew I was seeing what she had seen and I thought it was the most beautiful place in the world; and I knew that is what she would have thought as well for she was a beautiful woman who saw and loved the beauty around her of which she was a part. And I knew then how deep and how terrible was the wound Spalding had given her, because she was so beautiful, and this place was so beautiful, yet still she had chosen to die.

No one knew where Spalding was. They knew only that he had gone, and that he had gone with another woman, a French woman. He had met her at the boat club where Irene's father kept the motor cruiser he was letting Spalding use when he and Irene were in Freetown between their trips into the interior. The woman was a yacht-bum, crewing her way out from Europe, down the West African coast and then across the Atlantic to Brazil. Spalding had spent time with this woman at the club. He had been out to the boat she was on, and he had taken her with him on a couple of fishing trips. He was on his own a lot of the time when he was in Freetown because Irene wanted to be with her folks. One time he just didn't come back to the house and when Irene went out to the club to look for him, she found that the big yacht that had been there all the time since they had arrived was gone. Spalding had been seen on it as it left the lagoon on the evening tide. I remember Irene's father saying it was as if the sea had swallowed both of them. I spent a lot of time wishing that it had, and that it had treated him the way it had treated her, spat up on a beach with weed in her mouth and pieces of that beautiful face taken by the sharks.

I found him, not in South America, but a little way down the coast in Abidjan. I went down there and I faced him and I told him what she had done to herself because of what he had done to her. He did not once look at me all the time I was with him and all he would say was, 'I thought she was stronger than that.' He was like my own kid to me but when he would not look into my face and when he said that about her I hated him. I cursed him. I called his mother a bitch-whore because she had given him birth, and when he was gone I wept. I wept for that girl and her beauty, and I wept for him, I wept for him because he had robbed himself and he did not even know it, the poor, dumb bastard.

I saw nothing of him again. I heard nothing for almost a year, and then I got a card from St John's where, at last, he had fetched up. The French woman was gone. Seems she had left him in Bahia for another man; another boat. I felt that I should have hated her as much as I had hated him, but I did not. I had burned all that bitterness through the seasons that had gone since Irene's passing. It had left me, like a fever, and like a fever, it had left me weak, an old man too tired even to tear up his postcard.

I wrote him back, and I arranged the transfer of money that he asked me to arrange, and about a month afterwards he came to see me at the house in Maine. I had closed up my office in New York. I had retired. When he asked me why I told him it was because I was too damn old and too damn tired for the business anymore, which was true and was not true. I had quit because I was sick to my heart for the death of that girl, and I had quit because my doctors told me I should quit, unless I wanted my time to be even shorter than they told me it already was. They had found the cancers in me then, you see, eating their way out from the dark places of my lungs and stomach. I had lost Irene. I figured I owed it to my other daughter, my blood's daughter, to stay that little while longer with her before my blood betrayed me.

Spalding came to see me and he stayed, but he did not rest, and I knew he would not stay long. He was too close to the sea. I told him of how they had cremated Irene, and of how her mother and her father had taken her ashes out in their boat and given their daughter back to the ocean to which she had given herself. Spalding would not stay because he was too close to the sea. It was like he was sleeping beside her tomb.

Of course, he did not work, and he had not worked, not even lifting a pencil to draw a line upon a piece of paper, in all the time he had been away. And I knew he would not work, probably he would not work for the rest of the time he had. I knew that, even though I did not know how little time that would be.

He stayed a week, two weeks. I don't know, maybe it was two weeks, and then he said he would go. I asked him where and he said he did not know, but he would call when he got to wherever it was. Wherever it was was New York. He called from his apartment there. He said he wanted a place where he could be alone, and I told him New York was probably as good a place as any for that, but he had got hold

of this idea about the mountains. He wanted me to go up
there and talk about it with him, which I did and then we
flew to Colorado. The last time I saw him he was standing on
that canyon road, his canyon road, and the light was going
as I drove away. I looked into the mirror just once and he
was walking back along the road into the coming darkness,
back along the road towards the place where he would die. I
did not know that then, of course.


It was early April when they found him. I got a call from the
Alamosa sheriff's office; they still have sheriffs out there,
complete with silver stars and six shooters. At first I thought
the call was from him, that it was Spalding playing me an
April Fool's day joke, the way the English do. It was Jack
Nathan found him. He'd gone up to the cabin a week after
the snows began to clear because he had been expecting
Spalding to come into town for supplies. When he didn't,
Nathan got worried. He knew it was him all right, but the
Alamosa sherrif's office wanted me to come and officially
identify the body. Seems they'd found some papers he'd
prepared, naming me as executor of his estate in the event of
his death. They knew he was English, but not if he had any
surviving kin. I saw the body. I said he was who he was.

There was an inquest, and I stayed for that. A day or so
before the hearing I went back to the cabin with Jack
Nathan. The sheriff had the things he wanted from the stuff
that was there. I spent an afternoon putting the rest of it into
boxes for shipping back East. Later, when the body was
released to me, I had the same done with Spalding.

I'm all by myself here today, have been for a week. My
daughter took the kids and went back to New York to look
after her husband for a while instead of looking after me. I
feel as if I'm on vacation. If that sounds a little heartless, it
isn't meant to. She's a good girl and she takes good care of
me. I know it's hard on her, this time spent with me. Her

father is dying and there seem to be certain things she needs me to do, a certain pattern of behaviour perhaps. I don't quite fill the part. She looks like she wants to cry all the time but she doesn't and so her grief is turning to anger. I can see it. And she feels guilty about her anger.

I don't honestly know all that she expects from me. I think she wants me to express sorrow, or regret; but I'm eighty-three years old and although the doctors tell me that I have only a very little time left to me I do not feel sorry about it and I do not have any regrets. I think my daughter sees all of this as an act of prolonged and compounded selfishness. She may be right. It's funny how love gets all twisted around so easily and in so short a time. To her, death is a journey, and she figures I ought to be spending my time getting ready to go, getting ready for the saying of goodbyes. I'm not, because death is not a journey. It isn't anything. It is precisely nothing. That's what he knew, Spalding, I'm talking about Spalding, that's what he knew, in the end.

There was a tape he had made in the cabin, a diary. It was still in the tape-machine when I was clearing out his stuff. I don't know whether the people from the sheriff's office knew about it, or thought it wasn't important. I probably should have surrendered it after I had listened and knew what it was, but I didn't. It would not have affected things in the end, it would just have muddied the waters. The coroner's verdict of suicide would not have been changed, just made a little more sordid. The news people had enough to feed on with that. I did not feel I owed them anything more.

I listened to that tape the first night in the motel when I got back down from the mountains. I listen to it again now that I am on my own. I listen to it. I listen to his voice, and I think of him alone in those mountains, visited by the spirit he called unknowingly from the sea. I sit here, alone in this house by the sea, and am visited by his spirit that I have summoned from the mountains. I slip the cassette into the tape-deck, depress the 'play' key, and he speaks. It is the most elementary of seances, and guaranteed to work every time. Listen.

'What day is today? What date is today? I've been up here for less than a week and already my sense of time is beginning to go. I think it's a good thing, but I'm not sure. I think it's part of why I wanted to come here, but I'm not sure. Something else I'm not sure of is why I'm talking to a tape recorder. It's one of those things that seems like a good idea until you start to do it. Then you realize how bloody pretentious you are, thinking you might have something to say for — for what? Posterity? Probably not.

'So why did I decide to start? Because I have something to say? Not really. Because I have nothing better to do? It isn't that either. I have plenty to do. Nathan brought the lumber and roofing felt up from town this morning and I started the work on the roof this afternoon. I have enough to do. I'll really have to put the time in if I'm even going to get the place ready for the winter, and then there's still bits of business to do in the valley. Some time soon Nathan will come up with the big flatbed and take me logging. He claims it will be a three- or four-day job getting enough firewood to see me through. The truth is, Henry, I don't know why I started this. I was sitting with a drink and listening to music. The tape finished and instead of putting something else on I slipped a blank cassette into the machine and started talking. It was an impulse. And I've started talking to you, old friend, because I sound so implausible talking to myself, but even that conceit won't carry me very much farther so perhaps I'd better stop. Just one thing, this was just what I said it was. It was not intended to be, is not, and, in the highly unlikely event of its being continued, will never be, a confession. I have nothing to confess, Henry. But I've told you that before.'

'Henry, remember the old song, "I Didn't Know What Time
It Was'? Well, to coin a phrase. I know what time it is now. I
know what day it is too, and what date. It's Monday, 30th
October. It's evening, eight-thirty, more or less. I wasn't
intending to start this thing again, but now it seems like a
good idea. I came here because I wanted to be on my own,
but maybe I do need someone after all, someone to talk to
anyway. Jack Nathan was here a week ago. We went
wooding. I haven't had as much fun since I was a kid. I've a
stack of wood the size of which you would not believe, but
since Nathan left I haven't seen a soul, haven't spoken a
word to anyone but myself. So, here we are, well, here I am,
feeling an idiot again, but talking to you even if you aren't
talking to me. You always were a good listener, Henry, now
you're bloody near perfect, although I could do with a cue or
two from time to time. When I dry up I switch off the
machine and I never know when I'll switch it on again. You
probably won't ever hear this, you probably wouldn't want
to anyway, but I'm going to try and keep it going through
the winter so that I can tell you I got through the winter
when I do get through it. You think I'm doing this to escape.
I know I'm doing it because I want to. There is no other
reason, no other motive, hidden or otherwise. You think I
came here because of what happened to Irene. You're wrong
about that as well. You think I feel guilty about her. I don't.
Irene did what she did because it was what she wanted to do.
I don't have any responsibility in the matter. You think I do
because you think I should. You think I should because you
know that in a similar situation you would feel guilty. You
aren't often wrong, Henry, but you are wrong about this. I
did what I did, and she did what she did. That's all there is
to say about it, and because that's all there is to say about it
I'm going to switch this thing off.'

'Friday, 10th November. It snowed today, Henry. I went
down into the valley this morning to pick up some more

supplies and check my mail. People were talking about a big
snow coming soon and when I got back up here and saw it
coming down I thought they were right. I got back to the
house around four o'clock, but by seven it had stopped. Still,
the ground is white. It's beautiful outside, it's beautiful. The
air is so clear and the sky is filled with stars. I've never seen
the sky at night the way I see it here. I was always afraid of
the dark, afraid of being by myself in the dark. I don't mean
when I was a kid, I mean always. I've always been afraid. It
was something I worried about when I first thought of
coming here, but I seem to have forgotten my fear. I don't
understand it. Perhaps it is to do with the fact that the
darkness is different here from the way it is in the town. I
don't know. All I know is that here, alone in the darkness I
am unafraid. I go outside every night, before I get ready to
sleep, and I walk in darkness more extreme than any I have
ever known and I am unafraid. Sorry to disappoint you,
Henry, but nothing is haunting me, not Irene, not my
conscience — not even old man Nathan — nothing.'


'Sunday, 12th November. It's snowing again. That is an
understatement. It is snowing so bad I can't go out of the
house. I heard the snow warning on the radio last night. The
National Weather Bureau is now calling it the worst snow-
storm in twenty years. It looks like three or four foot of snow
could get dumped on the mountains, with big drifts because
of the wind. The wind chill could get the temperature down
as low as thirty below. I'm okay inside, of course, although I
go upstairs from time to time and check on the underside of
the roof. I keep thinking about that phrase from the Bible —
is it from the Bible — the thing about "the works of days and
hands"?'


'Monday, 13th November. It is still snowing. Blizzard
conditions here and all across the South-West, but you

probably know more about what's happening than I do, Henry.

'8.00 p.m. I've been passing the time reading. Surprised? I am. There's a box of books here belonged to the Nathans, mostly kid's stuff. I read some short stories by Nathaniel Hawthorne. He's one of your biggies, isn't he, Henry? Overrated. Boring. The sort of stuff parents buy for their kids because they think it will be improving for them, and either never read it themselves when they were kids, or did and forgot how bloody awful it was. There is a book of poetry here as well. American, of course. I quite liked what I read of it: Frost and Whitman. And there were a couple by Wallace Stevens that I liked, one about the snow. It seemed the right thing to read on a day like this. I also started into a bit of history, but stopped when I got to all this stuff about the Donner party. Is that true? It put the wind up me, not that I have too much to worry about, being here all by myself. I mean, no one is going to eat me, but I caught myself biting my nails a little while ago. Joke, Henry, joke.'

'Wednesday, 15th November. It stopped snowing. I've been out for the first time in three days, shovelling paths to the sheds. I've never seen snow like this before. It's dry. When I was a kid the stuff that fell where I lived was always wet and sloppy. This is like soap powder, flies about like fluff and feathers in the lightest wind. I feel I've moved onto a film set. I keep expecting Roger Moore to walk in. Amazing, really amazing! Oh yeah, Jack Nathan was right about getting out of here after a big fall. I can't. I'm snowed in, Henry. Don't worry, I'm not scared, I'm ecstatic. I feel like a kid. You know, Henry, when I was a kid, I used to daydream all the time, usually sitting on the lavatory. Ours was outside, the lavatory. It was next to the coal-place, down at the bottom of the yard. My sisters hated it, and at night, in the winter when it was dark, my Dad used to have to stand outside in the cold when one of them wanted to go. I was never scared, and I didn't hate it. Even in the dark I loved it. Going to the lav was one of the times I could find a bit of space to be alone in. I used to spend hours out there. I just used to sit and dream, not wankers' dreams, I was just a little lad, five or six years old, they were real dreams, and anyway, I always kept the door open. I needed the door open for my dreams.

'I used to have this favourite one, that the world got flooded, but I escaped and lived on a big raft. Then I would dive from the raft and swim around in what had become an undersea city. Everything was the same as it always was, even the apple trees in our garden still had leaves, but it was all under water. I had that fantasy for years. I worked on it, lovingly, making it better and better. They were the first things I made, those day dreams. I was lonely when I was a kid, you see. I had no one to play with, so I invented friends. I made them up from inside my head and the more I worked on them, the more real they became until I came to believe that they were true. My mother thought I was crazy. She was always hauling me off to the doctor, wanting him to get my head examined. Or the priest. She was convinced I had a devil inside me.

'There was something. Some of my imaginary friends used to get me into a lot of trouble. I was sick a lot when I was a kid. One year, it was the winter of — I don't know, I didn't go to school at all. It was supposed to be the scarlet fever, 'scarletina' the doctor called it. Whatever it was, I was sick for a long time, very sick. At one point my hair fell out, and then my skin began to drop off in huge scales, leaving me raw to the touch. The doctor, our family doctor, didn't know what to do. He wanted me in a hospital so as I could get special treatment, but my mother wouldn't hear of it. When he knew he couldn't shift her he brought the specialists to me, but they didn't know what was wrong either. I had blood tests, skin tests, all kinds of tests, nothing. Nobody knew what it was. Once, I remember, the school attendence officer came round to see why I wasn't at school. My mother, "me Mam", told him about the state I was in but the guy didn't believe her so she brought him inside to let him see for himself. Christ knows what I must have looked like, bits of hair stuck to my skull, my face all scabbed and scaled, but I remember his face when he set his eyes on me, it was fear. He left that room so fast he put tracks in the carpet.

'Then my mother heard that there had been some gossip among the other women down at my school and that this was why the attendence man, the board man we used to call him, this was why he'd shown up on the doorstep. Well, my mother wrapped me up in a blanket and put me in the old pram — that's a baby carriage — she used for wheeling the washing round to the laundry, and off we set through the snow for my school. It wasn't far, perhaps ten, fifteen, minutes, but I can still remember that ride so clearly. I was humiliated because of being in the baby carriage, and done up like a baby as well, and I was terrified in case we met any of my mates on the way, but as well I was exhilarated. I hadn't been out of the house in nearly two-and-a-half months and for most of that time there'd been more snow on the ground than I'd ever seen in my life before. I'd wanted to be out in it so bad, and then, suddenly, there I was. It was only seconds before I'd transformed the pram into a sledge pulled by horses, and I was tearing along through the darkness of a Russian forest with a pack of wolves snapping at the runners. In spite of the shame I was really sad when the pine trees turned into the school railings.

'We went straight to the headmistress's office, my mother sweeping by the secretary, who'd tried to stop her, with a "she'll bloody well see me" tossed out of the side of her mouth like a fag-end. Inside she put on one of the best performances I've ever seen, a bit like what's-his-name waving that bloody shirt in the Congress. She goes on about how she's heard this and how she's heard that, and how the "board man" has been round to the house because there's not supposed to be anything wrong with me, and then she whips off the blanket and there's that head looking like it should be on the shoulders of some kid from Hiroshima or somewhere. Then off comes the top of my pyjamas, and then the wrappings that were kept on my feet to stop them from bleeding and I'm standing there like the Visible Man. Miss Middleton, the headmistress of the school, backs off, just like the attendence man had, and says to my mother, yes, well, there has obviously been a mistake, and, yes, I am clearly ill, very ill. I must be taken home at once, at once. My mother wrapped me up again and did just that, and the last thing I saw of Miss Middleton, "Middlebum" we used to call her, she's at the little sink in the corner of the room washing her hands as if she had just put them into something indescribably filthy. My mother knew a woman who cleaned at the school, and this woman told her that Middlebum had fetched the Health Authority fumigation unit down that afternoon and had her office sealed and sterilized.

'Well, the snow seemed to stay and stay that winter, and it was still there when I began to get better and the doctor said I could go outside to play for a little while every day. My mother had me bundled up like a tea cosy, I had sweaters on, and a jacket, scarves, a woolly hat; I even had a bit of old blanket threaded through my belt at the front and back to keep my dick warm. It was this last bit that did it really, because as far as I was concerned the blanket was a dead ringer for a Red Indian's loin cloth, and as I'd been watching a television serial based on *The Last of the Mohicans* for the past few weeks, I was all ready to be let loose. Within ten minutes of me getting out into the yard the place was Canada, and I was surrounded by Hurons and Iroquois, or whatever they were, fighting for my life, hand to hand, with tomahawk and Bowie knife. I'd just sent six or seven of the best to the happy hunting grounds when I was caught with a cuff from my mother right across the back of the head. Then she hauled me up from the snow and back into the house, and I still didn't know it was her. I thought it was some big

Iroquois bastard had come up out of the snow and got me. That night I was in the doctor's surgery listening to my mother tell him that I was insane and ought to be put away. It was not the first time, and it wasn't the first time the doctor had told her I just had a very vivid imagination and there was nothing to worry about.

'He was right, that doctor. I did have a vivid imagination. I mean, I could see things that other people could not see, things that weren't there for them, but were for me. I suppose I must have seemed crazy. It's like, on a Saturday morning, when my mother changed the beds, I could go back upstairs and play because she always did my bed last. The sheets and blankets would all be turned back at the foot of the mattress and that way, to me, the bed could be anything and anywhere. It could be a ship, a pirate ship of course, and the blankets would be the side. So I'd be fighting from the side of my ship, falling into the ocean. The pillows would be sharks or enemies. Or, again, they could be my horse and I'm a cowboy or a cavalryman, the last survivor of Custer's Last Stand. Of course, my mother thought I was crazy: she'd come into the bedroom and there's her kid with his pyjama trousers tucked into his school socks, a scarf around his waist with a coat-hanger stuck through it, jumping up and down on top of two pillows. What else was she to think? She couldn't help what she could see any more than I could. She just saw a bed, but what I saw was wonder.

'Why did I tell you all that, Henry? I haven't thought about it, I haven't told anyone about it, for years, years, and suddenly it all comes out. I told Irene once, about my mother taking me to the doctor every week or so, one week to have him cure me of the latest infection I'd come down with, the next to have me committed to some institution, psychiatric, correctional, it just depended on her feeling at the time about what exactly was wrong with me. Irene said she sometimes wondered about me herself, and when I asked her what she meant she said that there were times when we were working she would look at me and I wouldn't be there. There'd just be this body going through the motions of making the work, but I wasn't there. I'd be off, somewhere, in another place, another world.

'She said it was like the wood-carvers in Africa. They looked and looked at the piece of wood they wanted to make into a mask, and then the spirit of the mask that was inside the wood called to them and they went to it to set it free. She said she'd watched them when she was a little girl and her father had taken her with him to the interior when he went on business. She said that it was the same watching me. You know, sometimes, in the beginning, when I was modelling and it was nearly right, it was nearly there, I used to have to fuck her, right there on the floor of the studio. And afterwards, after I'd finished fucking her, I would come back to myself on the floor and wonder how I'd got there, how she'd got there. I would have no awareness of what I'd done, nothing. You'll be shocked, Henry. You loved her. You loved her more than I did in the end.'

'It's — what day is it today? I don't know. It's been a while, a couple of days I think, since I taped anything for you. I could find out, I could work it out, but I'm too bloody lazy to run the tape back to the last time I recorded the date. Never mind. Listen, there's some other stuff I want to tell you about my mother. One Christmas I was given a gun, sort of a space gun really, that fired these rubber-tipped darts. They had a suction cup on the end, you know what I'm talking about, a suction cup so that if you fired at a flat surface the dart would stick to it. I got a target for the darts in with the gun, and I spent most of that Christmas in the front room, the best room, with this target hanging from a hook in the door, blasting away at it.

'It was an accident, it really was, just like the business with the snowball was an accident. I mean, I loved my mother, even though she knocked me about a lot when I was a kid. Anyway, one of my sisters came in to tell me I was to pack it in with the dart gun because the rest of the family is watching television and all they can hear is this thwack, thwack all the time from the other side of the door. I didn't, of course, so my sister came back again and said that if I don't, didn't, stop I'd catch it from our mother. I thought she'd be back again and I thought I'd get her this next time.

'There was a picture hanging right by the door, one of a set of four done by my uncle Pat, four seasonal views of the same bit of woodland. They were watercolours and framed behind glass. I reckoned that, if I moved quickly enough when I heard my sister coming back for the third time, I could get round behind one of the easy chairs and fire a dart off that would just miss parting her hair the wrong way round before it slapped up against Uncle Pat's vision of snow in Swithland Woods. I'd seen this sort of thing a thousand times on television: the careless intruder, the twang of a bow string, and whirr of the arrow's rush before it shuddered into the tree right in front of the guy's nose. I wasn't anticipating anything that spectacular, I just wanted to put a little bit of a fright up my sister.

'Somebody did come, of course they did, and had it been my sister it would have been all right. Well, I'd probably have got a thrashing for scaring my sister shitless and smashing the glass of the painting, but it wasn't my sister who came in through the door, it was my mother, and the flight of the dart was too low and it hit her on the ear. Have you ever hurt someone you both love and fear, Henry? I mean hurt them physically? It's like wanting to piss and crap at the same time. My mother was hurt, very badly hurt. She was a big woman, and strong and she had no fear in her. I had never seen her cry in my life. When that dart hit her she went down as if she'd been shot with a bullet. She was crying with the pain and shock, and I was crying because of what I'd done, because I hated what I'd done, because I wanted to tell her how sorry I was for what I'd done, and because I was so scared I was shitting myself. I was really shitting myself. I was jumping up and down and there was shit coming out of my trousers onto the carpet.

'My Dad sent my eldest sister out to telephone for an ambulance but she couldn't get one, I suppose, because it was Christmas and the operator didn't think what had happened to my mother was serious enough for an ambulance. She ordered a taxi and that took my mother to hospital. The dart had burst the eardrum, well, that's what she always told me. I don't know if it did or not really, but that's what she always reckoned. Certainly they kept her in the hospital that night, and she had abscesses in the ear for years afterwards.

'I remember my sisters telling me what a bad little bastard I was and that God would punish me for what I'd done to our mother. My eldest sister put me outside in the yard and I had to stay there in the dark and the cold until my Dad came back and fetched me in again. I was shivering. I knew there were terrible things out there in that yard at night, the things my sisters were afraid of when they had to go out to the lavatory, and I knew that these things would come and get me because my mother had died. I was sure I'd killed her, you see. In a way, I hoped I had killed her because, if I hadn't, I knew she would kill me just as soon as she got back home. But if she was dead, if I had killed her, then I knew her soul would come into the yard and make all the bad things there come for me. Well, she didn't die, and I didn't get a pasting when she came home, although I got plenty of others later.

'You know, Henry, I've lost the thread of this story. It's got something to do with the snow, but I can't remember what. I've been working my way down a bottle of Old Grandad and I'm a bit fuddled. Okay, I own up, I confess, honest injun, I have been drinking too much in the past few days, but be not afraid, Henry, your best boy has not yet consigned himself to the legion of the lost. It's the snow. I am not an alcoholic, nor am I drinking to forget — but I have forgotten the bloody story I was telling you. Like the divine Marilyn in "Some Like It Hot", I can stop any time I want to, only I don't want to. Anyway, I've seen you put more away in one night than I have over the last two days, three days.

'I was out in the snow today, by the way. I was trying to make a snowman but this stuff up here is no good. Too dry. Your boy was almost back at work for a few minutes there this afternoon, Henry. I actually wanted to go and make something with my hands again. I haven't wanted to do that for nearly three years. You think it all dried up when that stupid black bitch drowned herself. Sorry, Henry, the symbolism isn't that neat. I didn't want to make things even when I was making the last things I was making. You understand? Do you understand? I was tired of it. I was sick of it. She knew. It was all finished, you see, all of it. It wasn't just her, it was the work. I was done with the work before I was done with her and she knew it before I think I knew it myself. She knew what the consequences would be. That's why she decided to top herself. She was always — Irene was always so fucking dramatic. Christ, talk about my fantasy life, you should have checked hers at some point during all the years of your de-fucking-votion to us. She was an actress, playing the role of the spurned model, the old Lizzie Siddal trip or whatever the daft bitch was called, Jeanne —, anyway she was acting out a role, which was why she was so bloody good as a model but it finished us in the end, finished all of it for us in the end because — because it had to. You can see that, can't you? It finished us because it had to. No way out. No way out, man, no way out.

'I've remembered what it was I wanted to tell you about my mother and the snow. My mother had these abscesses in her ear for years after I hit her with the dart, every winter, as soon as it began to get cold. You know how the cold is in England, Henry, damp and chill so that it feels as if it's

about sixty below and gets right inside of you. Well, every
winter she would get these abscesses, and the doctors at the
hospital would keep her on a diet of penicillin and drain out
her ear every other week. Well, it snowed, you see, and the
first day it settled enough to be worth shit was a Saturday
and so every kid in the entire street was outside playing in
the stuff. Saturday was the big shopping day where I lived.
My mother had gone into the centre of town to do hers, and
it must have been about four o'clock, yes, it must have been
about four o'clock in the afternoon because it was dark, and I
was still outside with some other kids throwing snowballs at
the front doors of the houses. The idea was to aim for the
bell-push and try to set off the chimes.

  'I saw my mother coming down the street and she was
loaded up with bags. She'd carry these tremendous weights
of shopping home with her on Saturdays. I can still see her
hands when she came in to the fire from the kitchen, having
dumped the groceries on the kitchen table. Her hands looked
like the talons of some big bird. The fingers were all hooked
up and blue from the cold and carrying the dead weight of
the shopping. Sometimes she'd even have her bus-ticket
caught up against her wedding ring from having pushed it
down inside her glove, and the greeny-blue colour of the
ticket matched the colour of the veins that stood out under
the skin. The other kids in the street were scared of my
mother. They had reason to be. She landed out at anybody,
any kid, without fear or favour, if they were misbehaving,
according to her reckoning that is.

  'Once, when one of the neighbours came round to have it
out with her because she'd clocked his kid, she did him as
well. She was scrubbing the backyard when this guy came in
and I can see her now, standing there with the yard-brush in
her hands and her sleeves rolled up and this big bucket of hot
water steaming away in the cold air as he gives her the
business about what he'll do to her if she ever lifts a finger to
his kid again. And then, I don't know what he said to her,

but she fetches him a sharp one against the side of the head with the brush and the guy went down like a sack of potatoes. I don't know if she hit the guy again, or whether that first one was good enough, but the next thing I remember is she has him by the collar, pulling him down the yard and through the gate. Then, when she's dumped him in the gutter, she gets on with swilling the yard.

'Of course, the kids were scared of her. But I thought I'd do something to show them that I wasn't scared, although I was, I was more scared than any of them. We'd not long had a door-bell fitted ourselves and I could see my mother straining to get her finger up to it. I'd had a snowball in my hand all the time she was coming down the street and I let fly at the door, thinking I could hit the bell-push. I thought this would both help my mother and impress the other kids, who more or less had me down as a candy-ass, the kid that was always sick, always crying. I didn't hit the bell-push, I hit my mother, and I hit her on her bad ear again. The headscarf she had on must have slipped down to her shoulders while she was shopping and she took the full force of the blow directly on the ear.

'I didn't stay to see what I'd done this time. I ran and I stayed out until my Dad came to fetch me. My mother wasn't there when we got back to the house. I suppose she was at the hospital again. I asked where she was and my Dad hit me across the mouth, just once, very hard. That was the only time in my life he ever lifted a hand to me.'

'Thursday, 16th November. I'm snowed in, Henry. Stuck, as they say. I tried to get out from the property and on to the canyon road but it was useless. The drifts are taller than I am. I came back for the snow shoes, and I tried using them. It ain't as easy as it looks. I started clearing more of the snow away from around the buildings and off the roof. It was just for something to do, an excuse to get out of the house. Nathan warned me about cabin fever. I thought he was pulling my leg, you know, kidding me, joshing with the greenhorn. Now I think maybe he wasn't. It felt a little warmer towards noon today, and I thought maybe a thaw was setting in, but then, around three the temperature dropped again. It got cold enough to send me back inside, where I've been ever since, sitting by the stove drinking tea, not bourbon. Sorry about all that stuff the other day, Henry. I might just erase this tape. You would probably find it embarrassing. I would probably find it embarrassing. No personal revelations, eh, Henry? Let's keep it right and tight and business-like.'

'Sunday, 19th November. I made a snowman today. The consistency of the snow has altered since the blizzard, I guess with the temperature changes. It's a real snowman. I haven't made one since I was a kid. Then, we would use bits of coal for the features of the face. Here, I used twigs and pieces of bark from the wood store. I enjoyed making it. I haven't made anything for so long. I haven't enjoyed making anything for longer. You know, Henry, I might go out there tomorrow and play around with the snow. I have my cameras and a lot of film. I'll shoot the results. Don't worry, I'm not about to present myself to you renewed as some kind of half-assed minimalist/environmentalist by Goldsworthy out of Smithson. Look, I'm up here and I can't get out, and I want to do something with my time other than sitting around reading kids' books and drinking Old Grandad, or talking to a tape recorder and calling it Henry, Henry. So, goodnight Henry, and fuck off Henry, and Henry, over and out.'

It ends there. Nothing after that except the dry hiss of blank tape. I found the cassette in the deck just the way I said I did, and I put it in my pocket. I don't see that it would have changed anything if I had handed it over to the sheriff. The coroner would still have handed in the same verdict: suicide.

He didn't have a lot of choice in that. When he was found, Spalding was naked, face down in the melting snow. He froze to death. So, the tape would not have changed anything, and it would not have explained anything, not to them. To me, but not to them. And what it explained to me, explains to me each time I listen to it, is how he died the way he did, and why he died the way he did. If this was a detective novel and I was the detective I would probably come up with the line, The snowman did it. Only it wasn't a snowman, it was a snow woman, it was Irene.

I think of him there that last evening, I think of him starting to get excited because he is feeling he can work again. He was always like that with a new project. He used to start things, well, the real work, after the initial idea was formed, he used to start them very deliberately, very precisely. He was a man who savoured the pleasures of anticipation. So, I can see him, after so long not working, I can see him enjoying that evening, that evening knowing in the morning, or some time during the next day, the work would begin again.

And I can see him going out into the whiteness, from which almost any sign of any thing had been erased, to create. Did he start piling the snow into a mound, or did he return to the first figure, the snowman he had made? I don't know, but I believe that he began to work either on that first figure or another and as he worked something happened that he might not, in the beginning, have been aware of, but that came from him nevertheless. The figure in the snow slowly emerging was Irene. It could not have been otherwise. Nothing else can explain his death in that place, in that manner.

I can see him shaping the snow. I can see his cold hands, the gloves off now, finding themselves shaping breasts, her breasts, willowing out arms that were her arms, legs that were her legs, and the face, in spite of the whiteness, became her face. He could do it. I've seen him work with sand, once.

Once, we were in England at some seaside town. Cold as hell, it was. We were there for a personal appearance at an exhibition, part of a festival. Spalding knew the place, had been there on vacation with his family when he was a child. He had a photograph of himself standing by a huge sandcastle he had made for a contest. He took the prize.

He wanted to show us, me and Irene that is, where he had made the sandcastle, the precise spot. The tide had not long retreated and Spalding got excited, saying that this was the best time to build because the sand was wet but not too wet and, although we had to be at the gallery in an hour or so and he had on his good clothes and it was cold, real cold, he pulled off his coat and jacket and started digging the sand with his fingers. We stayed an hour, two hours, I don't know. We were late for the event at the gallery certainly. When, at last, we got him off the beach, he had left ornamenting the empty spaces of those wind-blown and godforsaken sands an image of Irene, nude, reclining upon her side: an imperial image of woman, African, sexual, looking out to sea, as if the soon-returning waves were lovers, for whose destructive embrace she waited.

I know what he could do. I can see that figure still, transformed now from dusky sand to pristine snow. A negative of Irene, but Irene nonetheless. I can see the heavy breasts and thighs, the slightly thickened lips and flattened nose, the slit and slanting eyes. Always, he would exaggerate the exotic in her flesh and face. I can see him working and as he works, as the day's light diminishes, I can see the figure in the snow begin to take on what light remains, drawing it in to itself.

At some point he must have stopped. He must have turned back towards the cabin, to the lighting of lamps against the darkness, the closing of doors. But he would have taken the outside with him this time. He would have taken her with him, or her memory, or her presence.

He would have pulled off his coat and boots, and taking the bottle of bourbon and the glass, gone to sit by the stove. Perhaps he would have needed to rekindle the fires, perhaps in his negligence the house had grown cold, cold as the figure in the snow just beyond the window. I checked that, the second time I went up to the cabin after he was dead. You could see, quite clearly and without effort, the spot where they found him, from his chair by the stove. That's where he made the figure, and that is where he died.

I imagine him trying to attend to the lighting of fires, the gleaning of warmth into his starving frame, the bourbon, a book even, or the sound of the radio perhaps. And I see his head turning, always turning from these saving tasks, to the window, and the figure which glistened in the darkness beyond the window. He would want to be out there with it — with her. It was the way he was when he had made something. His revelation of what he did to Irene when that fit was upon him was neither shocking to me nor was it a revelation; I had known about it for a long time. Irene told me, a long time before. It was when I first began to look upon him with less than love. He would have wanted her then, I know he would. And wanting her but not having her, he would have wanted the snow image. At some point his wanting became more than that and he put down the glass, and put down the book, and he pulled his clothes from his body. Then he walked naked into the cold and the darkness and he lay with what he had made in the snow until he was entirely spent, of his seed and of his life.

There was something Jack Nathan said to me, something he did not understand. I guess he must have mentioned this to the sheriff's people because they asked the same question. It had to do with the position of Spalding's hands and arms. When Jack Nathan found the body, his first reaction was to turn it over. He said it was as if Spalding had been holding something, or someone. It was as if his arms had been wrapped about something in an embrace, but now were empty. It was a mystery to me, as well, at the time, but now, I think, it is not.

The poems in the anthology he had been reading during the days and nights of the big storm were marked. He always had that very annoying habit of creasing down the corners of pages in books. One of the pieces by Wallace Stevens was called 'The Snow Man'. I had not come across it before, although I should have done, for I am myself a great reader of poetry. The final verse interested me, 'For the listener, who listens in the snow,/And, nothing himself, beholds/ Nothing that is not there and the nothing that is.'

I see now that what I feared at the beginning of our relationship — our time together — was true. He spent his life gradually emptying himself of his talent, his creativity. When he threw Irene away, when she died, he was left with nothing. He was a hollow space, containing only the echoes of what had once been there. It was an echo that called to him in the snows of Colorado, high up amidst the Sangre de Cristo mountains. Sangre de Cristo means the blood of Christ. The secret of Alan Spalding's death is that he died embracing his own creation, which was his sin and his guilt and his expiation. Alan Spalding died embracing nothing.

# HUNTING

They told me I'd had a good war, and I suppose that, from their point of view, they were right. After I got my commission I saw decent action in the desert with a good county regiment, my father's regiment, my grandfather's regiment. I got my wound and I got my medal, and, afterwards, I swanned about with David Stirling's shower for a couple of years until I was recalled and sent to the Balkans. There was another wound and another medal, 'from a grateful people', and then it was all over and I was back in civilian life where everyone kept telling me what a good war I'd had. I did the right things then: finished my degree, found a job, a wife. I thought I'd settle down all right, but I didn't. I lost the job, lost the wife as well, started to drink. I became a bit of an embarrassment really.

It was the war, you see, the good war. I couldn't seem to let it go. I wanted to, I did, I just couldn't seem to actually do it. In a battle, a proper battle, the sort of thing they used to train young officers for, most chaps, if they come out of it all right, never see the ones they've killed, never see them. They know what they've done, most of them; they know that they've killed, must have done, but unless they've gone in and cleared out a trench or some such thing, they probably never really even caught sight of the people they were fighting, the enemy. I know that for a fact.

It's different when you see what you've done. It's different
when you see what you're doing while you're doing it. It
leaves a mark which is worse than a wound because it
doesn't heal. You can't see it, of course you can't, and if you
don't know, if you don't know then, well, you don't know.
You could sit opposite me on the train and you wouldn't
know what I've done. You wouldn't know that I have shot
men, shot men no farther away from me than you are; or
that, once, I shot a man in the face, shot him and then shot
him again and then again because, even with pieces of his
head gone, he would not lie down and die. I was twenty-two
when I did that. But I had a good war, and I've got the
medals to prove it.

After my divorce I swanned about for a bit, quite a bit
actually and, as I say, I became something of an embarrassment. I tried to hold a job, but anything I turned my hand
to, well, I couldn't, I just couldn't seem to get the hang of. I
even went on the tramp for a few months, living rough in the
country. I knew how to do that. Then my mother died and
somehow the family got hold of me and tidied me up a bit for
the funeral, and afterwards it was made pretty clear that I
had to sort something out for myself. That was when I
started writing. I wrote about the war, of course; I had to.

There were a lot of chaps doing that sort of thing then.
Even with paper rationing the book clubs couldn't get
enough of war memoirs. I wrote down a lot of the stuff that
was bothering me, and some smart young girl at the
publishers' tidied it all up and it did very well. Of course
they didn't want the truth, but there was enough in what I
did write to sell it, mainly to chaps that had been too young
to fight. It isn't in print any more, but sometimes I come
across copies on market stalls, next to things about Tuck and
Bader. War memoirs. I started writing novels after that, and
then I went to the States.

I was married again by that time, to Susie. She was an
American and she had a bit of money, although why on earth

she was in London I never really knew. She'd come over with all the other Yanks in 1941 and just hadn't gone home again, though God knows how, and God knows why. When I met her she was involved in publishing in some way or another. Well, there were all sorts of odds and sods knocking about town then.

I thought we really loved each other at first. At first, perhaps we did, but it didn't last. I suppose getting married saw to that. I thought about a divorce, we both did, but, in the end, I knew I'd have to stick it out because a second divorce would have killed my father, I know it would. So we went to America. I got an offer to teach as a visiting professor at a place called Ruddock College in Colorado. The Yanks were up to their ears in cash then, of course, and they were more or less buying up any bit of European culture that took their fancy. Writers were as saleable a commodity as pictures, even chaps like me. I'd written four books by then, and I suppose I had something of a reputation. I got the offer through my agent and I was glad to take it. I was having a bit of a time living on my reputation, you see, and, anyway, I thought that getting away, to a new place, a new world really, I thought that it would help me let go, let go properly, of the war.

Susie went with me to America. I think she was as excited as I was, really. It wasn't that she was anxious to get home. She was happy in London, she always said that, but she was beginning to find that her happiness was starting to turn stale, like a bit of cake curling at the edges in the baker's window. She'd been born and had grown up in Arlington, Virginia. Colorado would be as new to her as it would be to me. A foreign country really. Perhaps, as well, she thought, like I did, that it might be good for us, for the marriage, that in this new place we might find the thing, the love, I mean, that we'd lost somehow in the old. She didn't say anything like this, of course, Susie wouldn't have. She wasn't that sort of a girl.

So we left England, and that morning, at the end of the
voyage when the ship came into port and all the towers of
Manhattan seemed to stand up like the sheaves of corn in
Joseph's dream, I thought that it was a sign. It was a sign.
But then we left New York, and the train took us into the
heart of the continent, and in Denver we left one train and
took another, and then we took a bus, and all the time we
were climbing higher and higher into the mountains and I
knew that I'd made a mistake. It wasn't a new world
anymore, not up in the mountains. Up in the mountains I
knew where I was. Up in the mountains I was back in the
war again. I used to dream about the mountains, you see,
dream about them and what happened there, what I did
there. I would close my eyes at night and I was back in the
mountains. Now I didn't even have to close my eyes. The
mountains were all around me.

The college was on the edge of what I suppose some
character in a Western film would have called a 'one-horse
town' up in the San Juan mountains. The bus set us down
outside of a cafeteria on the main street where a chap by the
name of Carmichael was waiting to take us out to the
campus, which was a word I was then unfamiliar with. He
was a tall fellow, and thin, with his hair cut short, but not
British Army short, you understand, this had been done with
a certain amount of care, of style, I might say. I supposed,
from my first sighting of him, that he had lived in the West
all his life, for he certainly dressed the part with his denim
trousers and high-heeled cowboy boots, but it turned out he
was from New Jersey, on the eastern seaboard, and had been
in Colorado for less than a year.

It was the same with almost all of the chaps I met at the
college. The faculty was predominantly young, many of
them still under thirty, and they had come from all over the
United States; there was even one fellow, a history teacher,
who had grown up on the island of Hawaii, although he was
as white as I was. Yet, to a man, they all wore these tight

denim trousers, blue jeans they called them, with tartan cowboy shirts and Western boots. Many even affected hats to go with the rest of the outfit, and the wives followed suit. It was odd, actually, though I dare say that Susie and I seemed as odd to them as they did to us.

They were kind though, these converted cowboys and their wives, very kind to Susie and me, and very kind to me after Susie left. She did leave. She managed a fortnight of it, the little town in the mountains, the welcome parties and dinners, the scenic drives, and then she said she really had to go and visit her dear old mother in Virginia and I knew I would never see her again. Yes, they were kind; after a month or so when everyone had guessed what I already knew, they were very kind. I suppose it was kindness made them want to take me out hunting.

I had not seen a gun since I came out of the army, but they were everywhere there, like the mountains. Carmichael had two of the things on a rack in the rear window of his car when he drove Susie and me out to the college that first time. I'd asked him about them and he'd said it was hunting season, as if that were a perfectly reasonable explanation as to why he should feel it necessary to go armed to meet a new member of the teaching staff and his wife. After that there were guns of one sort or another wherever I went; no home was complete without a set of rifles and shotguns, and, it seemed, no conversation was complete without talk of hunting. Indeed, it appeared to me that there were times of the year when very little that flew, walked or crawled was safe from the threat of death by gunshot in those mountains.

The talk was all of killing: deer, antelope, elk, partridge, quail, rabbit, bear, particularly bear. The president of the college had shot a bear the year before and the deed was still considered a worthy topic of conversation. I even saw the poor beast, or what was left of it after the taxidermist had finished turning the skin into a wall-hanging. It had been

pegged up over the mantelpiece, and I was at once led across
to inspect the trophy. I meant to offer my congratulations, to
profess my admiration, but all I could say was 'poor beast';
and my hosts — for my viewing of the rug took place at a
party given in my honour by the president and Mrs Donaldson — seemed a little taken aback. I suppose that, in the end,
they put my gaffe down to that innate sense of sportsmanship
with which the English are meant to be endowed; sympathy
for the vanquished, the fallen enemy. Only natural, after all,
in a former military man such as I was imagined to be.

I suppose it was this, too, that explained the sense there
seemed to be that I would be interested in hunting as well.
They had read the little biography my publisher circulated
about me, and they had seen the photograph on the back of
my books: the rakish tilt of the military cap, the battledress,
the ribbons. Poor, simple souls. They were all caught up in
the romance of the English officer, the chap on half-pay who
turns out with the local hunt, or shoots during the season, or
turns a rod on an English river, substituting the slaughter of
dumb beasts for the slaughter of men. I suppose I should not
have blamed them, even the men, those who had served with
the American forces and who really ought to have known
better. As I have said, even those who had fought had not
fought, probably, as I had. I had hunted and killed men in
mountains like these and I wanted no more hunting and no
more killing, but how could they have known, and knowing,
understood? It was as much to ask that pretty Mrs Carmichael should have known that I had as little taste for
loving a woman now, in the way she wanted loving, as I had
for killing, of men, or of beasts.

Susie knew. Susie understood. It was why she had stopped
loving me, and it was why, at last, she left me, there, in the
mountains.

Pretty Mrs Carmichael fell in love with me the first time
she saw me, I believe. I suppose I should say that she was
ready to fall in love with anyone who seemed to offer her —

what, romance? Yes, I suppose romance is the word I would use. It just happened that, on this occasion, the one who seemed to offer her the thing she craved was me. Or at least, it was her version of me, which was as much a fiction, I suppose, I know, as the version of me her husband and all the other hunters had taken up. The two delusions came together in the end, came together to send me up into those mountains where I had said I would not go, to do what I had said I would not do, to hunt bear. To hunt a bear.

The talk, when it was not of deer or antelope or elk, was all of bear. There were, it seems, a lot of bears in the mountains, mostly American brown bears, although some, particularly the man from Hawaii, claimed that there were grizzly bears, *ursus horribilis*, up there as well. Everyone, all of the men, wanted to shoot a bear, and everyone, all of the women, wanted a bear shot and spread out on their living-room floors, or pegged, like the Donaldson's bear, on their living-room walls. Pretty Mrs Carmichael wanted it more than anyone else, or, at least, that is how it appeared to me.

She voiced her desire at every opportunity, ridiculing her husband for his inability to satisfy her in this simple thing; suggesting, for those who would hear her, that there were other, simple, things in which he also was unable to satisfy her. As the first weeks of my time at the college went by, Mrs Carmichael began to embellish her complaint by turning towards me and speculating upon the ease with which I, a military man, one who still used his rank as title, a hero, decorated by a grateful people, might give her the thing she wanted more than any other.

It was then inevitable that, at some point, her husband would be required to ask me to join him and his party when the bear hunting season came; and inevitable, I suppose, that I would accept his invitation, for I knew that, were I not with him in the mountains, I should, in some way, whatever way she could and would contrive it, be with his wife in the town.

The way they went about their hunting was this: they baited the bear. By this I mean that the hunters would leave food out in the mountains, returning from time to time to see if any of it had been taken, and if it had, whether it had been taken by a bear. If such was the case they would continue to bait in that spot, and, at the same time, construct a hide in a tree from which to observe the bear they were now feeding. As the creature became used to being fed in this way it would grow lax and lazy and, one day, the men in the hide would shoot it. I did not say so, but it seemed no sport to me.

I went with Carmichael and the others of his party on these baiting expeditions, and, not often, once or twice perhaps, we came across the work of other hunters. They did not kill here for meat, the food they tossed so indiscriminately about the mountains for the poor, dumb beasts to eat was richer fare than any I had seen for fifteen years. No, it was not for meat they killed, it was for some form of pleasure so perverse I could not understand it.

We came across carcasses, decapitated, skinned and then left bloody in the forest. I had seen sights not entirely dissimilar before, and I looked to confirm memory. The butchering, more often than not, had been as botched with the rifle as, later, with the knife. Three, four, sometimes five shots to despatch the poor creature, and I thought of it, of how slowly death can come to the living in spite of all the mechanical violence our civilization has given us to visit upon sensiate flesh. I thought of that man I had shot who would not lie down and die. I thought of all the men I had shot who would not lie down and die. I thought of these creatures, slaughtered for a whim, a ritual, a conversation piece. I asked Carmichael whether it did not entirely ruin the trophy for it to be so holed. He told me it did not, that the taxidermist in the town was well-used to dealing with such things and generally made a pretty good job of them.

Well, we found our bear. It had been taking the bait for a week or so before we had the first sighting of it. I had helped build the hide, it was something that I knew how to do, and I was there with a man called Frank Hildy, watching when it came and we were able to see it. The bear was a young male, two or three years old, Hildy thought. It was small for its age, and evidently unwise in the ways of the world in which it must live perforce, yet Hildy was not unsatisfied. He ventured the opinion that we would, one of us would, be able to shoot it well before the end of the month.

We went armed now when we baited the bear, armed to the teeth, and we stayed in the hide for longer and longer periods. At weekends we took to sleeping in the forest, in the high, cold air. There were four of us, Carmichael, Hildy and myself, and a fellow called Carl Watson. They carried powerful hunting rifles with telescopic sights, not unlike the sort of thing unit snipers used during the war. I had never had much time for snipers, even our own, ever since I had heard one boasting that he had shot a chap who was in the act of relieving himself. It seemed such a dirty trick, as dirty as the trick we were engaged upon now. There was not very much to choose, it seemed to me, between shooting a man as he defecated, or a bear as it fed.

I had no gun of my own and would not buy one, so I was given the loan of an old lever-action Remington, a .32 calibre weapon which sighted along the barrel. I fired it several times to adjust the sights for range and knew that it would kill as well as anything else. I carried it, loaded, each time I went with the others into the mountains, and I carried as well my pack and two shotguns owned by Hildy. I served as porter because I could not be trusted as a gun. That much was evident, and yet, in the end, it was I that shot the bear.

I shot it because I had seen the others shoot, had seen their special ineptitude, and because of the men that I had shot, and the face of the one that would never leave my memory or my dreams, the face I shot again, and again. I shot the bear for him, I think.

We were in the hide, and it had been decided that the bear

was to be taken that day if it appeared, if it presented itself as a target that might be hit. It did appear, and it did so present itself, and I knew then what I should do, and I knew that I should do it at once. It was a single shot to the base of the skull, executed while the others were wrapped in a fever of anticipation, sighting their rifles, drawing their eager, anticipatory breaths. The creature went down at once, more easily, more easily by far, than any man I had ever seen go down. I know that it was dead within seconds, and that it had but a short suffering, if it had any at all.

The others were out of the hide before I was, carried away before me by a great wave of euphoria at the kill, euphoria so great it eclipsed the shock of the fact that it was I who had done the killing. But they were hunters, and they had their kill. It did not matter how and, even had they wondered, it did not matter why. They were more or less performing a dance around the slaughtered beast when I came up to them, checking the loads of the shotguns, and they were at first bemused, still with the excitement of the kill pushing reason from them, when I ordered them to stand clear of the carcass. It was the first time I had given a command since leaving the army.

I do not believe any of them, not even Carmichael, quite understood what I was about until I fired off the first shotgun into the bear. The blast tore a massive piece out of the shoulder and left the hair around the wound singed and smoking. I fired the second gun into the spine, and then I reloaded both weapons and fired them into the beast again, and then once again.

They understood then, even Carmichael. He threatened to shoot me. He actually levelled his weapon at me and put a bullet into the chamber. I told him that if he did shoot me, and if he shot me right, then he would be visiting upon me an act of the greatest kindness imaginable. Of course he put down his weapon. He would have had to watch me die, you see. It is one thing to shoot a bear as it is feeding, particularly as it is feeding. It is something quite other to shoot a man who is looking at you, his eyes levelling with yours along the barrel of your gun.

They left me there in the mountains, amidst the trees and the high, cold air. They left me alone with the ruined prey. I let them get an hour or so's start on me, and then I began the long walk down the mountain myself and the road leading to the little town and the college campus beyond. It was dark before I arrived at the house where I was living, and as soon as I got inside I began to pack my bags.

That night Mrs Carmichael, pretty Mrs Carmichael, came to see me. I had imagined that she would. She wept. She raged. She asked me why I had done what I had done. When I did not, when I would not answer her, she said I could have her, I could have her then, there, and she began to pull at her clothes until she stood, undressed, before me. When I did not do as she wanted, when I would not, she raged at me again, and gathered her clothes about her again. She said she would run out into the night as she was, half-naked as she was, and she would cry out that I had torn the clothes from her, that I had attacked her. It was only when I told her I did not care that she grew quiet and put herself in order again, in some semblance of order again.

And when she was dressed, and as she made to leave my house, she said I would not take her for the same reason that I had despoiled the bear, which was because I was not, in any real sense of the word, a man. I said I agreed with her, I was not, in any real sense of the word, a man. I was not.

It was the first time in such a long time since I had spoken even this approximation of the truth. And it was the first time in such a long time that I was entirely happy.

# A SLIGHT MISUNDERSTANDING

*I* remember the first time I fell in love because it was exactly one week and two days after my thirty-fifth birthday. I was married, with two children: Osamu, who was fifteen, and Mari, the baby. She wasn't a baby really, she was six then, but I always thought of her as the baby, as my baby. Her birth was difficult. I was in labour for seventy-two hours and in the end I went from the midwife's house to hospital and they took her out of me. Afterwards they told me I oughtn't to try and start another child. Well, I didn't try to start Mari, but I had her and because I knew there would not be another, she was always the baby to me, my baby. She still is.

I'd been married for fifteen years when it happened, when I fell in love. I know, I know. I was well pregnant with Osamu when we had the reception. It's one of the things my husband has never forgiven me for. He's always said I did it on purpose to trap him into marriage and make him take on my father's business. I'm the only child you see, so I had to find a husband to keep the shop going, but I didn't mean to get pregnant. It was an accident. Both of the children were, and the first was even more of an accident than the second. I mean, we only did it the once, and it was my first time. I wasn't the sort of girl that went with men, well, not like that, not in that way. I didn't even enjoy it. I never have. If anyone was trapped it was me. I didn't want to get married. I certainly didn't want to marry my husband. It was just one of those things. I was unlucky. It was my first time and it should have been my last, with him anyway, and it would have been if I hadn't fallen pregnant.

It isn't even as if we did keep on my father's business. My father was a butcher, but my husband couldn't learn the trade, or wouldn't learn it. So we turned the shop over to what he did know, which was boxed lunches. That had been his people's business, you see, so naturally enough it was what he knew. It's what I know now. I've had fifteen years of it, standing over the vats frying up bits of fish and vegetables, scalding myself with the steam from the rice cookers. We still do a bit of meat. My father looks after that side of things, although he's over seventy now and my husband is always saying that he gets under people's feet in the shop. It isn't much he puts up these days, just a tray or two of beef and a bit of pork and chicken. He still has one or two customers from the old days. I think they come more for the talk than the meat.

My husband complains about that as well, of course, especially when we're busy with the lunch-time rush. He says that the old women, it's nearly always old women that come for my father, he says they take up space and put off the real customers. He's probably right, but my father hasn't got anything else now. He's been an active man all his life, you see, and I know it would kill him if he lost this last little bit of independence and the contact with the old days.

My family have had a shop here for as long as anyone can remember. We were here during the great earthquake, and we were here in the war through all the bombing. We haven't always sold meat, but we've always been here and we've always sold something. I won't let my father be pushed into the back like something that isn't wanted anymore. He means too much to me to let that happen.

He does mean a lot to me, my father. So do my children,

and yet, and yet, I'd have walked out of that door, I would,
I'd have walked out of that door and down the street and I'd
not have looked back, I'd not, if Satoko Inoue had told me
once, just once, that she loved me as much as I loved her;
even if she'd have told me that someday, one day, she might
love me. Even that would have been enough. She never did.
So I'm still here, as you can see, putting the boiled rice into
the boxes with the shrimp and the pickles, a bit of salad, a bit
of egg sometimes, sometimes a bit of something else.

Like I said, it was a week and two days after my birthday,
which no one round here except my father remembers, that
she came into the shop for the first time. We get all sorts in
here, you know, all sorts: people from the bank, people from
the supermarket across the road, builders, travelling sales-
men, the girls from the pharmacy round the corner. We even
get the occasional foreigner come in because Tokyo's
changed so much in the past few years, but I'd never seen
anyone like her in the shop before.

Well, to be truthful, I'd never seen anyone like her before.
She was a beauty, but that wasn't it, not really. There's so
many pretty girls nowadays, beautiful girls really: the girls
from the bank, even one or two of those that work on the
check-outs at the supermarket. They're all pretty and, like I
say, some of them are really beautiful, but none that I can
think of have what she had, what Satoko Inoue had. You
might call it style, but even that wouldn't be quite right. It
was more than style like it was more than just beauty.

She was tall, well, even that isn't unusual today, is it? A lot
of girls are tall now. I was reading in the paper that it's all
the protein they eat, all those hamburgers and chicken
nuggets and the like. Well, she was tall, and she was thin, a
little bit too thin, you might say; as you might say she was a
little bit too tall, to be honest. She had very long hair,
although I didn't know that, not the first time I saw her,
because she had it all coiled up tight at the back of her head
like a dancer, just like a ballet dancer. That was part of what

made her stand out. The very moment I saw her I thought to myself that she was like a dancer, a ballerina. It was because she was so tall and thin, and the way her hair was done, all scraped back off her face and wound into that tight little bun on the back of her head. There was that air about her, of grace and beauty, just like a ballerina.

It was the clothes as well. No, she wasn't wearing a long white frock or anything of the sort. She had a grey suit on, in fact, but it was beautiful. It looked expensive, do you know what I mean? You looked at that suit, and it seemed to look right back at you and say the word 'money', ever so quietly, and ever so politely, but ever so insistently as well. I remember thinking that it must have cost a packet and that she shouldn't, she really shouldn't, have come into the shop in something like that because the smell of the cooking would settle on it. It gets everywhere, you see, the smell of the cooking does. It gets onto your clothes, and your hair and your skin and it never comes off no matter how much you scrub. When I go shopping on my day off I start getting ready at five in the morning. Well, even though the shop is closed I've still got to make the children's lunch-boxes, and then leave something for my father and my husband as well, if he's staying at home. Mainly though, I get up that early so I can give myself a good scrubbing. I wash my hair and I wash myself; I give myself a really good scrubbing; I don't put my best clothes on until I'm ready to leave the house; I use perfume, expensive stuff, Chanel. It's no good; people still move away from me on the train. They can smell the food, you see. I know they can.

Well, I didn't want that smell on her, or on her clothes. That suit was beautiful. It was beautiful like she was beautiful. I'd never seen clothes like that round here before. That suit — it was like something you might see on television, from the Paris fashions. She had this little leather bag as well — no, not a bag, it was more like a briefcase, like a gentleman would carry, a real gentleman might carry. Not some office worker, you understand, something one of the bosses might carry. The bag was made from the same leather as her gloves, and her shoes.

She wore dark glasses as well, that first time. I remember exactly how she came into the shop. It was after one, so we weren't busy. In fact, we hadn't got much left and I'd started cleaning up so we could get ready for the next rush at five. Anyway, she comes in and she comes up to the counter. I was on my own, doing the sink up a bit. She comes up to the counter and she pulls one of her gloves off, the right glove it was, and then she took off her dark glasses and I think I fell in love with her then. She looked at me and she asked me for something we'd sold right out of and, normally like, with anyone else, I'd just have said that it was all finished but, in fact, I told her that I was just about to put a new batch on the gas. It was a stupid thing to say, really. I mean, it was obvious that I was cleaning up after the lunch-time rush, and anybody with a bit of sense would know I wasn't about to start cooking stuff for the five o'clock crowd at that time in the afternoon, but, there we are, that's what I told her. I said it would be about ten minutes, and would she mind waiting.

She must have known, she must have, but she didn't let on, she just said she had some messages to get and she'd be back. When she looked at me then, when she spoke to me, I — it sounds stupid telling you this, like something out of one of our Mari's comics — well, I came over all funny. I went hot all of a sudden and I couldn't get the right words out. It sounds really stupid, but that's what it was like. I don't know if she noticed. She didn't say anything. She just put her dark glasses back on and her glove. I watched her putting it on her hand. It was so lovely her hand, lovely long fingers and bright red varnish on the nails. She put her glove on and she smiled at me, and went back out into the street again.

I watched her go, and I was shaking, I was trembling all over. I was shaking so bad I couldn't even get started on her lunch-box. I had to sit down on the little stool we keep by the fryers, it was so bad. I told myself I was being stupid. What would someone like her want with someone like me. Funny, even then it wasn't that she was a woman and I was a woman. I didn't even think about that side of it. No, it was her clothes, and her hair, and those long fingers with their painted nails. I thought about all of that, and then I thought about me, about my clothes, and my hair. I held my hands up in front of me, as if I'd never seen them before, as if they weren't mine. Even if they'd been decently looked after they wouldn't have stood comparison with hers, but they hadn't been looked after, you see, now had they? My fingernails are so short you can hardly see them, well, if you work in catering you have to keep them like that. It wasn't what upset me though, it was the fat burns all over the backs of my hands and all up my arms. You get burned a lot in this trade, well, it's only natural, isn't it? I mean, you're dropping stuff into the fryers all day long, day in and day out, you can't expect not to get splashed, can you?

What upset me was, well, I looked at my hands, and then I shut my eyes and I thought about her hands. I thought, I don't know why, I really don't, it just came to me like, I thought about her hand touching me, stroking me, and then I tried to think about my hands touching her, stroking her, touching her skin and her hair and her clothes, and it was impossible, I knew it was impossible. So, I had a bit of a cry and then I started getting her order ready.

Of course, I'd got all behind with things and the shrimps weren't ready by the time she came back. I told her I was sorry, but she said it didn't matter, not to worry and that was it. I wanted to ask her things — you know, who she was, what was she doing round here, but I didn't. I got the shrimps out of the fryer and finished the box, wrapped it, and that was it. Oh, she said not to bother with any throw-away chopsticks, we had to think about the environment, which I thought was funny. The foreigners won't use disposables, but it was the first time I'd heard that sort of thing from a Japanese. Anyway, she gave me the money, and just for a moment, I touched her hand. Then she was gone, and I went back to scrubbing out the sink. I didn't think I'd ever see her again. I mean, I'd never seen her before, so why should I see her again? She obviously wasn't from around here, probably on business in the area and wanting a quick lunch. Then she came into the shop again the next Saturday. It was right at the busiest time when she came, and my husband served her.

I wasn't behind the counter when she came in. I was with Dad at the back of the shop. He was supposed to be sorting out a consignment of wrapping paper that had just come in, but he'd got into a mess with it, so I'd gone to help him. I couldn't see the door from where I was, but I knew when she came in, I knew it. I can't say how I knew. I just did. I stopped what I was doing and I went back into the shop and there she was. Like I say, my husband served her, but she saw me and she smiled at me when she took her change. I went back to what I'd been doing, and when I'd got Dad sorted out I had to go and help with the serving because we were so busy, but I was useless for the rest of the afternoon; I got the orders wrong, I gave out the wrong change twice, and I couldn't seem to make my fingers work right when I was wrapping up the boxes. I knew it was ridiculous, I knew it. I just couldn't help it. That's the way love takes you though, isn't it? Well, so they say. It was all a new experience for me.

We're open all day on Saturdays and Sundays, but there's always a quiet time from about half-past three in the afternoon until just before five. I told my husband I wasn't feeling well as soon as things went a bit slack — I said I had a headache. What I wanted was to be on my own for a bit. I wanted to think about what had happened.

What had happened was that she'd come back when I'd thought I would never see her again. What had happened was that she had smiled at me. What had happened was that she had taken off her lovely grey suit and put on a pair of slacks and a sweater and a blue jacket, and she'd uncoiled her hair. What had happened was that I knew she must be living round here. She had to be living round here, because she wouldn't have come into the shop dressed like that if she wasn't. I mean, we weren't famous or anything. People didn't travel across the city just to buy one of our boxed lunches. Our trade was local, and she'd come back, on a Saturday, dressed in casual clothes, so she was local. And she'd smiled at me. She'd remembered.

I was right. I saw her again the next week. I saw her twice: once, early in the morning, I was in the shop cutting up and I saw her go by the window on her way to the station, on her way to work, I suppose, because she was carrying that little briefcase and a big, flat, black bag, and she was dressed beautiful again, beautiful. Then I saw her when I was out doing some deliveries. That was at night. She was all dressed up in sports clothes. She was running along by the side of the road and I went by her in the van. I watched her for such a long time in the mirror. I watched her until she faded into the darkness and the lights of the traffic behind me. When I couldn't see her anymore, when I got out of the van to drop off an order, I stopped for a minute and I said a prayer. I said, 'Please let me see her again. Please let me talk to her properly. Please make her love me.'

She came back into the shop on a Wednesday about ten days after that. It was the same time as when she'd come in before and I was on my own again. We were right out of everything that day so she took some little bits of the different salads that we do: some macaroni, some potato salad, some coleslaw, the last few bits of fried chicken. I weighed everything and put it all into containers and wrapped them up for her. All in all it came to less than eight hundred yen but she handed me a ten thousand yen note. Well, I didn't have any change. Like I say, we'd finished the rush, and my husband doesn't like leaving a lot of cash in the till so he usually clears it all out as soon as he can and takes it to the bank. We don't put a float back in until we open again for the tea-time trade. If we do get the odd customer come in, whoever's behind the counter makes change out of their own purse and then gets it settled up at night.

Well, I didn't have enough in my purse to give her her change and so I had to leave the shop and go upstairs to see if my father could help me out. There was nobody else in the shop, and I knew my husband would be furious if he came back and found a customer waiting in front of an empty counter, but I didn't know what else to do. I was in a terrible state as it was, being on my own with her and then not having what she wanted, not being able to give her her change. I think my Dad knew something was the matter, but he didn't say anything. He just counted out the notes and the coins and put them in my hand, and then I went back down the stairs.

She was waiting for me, of course. I gave her the money and the food, and then, do you know, there was this moment, this sort of hole in time, when she was just standing there, looking at me. I didn't know what to do. I kept thinking to myself, what should I do? There was this silence and her looking at me and saying nothing, just looking at me. My heart was racing, so it was, just racing and I thought, please go away, just go away before you see how ugly I am, before you find out how stupid I am. Then she smiled at me and she said how much she liked the food we made, and all the clocks started ticking again and I said something, I can't remember what, something, and we started talking, just like that.

She must have stayed for twenty minutes that day, just chatting, asking me things about the shop, about myself, telling me things about herself. She had just moved into the neighbourhood. She'd got one of the flats over the new bank that had been built where the grocery store and the umbrella shop used to be. She was working just three stops up the line in some sort of studio place. Well, I assumed she must be a hairdresser because a lot of them have studios, don't they, but when I said she had lovely hair and that must come from being in the trade she laughed, in this lovely way, like music really, she laughed and she said not that sort of studio. It was a design studio. I didn't know what she was talking about, really, but I said something about how interesting that must be, and she laughed again because she must have seen that I didn't understand what she'd said, and she told me she was an architect. She gave me her card, and when I took it from her I looked down at my hands again and I was so ashamed I could have just run away from her then and there. It was beautiful, that card, like everything else about her, and I held that beautiful card in my fingers. It seemed a shame to me. It still does.

I held that card for a long time after she'd gone. I kept looking at it, and I kept reading her name, Satoko Inoue, and her address. I had to tell her who I was because the shop cards just have my husband's name on them. It's funny, but when I told her I used my own family's name, my Dad's name, I did it deliberately. I didn't want anything that connected me with my husband to come into contact with her.

So there I was, all by myself in the shop, holding her card, thinking about her name, and what she'd said to me. What she'd said to me was, 'See you again.' I must have been in a trance because I didn't hear my husband come in, not until he shouted at me and even then I didn't really hear him. I just heard her saying, 'See you again', and I kept thinking, yes, see you again, see you again.

She started coming into the shop regular after that, and she always had something to say to me, even if the place was full of people. Mostly she came in when things were slack and then we'd have a proper talk, but even when there were people lining up in front of the counter she would have something to say. It was like she wanted me to know that we were friends, and that it didn't matter how busy things were, there was always a bit of time that was just for us. I was so glad she did that because we were becoming friends, it wasn't just me, it wasn't just my imagination. I loved her, of course, I really did, but I knew for her it wasn't like that, even though I wished it was, but we were becoming friends.

After that first time when we'd talked, everything seemed really easy. I found it was easy to talk to her, and it was easy to say things to her, all sorts of things. I've never been one for talking, me. I've always had trouble putting things into words, even with people I really like. When I was little everyone used to say that I was the quiet one in the family. I suppose I was, but it wasn't because I wanted to be like that; I didn't. There was lots that I wanted to say, that I wanted to talk about, I just couldn't, that was all. Like I say, I couldn't put things into words.

It was different with her. I found I could talk to her until the cows came home, really, and I could say things to her that I couldn't have said to anyone else, ever. I don't know why it was like that, I just know that it was. It was easy. Perhaps it was because I loved her. I did love her and even though I knew she didn't love me it was still all right. She came into the shop and I could see her, I could talk to her. I was quite happy with that, but then something happened, not a big thing, but it changed everything else and I knew I couldn't be happy any more. I knew I had to have more than seeing her over the counter, and chatting to her for ten or fifteen minutes once or twice a week. I knew that I had to be with her all the time, and I knew that I had to make her love me as much as I loved her. Like I said, it wasn't a big thing that happened, it wasn't a big thing at all. It was just that I went out one morning and I met her on the train.

It was my day off. I had some errands, as usual. I could have done them local, but I thought I'd like to get out of the neighbourhood for a bit so I decided to go to the big shops in Nihonbashi. I got myself ready and went down to the station and I was standing on the platform, miles away, I was just thinking about this and that, when I heard somebody talking to me and it was her. It was Satoko Inoue. I panicked for a minute, I really did. I didn't know what to do. You see I'd got used to talking to her in the shop, but this was different. There wasn't a counter in between us and — and well, it was all different and unexpected. What it was really was the way I was dressed. I mean, there she was, looking like a fashion model, and there I was. I just felt ridiculous. I've never really had the money for clothes for a start, and then, I've never known what to buy when I have had a bit to spend on myself. That day I was wearing — well, I don't want to think about it really. I just looked really stupid and she looked so beautiful, like she always did, and when I realized who it was that was speaking to me I kept thinking that I wished it was anyone, anyone except her; which was stupid really, because ever since she'd started coming into the shop regular I'd been dreaming about this. It was just that, in the dreams, I was dressed like she was dressed, and I wasn't little and ugly, and my hair was done nicely, and my fingernails were like hers and — oh, everything.

She saw something was wrong as soon as I looked at her because she asked me if I was all right, and she still seemed concerned even when I said that everything was fine. She asked me where I was off to and when I told her she said that, if I didn't mind, she'd come along with me, which made me feel even more uncomfortable. I asked her about work and she said she'd telephone her office. She was late anyway, she'd been up late the night before trying to finish something and she'd overslept. She still hadn't got the work done so she thought she might as well take the day off, come shopping with me, and then start working at home again in the evening. I asked her if she wouldn't get into trouble doing something like that and she said she didn't really think about trouble. She said that she believed you should do what you wanted to do, trouble or no trouble. She said you just had to want to do whatever it was badly enough, and then you could do it. You could sort out the trouble afterwards. If you let what might happen stop you living your life then you were not living your life, other people were living it for you. That's what she said, more or less. It didn't mean a lot to me at the time, I was just embarrassed at the thought of her being seen with someone like me in a posh shop like Takashimaya.

I can't honestly say that I enjoyed myself that day. I was too nervous, and, in fact, I ended up having to get all my shopping local anyway, because I didn't want her to see the sort of things I needed to buy. Still, when I think about it now, it was all a bit of an eye-opener for me. I mean the way she acted, and the things she told me, the places she took me — well, it was all new, to me anyway, but she just seemed to take it all in her stride, as if to say, look, this is the way I live, and if you want to, it can be the way you live.

It was like, when we wanted to get something to eat, we went to this French restaurant in a big department store that I'd never even seen before, and there was a foreigner, a real Frenchman in fact, to take us to our table. I felt out of place there. Well, of course, I would, wouldn't I? I mean all those women in their expensive clothes, and that foreign man pulling the chair away from the table for me, and all the knives and forks and spoons that I didn't know one from another. I think if I'd have been there with anybody else I'd have run out into the street again; or I would've sat there blubbing. But I wasn't with anybody else, I was with her and she made it — well, if not all right, then tolerable, if you see what I mean. She saw when I was in trouble and she helped me get out of it, like with knowing what to order and which spoon or fork to use with what, that sort of thing.

I felt terrible when I finally got home. I mean I was worn out with it all, all that strangeness. I felt I just wanted to get into the house and take my clothes off and have a bath, and a cup of tea, and then go to bed. Yet, there was something else there as well, something inside of me like, a feeling sort of

thing, as if I'd done something that day, something important. I felt that something had happened to me that day and
even if I wasn't sure what it was, and if I wasn't sure that I
quite liked whatever it was, at the same time I felt that it was
important. I wanted a bit of time to myself to try and
understand it. I wanted to get into the bath and just stay
there thinking about the day, and the things I'd seen and
done, and all the things she'd told me about herself and her
life, because I knew it was all affecting my life. I knew it was.
I could feel it. Of course, I didn't get into the bath until
nearly midnight, and by that time I was too tired to think.
Still, I knew I wouldn't be the same after that day, and there
was something else I knew, that I was going round to Satoko
Inoue's flat the next week. She'd invited me.

It was lovely where she lived, really lovely. It was all new,
of course, the building and that, so it was ever so clean. I
liked that, and I liked the way she'd got everything set up.
She had three rooms and a dining-kitchen, so there was a lot
of space, and because she didn't have very much in the way
of furniture, and there weren't any kids running around
making everywhere dirty, the place seemed even bigger than
it was. I was really envious and I told her so. I didn't mean
to, it just slipped out sort of a way. I thought she might be a
bit offended with me but she wasn't, she just smiled and said,
well, there were a lot of things that I had she was envious of.
Of course, I said I couldn't think what they might be so she
told me: a family, she said, you have a family.

Now, thinking about that, I don't believe she meant what
she said, although, as it turned out, she didn't have a family.
She was quite alone in the world when I knew her; her
parents were both dead, and she'd been their only child. She
didn't have a boyfriend either, we talked about that later; she
said she wasn't interested in men at all, except as friends.
The men she knew weren't interested in being friends, they
wanted more, what my mother used to call 'privileges', you
know. Perhaps she did envy me in some ways, although I

couldn't think why then, and I still can't now, but perhaps
she did, in some ways. Really, though, I think she just said
that — about envying me — to get me talking because, you
see, she'd told me such a lot about herself, how she'd gone to
the unversity and then lived abroad all by herself for three
years, and working in that studio and everything, she'd told
me all of this, but I hadn't really told her anything at all
about myself and it was time, I knew that myself, I knew it
was time.

Well, I told her. I told her about the kids, and I told about
my Dad. I told her about growing up around here, and how
different everything was then. I told her about my husband,
about how I'd met him and why I'd married him. I told her
about the shop; about what it was like frying shrimps and
bits of whitefish and battered vegetables all day long, and
being on your feet from six o'clock in the morning until after
eleven at night six days a week, fifty-two weeks a year — not
counting the four days we closed in the summer and the four
days we closed in the New Year. I told her what it was like to
do that year in and year out, from when I was a young girl,
year in and year out. I told her, and she listened and then,
when I'd done, she just asked me why I didn't leave.

I tell you, that question, that question really shook me. I
sat there, looking at her, looking at her waiting for an
answer, and I could hear myself and all that I'd just been
saying, and it was so obvious what she'd asked me, it was so
obvious, but I'd never thought of it before. In the end I knew
I couldn't think about it and so I just said that I couldn't and
when she asked me why not, I said that I couldn't because of
the kids and because of my father.

She didn't say anything else about it after that, as if the
matter was closed. It wasn't. Even I knew that, but she acted
as if it was. She gave me some more tea, and another piece of ·
cake, and she started talking about something else. After
another hour or so I said I'd have to go, and she said all

right. I got up, and then she got up, and she went to the door with me. She didn't say she'd see me again when we said goodbye. She didn't need to. She knew and I knew she would see me again. We didn't need the words anymore.

I went home and I tried not to think about that afternoon and what had happened, but I couldn't help it. I had to think about it. I had to think about her, and where she lived and how she lived. I was jealous, I think. I had this little hard stone of envy in me that I'd never had before. I was envious of her — not the flat, although it was ever so nice, no, it was her I was envious of, the way she lived. You see, there was inside of Satoko Inoue this idea, this idea she had about herself, and it was so completely different from the idea that was inside me about myself that, well, we might have come from different countries, different worlds even. She explained it to me a bit later on, when things got so bad for me that I had to talk to her about what was going on: she said that the difference between us was that she looked at the world and said, yes, I can, and I looked at the world and said, no, I can't, or no, I shouldn't, or no, I daren't. And she was dead right, that's exactly what I did do, when I looked at the world at all, that is.

Well, the days went by and I got through them because I knew that on such and such a day at such and such a time I would see her, I would be with her, I would talk to her. I knew I was in love with her. I lived just for her, just for her and the times when I saw her. I loved her and I needed her, and I began to neglect them that loved and needed me. I mean the kids, of course, and Dad. It wasn't anything you could see — I mean, I still got up to make the kids their lunch boxes and see that they were fed and washed and dressed nicely for school, and I still sat with Dad and listened to him talking about the old days. It wasn't in that sort of a way I neglected them, it was much worse than that because it was in my heart. I don't think the kids ever knew, but Dad did. I could see it in his face sometimes. You know,

I'd be doing something, and not really thinking about what I was doing because I would be off somewhere in my head with Satoko Inoue, and then I'd catch myself and I'd see Dad looking at me. I think he knew.

I used to think about her all the time. Well, you do, don't you, when you're in love the way I was in love, you do think about the person all the time. I thought about her, and I worried about her, as well, but then, you do that, too, when you're in love. I don't mean I worried about her in the way I worried about the kids, or even about Dad — is she getting enough to eat, did she put a good warm coat on this morning — it wasn't that sort of worrying at all. No, it was more, will she really meet me next Wednesday afternoon, or will she come into the shop on Saturday, and what will I do if she doesn't, if she doesn't meet me, if she doesn't come into the shop on Saturday? It was worrying about that and about what she felt for me and why she felt whatever it was she felt for me, and it was worrying about losing her, about her meeting somebody else she liked more than she liked me, some man, or some woman. More than anything else it was worrying about that.

I think it was the worrying made me do what I did, in the end. I mean, run away, run away from home, run away to be with her.

It wasn't anything at home made me do it, I know that. I mean, nothing changed there. There wasn't any big scene or anything. It was just that I couldn't bear being apart from her anymore. I didn't hate my children, and I didn't hate my Dad. The night I walked out I thought my heart would break when I looked at the kids' faces just before I went through the shop and into the street, because then they knew, they really knew that something had happened and that Mummy was going away. I didn't even hate my husband. I didn't have any feelings about him at all, not one. It was her. It was being apart from her. I couldn't stand it anymore, so I just stopped what I was doing, I just stopped. I walked into the back of the shop and I took my overall off.

I took my overall off and I went upstairs. I got some of my clothes and put them in a little bag: just some underwear, and a sweater and jeans, I got my few bits of make-up and my toothbrush, and washed my hands and face while I was about it. I got all the things I thought I'd need for a couple of days into the bag, I ran a comb through my hair, and then I went.

I walked out through the shop, and my husband just looked at me a bit strange like, you know, where's she going at this time of night, but that was all. He didn't say anything, nothing. He just looked and then went back to serving, because there were customers waiting. Dad was there, he'd just opened up one of the big rice cookers, but I could see him through the steam. I know he understood that something had happened. I wished, just for a minute, that I could have told him. Then I opened the door and I was out in the street and turning in the direction of Satoko Inoue's flat. I was crying by that time, but whether I was crying because I was leaving my kids or whether it was because I was going to her I didn't know, and I didn't want to know.

She didn't seem surprised when she answered the buzzer. I just said it was me, and something had happened and could I stay with her for a few days. It wasn't what I wanted to say, but even I wasn't silly enough to tell her I loved her and that I'd left my family for her through a door-phone. She let me in, and she took my coat and the bag, she put a kettle of water on to boil, and when it was ready she made a pot of tea. A bit later she asked me if I wanted something to eat and although I hadn't felt hungry before then, when she asked me I had this sudden desire for food. It's funny now, looking back, all she had in the house was one of our box-lunches that she'd bought the day before and never touched, so we shared that. About ten o'clock she said she had some work to do for the next day, and she'd probably be working until late.

So she showed me where I was to sleep and where the bathroom was, and the lavatory, and she left me to it. She said she'd see me in the morning, and I thought, yes, in the morning, and in all the mornings to come, although I think that even then I knew I wouldn't, I wouldn't see her in all the mornings to come, and, of course, I didn't, so I was right about something, after all.

I stayed in the flat for four days, and in that time I never once went outside. I daren't. If I had someone would have seen me. I mean, I was only ten minutes' walk away from the place where I'd been born and lived all my life. Someone would have seen me, and then they'd have told my husband. I couldn't go out.

I didn't see that much of Satoko Inoue in the four days I was with her. It was a very busy time at her studio, she said, and she had a lot of work to do. She used to leave before eight in the mornings, and it was sometimes nine and later when she got back at night. She'd sit with me for a bit then, and we'd eat together, I'd always be famished because I'd have eaten next to nothing all day long, but then she'd go off to where she had her work all set up and I'd go to bed.

We went through three days like that, and then, on the fourth day, it was a Saturday, Satoko Inoue came back from work around midday and we sat down together to have something to eat and she asked me if I wanted to talk about why I was there. It was that way she had, you know, of asking you the most obvious questions straight out so that you couldn't find the answer you wanted, and you just said the first thing that came into your head, and it was never quite the right thing. It was never entirely wrong, but it was never quite right, either. I said I was there because I loved her.

It was another of those times between me and her when all the clocks stopped and there was this sort of emptiness in the air, like when you pull the plug in the bath and there's always that moment when the bath is emptying but it seems as if it isn't, and then suddenly the water starts to make a noise as it goes down the drain and everything starts up again, you get out and you dry yourself and you get dressed, and start your life again. That's how it was when I told Satoko Inoue that I was in her flat with her because I loved her. Everything stopped, and then she spoke and everything started again.

She spoke, and she told me that what I'd just said was one of the loveliest things she'd ever heard and I thought, it's all right, it's all right, I've told her and it's all right. It's the loveliest thing she's ever heard, I've just told her the loveliest thing she's ever heard. I wanted to kiss her then. I wanted to touch her and to hold her and do all of those things that people want to do when they love somebody. I went to where she was sitting, and I knelt in front of her and touched her hands, her lovely hands, and I put my face close to her face and I closed my eyes and I kissed her.

I kissed her. I kissed her. I kissed her, and that was all. I kissed her face, but she did nothing, nothing at all. She didn't kiss me back: she didn't not kiss me back. She just did nothing, and doing nothing she told me that I had made a mistake, so I opened my eyes, and I let go of her hands and I went back to the place where I had been sitting such a long, long time before. I'd made a mistake.

We had a drink of wine. She fetched a bottle from out of the fridge. It was cold, and tasted sour, but then I wasn't used to drinking wine. I drank it anyway, watching how she did it and copying her. When we'd both had a glass she asked me if I was all right. I said, yes, I was all right, and then she asked me if I understood, and I said, yes, I understood. Then I said that I'd made a mistake and I tried to tell her how sorry I was but she stopped me by saying that it wasn't a mistake, it was a misunderstanding, a slight misunderstanding, and I said, yes, a slight misunderstanding.

She asked me if I wanted another glass of wine, but I said

that I didn't. I said I would get my things and I'd go home, and she asked me if that was what I really wanted to do. I said it was, because I had to look after the children, and then there was my Dad. She said that just because some things were impossible it didn't mean that everything was, and I said I knew that, but I wanted to go back to look after my children; and it was true, I did, it was just that I didn't want to look after my children as much as I wanted to be allowed to love her, even though it wasn't possible, not the way I wanted it, even though we'd had a slight misunderstanding.

So, I went home. I went back to the shop, and my kids, and my Dad, and my husband. I had a good cry that night in the bath, and then I got on with things again. It was Sunday, of course, the next day, our busiest time in the shop, which was probably just as well. My husband didn't say anything; nobody did. It was as if nothing had happened. Life started again, just like that, and I had to start again with it, or, at least, I had to try. It wasn't very easy in the beginning, but it got easier in time, although it was a long time.

I still saw Satoko Inoue. She came into the shop sometimes, and once or twice we went out shopping together. Then, about eight months after it had all happened, she had me over to her flat again for tea and she told me she was going away. She said she'd been given the chance to work abroad for a year and that she'd decided to go. Again, I didn't know what to say to her, so I just said that it all sounded very nice, very exciting. And then in a month it was all decided. She was packed and ready to go; the flat was up for rent again in the estate agent's window. She came by the shop to say goodbye the day before she was due to leave. I'm glad she did it like that because I couldn't have got through a goodbye if there'd just been the two of us on our own somewhere. My husband was there, in the shop. He was cleaning shrimps for the evening rush. When Satoko Inoue was gone he asked me who she was, and I said she was just a customer I'd got friendly with. He didn't ask anything else.

I thought she'd write from abroad, but she didn't, and she didn't get in touch again when she came back. I bought myself a little diary when she left, and I marked off the months that she'd be away, so I knew when she was supposed to come home. Perhaps she liked it where she was and didn't want to come back. I don't know. Once I thought I saw her in the subway, and I called out but it wasn't her, it was just me wishing that it was.

# A FLOATING WORLD

Eiko was afraid of the city even before she saw it. At the airport she had been drawn with the crowd into the narrow funnel of the immigration zone and only the hold she had on her husband's jacket assured her that she would somehow get through this fresh ordeal. Jun towed her behind him, his own hands filled with the bag she had declared herself incapable now of carrying, and their passports. The passports were more important than the bag. They were caught near the front of the crowd of passengers when the shouting had begun, and Eiko's tremulous courage failed.

It had been impossible to know what was happening. In the narrow space people tried to break from the crush and for a moment she felt her hand lose its hold on her husband. The shouting seemed terrible to her, and she began to sob, her eyes closed, until Jun's familiar essence, his cologne, the faint musk of tobacco that came from his clothes, from his hair, brought her back to herself. He was with her, strong and living by her side, and when she opened her eyes again she tried to quiet her emotions.

A woman with red hair was shouting, screaming almost, at a fat, unshaven man in some sort of uniform. The woman took a passport from the table and pushed it at the man, who snatched it from her and tossed it onto the table again.

Again, the woman picked it up. Again the man threw it down.

There was a boy with the woman, very young, and very pale, with long hair that was combed back and plaited into a braid, like a girl's. He seemed to be trying to reason with the man. Of course, Eiko could not understand what was being said, any of it, but the sounds the boy was making seemed to her ears soothing and placatory. Then the soldiers came and the red-haired woman and the boy were taken away.

Another table had been set up on the other side of the narrow corridor and the business of checking and stamping passports began again. Eiko hoped that they would be able to go to this new table, but accepted that fate would not allow them this, even this, small favour, and she was right. They came before the unshaven, angry man and he pulled the passports from Jun, shifting his staring eyes from the photographs to their faces again and again before he let them go through to wait for their suitcases.

Even then it had not ended. There was some delay in getting the baggage off the aircraft and, while they waited, Jun had left her to go up to the girl behind the desk marked 'Informazione'. Eiko followed him because she was so afraid of being left on her own.

He wanted to ask the best way of getting into the city, but the girl's face remained unmoved by his question. When he repeated it, the girl seemed impatient with the query and waved her hand at Jun, as if telling him to go away. When he spoke again, she shouted at him, and Eiko hoped that he would shout back but he did not, instead he turned to Eiko and shouted at her. She had forgotten the bag he had entrusted to her; she could see it, where she had left it, pushed underneath the bench on which he had told her to sit.

He was angry with her, as if anger were a disease one caught too easily here, but whether his anger was because of her carelessness in a country of thieves, or her carelessness in a country of terrorists and bombs, she was not sure, and her uncertainty made her cry again.

Afterwards, in the taxi that took them across the causeway, he was gentle and consoling. He need not have been. He had explained to her again and again how vigilant she must be in Europe. It was not only the thieves. The Red Army terrorists had become active once more that spring, and all Japanese must be suspect to the foreigners they moved amongst in such great numbers now. He was gentle and consoling as they drew near to the city, and when the taxi stopped and they got out her apprehension was all but forgotten.

Eiko found herself standing in nothing more extraordinary than a car park. And then Jun picked up their bags and they set off in the direction the driver had indicated and it seemed the city rose up before them suddenly, like a spectre, its domes and towers floating, insubstantial and unrooted, above the water, the water.

They had come to Europe, and for Eiko it was the first time to travel so far away from her home and to such foreign places. She had been unsure when Jun first suggested the scheme. Of course, she had been to Hawaii, but somehow that had not seemed foreign at all, or, at least, it had not seemed foreign in the way London was foreign, and Paris was foreign and Munich, and, now, this place. They had gone to Hawaii for their honeymoon, with a party of fifty other newly-married couples. They had flown on a Japan Airlines charter flight, and the first foreigner she had seen was a lady from the American Customs and Immigration service, a fat lady, the fattest lady she had ever seen, so fat she seemed like a large and jolly baby, who waved all of the couples through behind the banner of their tour guide. And in the airport at Honolulu there were so many other Japanese behaving just as they did at home, that it was hard for Eiko to believe she was not still in Japan.

It was the same in the hotel. Sometimes one of the waiters would be an American, but not often, and once, once she had gone back to the room to collect something and surprised the maids and they had spoken to her in English, but she had laughed and said, 'Yes, yes, thank you very much', as Jun had taught her, and run away again. Whenever they went out of the hotel it was with all the others, so it seemed that they had not really been to a foreign country at all, they had simply borrowed a little part of one for a short time. It was not like that here, and it had not been like that since they had left Japan ten days before.

It was in London that Eiko knew she had made a great mistake in agreeing to Jun's plan, but she had become caught up in his excitement and enthusiasm for the scheme and had quite forgotten her usual caution. He had come home early one evening and unannounced, so that nothing was ready and she had not bathed or done her hair or make-up. It had not mattered; he had been so excited he had not noticed her paled lips and shrunken eyes, or the unwashed dishes in the sink, or the bed still as it had been when he left it that morning. He had his plan to tell her about.

He had read the results of a newspaper survey as he stood in the train on his way to the office, and it was as if what he read had put a fever in his head. He could not work; he could not work because he could think only of what he had read, and the idea that had spawned from his reading.

The survey had investigated the hopes and dreams of what was already being called the 150 generation, the youth under the age of thirty who had been emancipated from the necessary servilities of their parents and grandparents by the new-found power of the yen, trading with ever-increasing advantage now against the American dollar. The survey questioned a representative section of these new Japanese as to their most secret desires; one, the one that occurred again and again, was to travel abroad, independently.

And as soon as he had read this, Jun told her, he had known what he had not known before, that this was his own most secret desire, so secret, his mind had held it in its deepest levels, until, released, it had surged to consciousness like a swimmer desperate to break the surface of the sea for air. Once known it could never be forgotten; once set free it could never be taken captive again, and returned to the place in which it had for so long been imprisoned.

So, they would go, he said. They would go soon and they would go alone. He was so strong in his convictions and, as he spoke, as he outlined the many justifications he saw which supported them, she began to see with his eyes, and she began to see that he was right. They were modern in so much else. They had been married for five years and had no children, not because they could not, but because, in spite of the questions from aunts and others — married friends, even now their own parents — they would not. Jun said he did not want a child littering their apartment with toys and leaving its fingermarks upon the windows and the television screen, and Eiko was glad because she did not want to look like the other women in their building, dragging to the supermarket with the little ones on their backs, their figures gone, their nails gone, their hair hidden in the hasty wrapping of a scarf. Eiko was proud of her figure, and jealous of the power her body gave her over her husband, the power that made him come home, always, always come home, no matter how late, to her and only to her.

They were modern. They went to jazz clubs on Friday nights, and French restaurants on Saturday evenings. Eiko smoked, occasionally, and in public, and had her own gold American Express card. On Sundays, they spent much of the day in bed, although of course, Eiko woke early to attend to her hair and make-up, for, with the exception of that one occasion already mentioned, Jun had never seen her except at her best. When, finally, they did get up, they dressed themselves in silk pajamas, sent out for pizza, and drank wine, French wine, until late into the evening. They were modern, and if Jun said they should go abroad on their own, then they would do so.

But her certainty had not survived for very long. They had gone first to London, Jun deciding that they would use a foreign airline for the flight, beginning, he said, as they intended to go on. It was awful, even though they were in First Class. They were the only Japanese in that section of the aircraft, except, that is, for the two Japanese stewardesses, who were obviously and quite pointedly rude to Eiko. It is true that the British cabin crew were friendly, kind even, but because Eiko could not speak to them, their friendliness was often almost maliciously besides the point. And Jun could not help her because he slept through most of the long flight.

Jun had a weakness, the only one she had discovered in all the time of their marriage: he was terrified of flying. He dealt with his fear by drinking excessively before boarding the aircraft, and then, as soon as he was seated, taking two of the sedatives his father, who was a very successful doctor, provided him with each time he travelled. He was usually unconscious as the aircraft left the ground.

Alone then, or as good as alone, Eiko had endured the comforts of the forward cabin, and longed for the friendly fug of deprivation in the Tourist section, with its full complement of recent graduates and newly-weds, and circles and clubs and associations.

London, where they were for three nights, distilled itself down into three or four shops and a sequence of increasingly uncomfortable and, Eiko was convinced, unhygienic, theatre seats. The shop assistants were unfriendly, snatching at the money they were offered, and anyway, all of the things on sale were easily available at home. It was true that they were cheaper here, but it was only when Jun found the Mitsukoshi store in New Bond Street that Eiko knew a small sense of ease. Even this was vitiated by the fact that the Japanese assistants were very common types, who would most certainly not have been considered for employment at the Tokyo store. So they spent the mornings shopping, and the afternoons and evenings sleeping through musicals they had already seen, but which they felt they had to go to in London for the pleasure of being able to display the stubs of their 'unobtainable' tickets to their friends when they returned home.

Even their attempts to eat out were disasters. They were humiliated by the waiters in the Café Royal when they tried to have an English tea there, and although a dinner at Simpson's in the Strand — where they were entertained by a friend of Jun's who was with the embassy in London — met with much greater success, the meat Eiko ate did not agree with her and she vomited in the taxi on the way back to the hotel. Thereafter they took all their meals in the hotel's restaurant, although Eiko ate almost nothing, finding the food too rich for her.

Paris was better, a little. They had learned certain lessons in London, and anyway, there were more friends to see who lived in the city and spoke the language. For one day Eiko felt that Jun had been correct after all in what he had done, but then she had gone to an exclusive leather goods store and suffered the indignity of having her hand stamped with an admission number to make sure that she did not enter the store again that day after she had made her permitted purchases.

She saw almost nothing of Munich because both she and Jun came down with a stomach virus on the first afternoon and were confined by necessity to their room. Now they were in Venice, where, Eiko was soon to find, they did not even have the comforts of a decent hotel.

They had not meant to visit Venice. It was not on the itinerary Jun had prepared. He had been persuaded by his friend, the man at the embassy in London, who had recently returned from a short secondment to the consulate in Milan.

It was he who had recommended that they cut short the time they had planned to spend in Germany and go to Venice. He said it was a city of dreams.

Jun had made the additional travel arrangements, but the time when they would be there was the festival of Easter, and there was not a room to be had at any of the hotels the guide books recommended. There were hotels with vacancies on the Lido, but Jun's friend counselled against staying there. They had to be in Venice itself, or abandon the visit altogether. Jun, with the idea of this shimmering, insubstantial place inflaming his will, would not be deflected from his goal. At last the travel agency he was dealing with telephoned to say they had a double room at a small hotel on the Lista di Spagna. Jun would not listen to the agency clerk's reservations about the quality of the hotel. He secured the room at once, and then arranged for the flight from Germany.

They stood now, looking at the seeming mirage of buildings, domes and towers, palaces and churches, and two men with a little cart approached, asking if they required porters to take their luggage to their hotel. Jun, the realization of whose dream had made him strong again and still, indicated his acceptance of the offer, and the men put the two suitcases, and the smaller bag that had been the cause of his anger at the airport, onto the cart and set off across the first bridge. Jun and Eiko followed behind.

The hotel confirmed all the doubts that had swollen in Eiko as she walked into the city. It was set back from the Grand Canal, in a long street of souvenir shops, leavened here and there by a pharmacy, a tourist restaurant. The lobby was small, so small that the couch which was its solitary furnishing seemed too much, and the chest of drawers serving as a reception desk could hardly accommodate the man who answered Jun's ringing of the bell.

Their room, when they saw it, disappointed them again.

The air was stale, and the sheets on the bed — which, upon investigation was not a double bed at all but two single divans covered with a thin double mattress — though clean, were patched and mended. There was no bath. There was no lavatory. There was a washbasin, but for all the more intimate requirements of her toilet Eiko realized she must cross the wasted space of the vestibule that lay beyond the door, and she did not know how she would manage this, in the mornings and in the evenings, particularly in the evenings.

It was almost evening now, and Jun, the door shut, went to open the windows that ran along one side of the room, ensuring privacy by closing the green slatted shutters immediately afterwards. The noise of the pedestrian traffic in the street below, an ill-mannered mongrel of sound, came bounding, unwelcomed, into the room, crossed the bed to where Eiko sat, and circled round and round her. Jun went to open the doors of the shallow cupboard that must serve to hold their clothes, and then, having done so, lacked the heart to begin the process of unpacking. He sat by his wife instead, and together, without moving, without speaking, they began to serve out the time they had condemned themselves to spend in Venice.

It was after eight before they went out again, and then it was hunger, not curiosity, that drove them. Jun had made the journey across the hall to shower. Eiko had not. She had managed a sort of ablution at the small sink in the room. She had not emptied her bladder, however, since just before leaving the airport in Frankfurt. She had a certain modesty in such matters which, allied to a natural reticence and particularity, meant that the only spaces in which she could relieve herself must be spotlessly clean, and designed to secure her against any possible embarrassment. In practice, this meant she could only properly indulge her bodily functions in her own or her parents' home, and then she would continually flush the lavatory as she used it. She really did not know how she would manage in this place and she was at the extremes of her endurance as Jun led her out into the street in search of a restaurant.

They turned to the left as they went out of the hotel, walking along the Lista di Spagna to the point where it feeds itself into the Campo San Geremia. They were intending to walk to a trattoria somewhere along the Fondamenta degli Ormesini, but it was dark now, and a light, cold rain fell on them. Walking on the greasy, trash-strewn stones, they decided, when they came to the Ponte delle Guglie and saw its shroud of steel pipes and the attendant barges moored beneath, and were scared by the uncertain footing of the wooden structure they must cross alongside it, to turn back, preferring the lesser uncertainties of the tourist menu three doors down from their hotel. There they were not deprived of anything that might have added to their disappointment, and the sense they both had of having made the wrong decision in coming to this place of cold, wet streets and dull canals.

Eiko did not sleep and, in the early morning, she wept. It was not her first time of weeping, nor the second. Jun had sought to console himself with her when they returned from the restaurant, but she had denied him. She was in such a state herself, still not having found a toilet she could bring herself to use, that it would have been impossible for her to have done anything else. Jun, of course, could not know this because she could not tell him. He had gone to sleep hurt, and angry again with her.

Eiko wept and waited, waited until she thought no one, no one, could possibly still be awake, and then she put on her raincoat, the one she had bought in London, over the negligee she had bought in Paris, and went with cautious desperation across the cold and dark expanse of floor towards the dim lights of the lavatory and shower. When she got there the lavatory was engaged, so she hid in the shower, listening with increasing despair to the sounds of a man, a foreign man, emptying his bladder and his bowels. She relieved herself at last when he had gone, choking on the stench the man had left behind him as she first wiped the seat and floor with one of the alcohol towels she always carried with her, and sprayed the tainted air with the tart scent of citron.

When she was finished she had to hide again. She used the shower to clean herself, she had no other choice, and the sound of water must have roused another of the guests because she heard a door open, saw a light come on, and heard the rumbled tones of anger, like thunder, in a foreign tongue. Of course, she wept through the sleepless hours of the night until dawn came. There would be another nine days of this to endure before she could begin the long journey home.

She got up before Jun and crossed again to the small shower-room and the lavatory next to it. This time both were unoccupied. She attended to what was necessary, and then, after her shower, applied her make-up, wiping the steam from the mirror in the shower-room. If she had been able to rid herself of the fear that someone, some stranger, or, worse, her husband, might knock at the door before she had finished her face, it might have seemed almost as if she were back in the routine she followed in Tokyo. But she could not rid herself of her fear, and so, when she was satisfied that she was ready, or, at least, when she was satisfied that she was as ready as she would be, could be, she belted her raincoat tightly about her and fled again to her room, placing the key into the lock with as much stealth as she could manage in the dark and with her shaking hand. Then, in the room again, she slipped the raincoat from her shoulders, and got back into bed, carefully, so that she would not disturb either her hair or her husband, or leave traces of powder on her pillow. She would not, she could not sleep.

The weather was bad again. Not the chilling drizzle of the

night before, but heavy, soaking rain. Jun caught Eiko's arm as they stepped out of the hotel doorway, pulling her further under the big, green umbrella. It was cold, and her famished body felt it, felt the cold, felt the damp, at once, like a cloud, a mist, seeping up from the pavements, seeking the flesh beneath the layers of clothing. They had missed by half-an-hour the breakfast the hotel served, and, in the restaurant the night before, faced with the mess of greasy batter which had arrived in response to their order for *frito misto di mare*, Eiko's stomach had revolted after the first mouthful, so that, for nearly twenty-four hours she had taken nothing but coffee, a small cake of such cloying sweetness she had been unable to finish it, two glasses of wine and a little bread. Jun caught her arm, pulling her further under the big, green umbrella and led her over to the café, whose bright and steamy windows he had seen from their room a little earlier.

She did not want to go. What she wanted to do was return to the room and throw herself down on the bed they had left just a little while before, and continue her weeping. Jun would not let her, and not letting her, he saved her.

There were no tables or chairs inside the café. Facing the door was a marble-topped counter which fronted a row of shelves containing a variety of cups and saucers, and an impressively angry Gaggia spitting steam from a bewildering display of chrome pipes and grills. Along another side of the shop, forming the second side of an unfinished square, was a series of glass cases, each filled with one or two kinds of pastry: croissants smeared with chocolate, or spattered with almond flakes, iced whorls, tarts, folds of baked dough oozing cream or custard or marzipan fillings. The couple stood transfixed, as if the moist warm air, ripe with the smells of boiling milk and coffee, marzipan and cinnamon, were narcotic to them. But it was not this that prohibited movement. With Jun it was confusion. With Eiko it was fear, still it was fear.

Human voices called out. A fat man in a white coat, the Gaggia's guardian, or servant perhaps, spoke to them, a question in any language, and gestured that they should approach the white expanse of marble. Movement cleared Jun's confusion, and he pulled out his phrasebook, already open, bent double, at the section for beverages and confectionary. Emboldened by the power of words, Jun ordered coffee — cappuccino for Eiko and espresso macchiato for himself — and then they were taken over to the rows of pastries to choose their breakfast.

Eiko could do nothing still; she was catatonic. If her husband's strong fingers had not maintained their grip upon her arm she might not have been able to prevent herself from sliding to the floor, wet with rain from coats and umbrellas, soiled by shoes. Certainly she could not answer Jun's queries as to what she wanted to eat, and so he chose the cakes for her as he had chosen the coffee for her: an almond croissant, a round bun filled with cream.

She ate, although she thought the first mouthful must choke her, and she drank, sucking the sweet, dark coffee through its beard of milk. And suddenly her fear lifted, and the despair that had all the while kept company with it, fled. She felt the sweetness of the cakes, and the stimulating warmth of the coffee and the milk flood into her bloodstream. Her face flushed, she felt a sudden flash of heat beneath her clothes. She was restored.

They drank another cup of coffee each, and Jun swallowed more of the pastries, before leaving the café for the soaked streets. Jun was strong again and he was certain again. He had the guide to Venice; he had the first day's itinerary that they had worked out together with their friend in London. He knew exactly what he was going to do and because of the sureness of this knowledge Eiko felt safe again, in spite of the rain and the unfamiliar quiet of the streets. Jun would lead her, and she would follow, safely, behind him. It would be the way it always was, and, in the time she had known her husband, always had been. She would not be afraid again because there would be no need for fear.

And it was so. They achieved all that they had set out to achieve that day: the water-bus to the Accademia bridge, the Gallerie dell'Accademia, and then lunch, successfully negotiated at a restaurant on the Calle Lunga San Barnaba. Jun found that he could carry out most of the necessary transactions in English, and, when this was not possible, the phrase-book provided the keys necessary to understanding, in spite of his tongue's reluctance at the softness of the words. He was happy with his prodigiousness: protector, provider and guide to his wife. She was happy to be protected, to be provided for, to be led, along narrow alleys and across broad squares, over bridges and onto boats, all the time without any understanding of their, or her, ultimate destination. In the afternoon, when they had arrived back safely at the small hotel in the Lista di Spagna, Eiko let her husband undress her, and undressed, she took him into her body as an act of gratitude.

She had wanted Jun for her husband from the first time she had seen him, when she was seventeen, and still a child, a silly high-school child. He was twenty-three then, one of the small annual intake of graduates into her father's company. He had been required to call upon her father at their home, not a usual practice, for her father maintained a wall of distances and strategic separations between his family and his business, but not so entirely unusual as to make this particular breach unique. From time to time small crises arose at the company, and from time to time it happened that her father was at home when they arose. If a telephone call to him was not in order, and the crisis was not at all severe, yet still a crisis, then someone at the bottom of the office hierarchy would be sent to bring the boss back. On this particular occasion it was Jun who came and he was so entirely unlike the few others that had come before, Eiko could not help but remember, and, remembering, could not help wanting him.

He was polite, of course he was, and able to show that he knew his place in the scheme of things, of course. Yet, there was something in him that had to do with a certain pride. The others, the ones that she had seen before, were young men in haircuts as unfortunate as their suits. In the boss's house, in the company of the boss's daughter, they were self-conscious and they were miserable.

Jun was not like that. She remembered the sleekness of his hair. She remembered his clothes. It was summer when he came, and he wore a loose suit of grey linen, with a grey shirt and a silk tie, a green silk tie. His skin was lightly tanned, and there was not a blemish on his fine-featured face. When she had stooped to offer him a pair of slippers and straighten his shoes, she could not help but notice that his socks were of the same thread as his tie, and the loafers he wore were imported. Of course she wanted him, but she kept her wanting secret for six years, until she was in her senior year at the University of the Sacred Heart.

She kept her wanting secret for six years, until she was in her senior year at the University of the Sacred Heart, and then, at the beginning of the second semester, her last semester, she spoke to her father. In less than a year, when all the necessary rituals and requirements had been properly settled, she married Jun. He took her father's name, in spite of his own father's standing in society, and entered her father's business.

The sun shone over the weekend of the Easter celebrations. The streets and bridges, the waterbuses, were choked with people. The city seemed to Eiko as if it must sink beneath the weight of them all. She had already asked Jun whether it was wise to tarry long in a place so precariously fashioned upon the water. Jun, seeing the worry in his wife's pretty face return, explained what he knew of the city's construction: the

piles of Istrian pine driven down deep into beds of com-
pressed sand and clay, the foundations of the buildings laid
with sandstone impervious to the corrosion of the sea, the
careful watches kept upon the tides. When his words failed to
ease her mind he took her away, to Chioggia.

On the bus from the Lido Eiko's mood improved enough
for Jun to tease her a little, asking how she could worry that
Venice might sink during their short stay when they lived
their lives in a country which rested on the back of a large
and recalcitrant catfish, a single flick of whose tail would
send the towers of Shinjuku tumbling into the abysses of the
suddenly broken earth. She tolerated his teasing, but he
knew how she worried about the earthquake that one day
must destroy Tokyo; how, each autumn, she duly checked
their knapsacks of dried food, the small supplies of bottled
water, batteries and emergency clothing. They completed
that part of their journey in silence.

In Chioggia they walked along the Corso del Popolo to the
piazza. For the young Japanese couple it was not crowded,
and they were unaware of the good-natured curiosity their
presence engendered amongst those with whom they shared
the warmth of the sun, and the light which came from the
waters. Eiko enjoyed the excusion but, on the steamer to
Pellestrina, as they began their return to Venice, Jun pointed
to a woman with flaming red hair. It was the woman from
the airport, the one who had been taken away by the
soldiers.

She was with a man, a small, dark man, with closely
cropped hair and an unshaven, but not yet bearded, face. He
wore a raincoat, unbuttoned, over a dark blue suit, and, Eiko
could not help but notice, his trousers were too long for him,
so that, at the back, the hems had been trodden under the
heels of his shoes until they were shredded, and thick with
the filth of the streets.

The woman was laughing at something her companion
had said, but then, as if she became aware that other eyes

were watching her, she looked across the deck to the railing where Eiko and Jun were standing. Eiko could not return the stare and turned away. After a few minutes she looked again, but the couple had gone and Eiko did not see them board the bus after the ferry had docked. She was relieved. That night at dinner, she asked Jun how it could be that the woman had been allowed into the country after all, and wondered what had become of the boy she had been with at the airport.

The rain began to fall again. It grew cold again. Jun sought to hold back the effects of the weather with his plans. Each evening, while Eiko showered and dressed before they set off to the place where they had arranged to take their dinner, he would write out a time-table for the following day. The planning had become simply another part of a routine with which the young man hoped to make familiar his wife's now daily encounters with an unknown world. He understood that what she was afraid of was experience itself, and he did his best to ensure that when she must confront it, she should do so only within a space and a time of his own choosing.

Their days began, always, with breakfast at the little café across from the hotel, the place where they had gone on that first morning. They were expected now, and the fat man with the grey hair and the white coat would prepare their coffee as soon as he saw them enter his shop, just as the girls who attended to the pastries and the cakes would have their croissants and cream buns on plates by the time they reached the marble-topped counter. From the café, they would set out into the rain towards the first item on the agenda that Jun had prepared.

There were certain places where they lunched now, and certain cafés where, after lunch, they would take coffee and perhaps a liqueur, and smoke. Then, afterwards, they would return to the hotel to make love and to sleep, and after sleeping go out again for tea at one of the better hotels, the

Gritti, or the Danielli or the Cipriani. At six they returned
again to their own hotel so that Eiko might get herself ready,
while Jun sat with his notebook and his guides and his map.
At eight they would go out to dine.

Jun did not speak Italian, but he was not afraid to stand
with his phrase book in his hand, and over the course of the
passing days, he found himself becoming increasingly familiar and at ease with the necessary words for this and for that.
Much of the time, of course, he spoke English. Eiko was
surprised at first by the number of people in restaurants and
museums who knew what for her, in spite of having gradu-
ated as an English major, remained an obstinately obscure
language. That Jun spoke it, and spoke it well, something
she had not fully been aware of until their honeymoon in
Hawaii, only added to his attractiveness. She had loved to
see him then, as she loved to see him now, at ease in the
foreign world, conversing easily, intimately almost, with
foreign people in a foreign tongue.

One day he further amazed her by purchasing a Venetian
newspaper, and sitting, during the hour after lunch when
they took their coffee, with a dictionary, patiently going
through the entertainments section. Eiko puzzled the words
of the headlines on the outside pages, which seemed yet more
items on the menus they encountered each day at luncheon
and at dinner. Only the photographs made sense to her, the
punctured metal of a car, the shattered windows, lines of
white tape and police in leather coats, the indistinct shadows
at the side of the roadway that were, she knew, even she
knew, not shadows but the shrouded broken pieces of human
beings. Next to the pictures of what the bomb had done were
the faces of those who had, perhaps, set it off: the familiar
faces of a man and a woman, familiar because she had to
look but once to know them for what they were, Japanese.

Jun was not interested in the bombing of an airline office
in Milan; he had discovered that a new season of opera was
to begin at La Fenice the following day. There was no

question, of course, but that they should go. It would make
the holiday.

The day began, as all the days seemed to here, cold and
with a heavy drizzle that promised nothing but an even
heavier rain to come. They were a little late in leaving the
hotel because Eiko found that she had a sore throat when she
woke, and Jun fussed, searching through their luggage for a
scarf to keep her neck warm. All he could find was the
woollen Burberry they had intended as a present for one of
Eiko's aunts. Not only would its use have required the
purchase of a replacement gift, but, Eiko protested, although
she was chilled, she could not bear the thought of wearing
wool against her skin in what was, after all, the spring. So,
when they crossed to the little café for breakfast, she had one
of Jun's handkerchiefs held at her throat. Perhaps it was this,
and not the slight deviation from what had become routine,
which caused the first quizzical looks from the people behind
the counters.

Immediately after they had finished eating Jun insisted on
a search for a silk scarf in the small boutiques along the way
to the Ponte di Rialto. It took most of the morning to find
something that was suitable. In the shops the assistants
raised their hands in dumb expression of the fact that they
did not have what Eiko wanted, and finally, all she could
find was a large square of polyester, printed with a design of
hounds and dead game birds, and that was in a supermarket
they came upon by accident after going back along the route
they had travelled from their hotel as far as the Rio Terra
Della Maddalena.

By lunch-time they had seen nothing of the two churches
Jun had decided they would visit that morning, and Eiko
worried in case his silence was caused by anger with her, as
well as the wet and the cold, and the wasted morning.

They had reservations at a new restaurant they had visited
briefly just before the Easter weekend, but there was no
possibility of reaching it in time now, so they ate, poorly, in a

sandwich place not far from the Rialto bridge. Eiko tried to make conversation, but Jun would say only that they could not visit the restaurant again because he had been unable to cancel their table, and he would be too ashamed to go there, having let the owners down this first time.

Eiko knew that this was true. She also knew his pride was hurt because he had been forced to point to the sandwiches they wanted for lunch, just as the foreigners at home did, pulling the waiters out into the street in elaborate dumbshow and waving with uncertain fingers at the plastic replicas of the food in the showcase outside.

Yet the food, if indifferent, nourished, and the coffee and the wine they drank with the sandwiches warmed their bodies and cheered their spirits. Jun began to regret his mood, the unreasonableness of his behaviour towards his wife; and, if he did not openly apologize to her, his behaviour, like that of a little boy, his bashful expression when he looked at Eiko over his coffee cup, spoke of contrition with a certain precise eloquence. In a spirit of reconciliation, they decided to abandon their plans for the afternoon, and go instead to La Fenice, to purchase their tickets for the opera.

It would have been easier to take the vaporetto to Santa Maria del Giglio, but Jun decided that they should walk. It really was not so very far, but the cold rain, and the wet, close streets oppressed Eiko, and she remembered the fears she had carried with her during the first days in this city which rested upon the waters, darkness falling, the sound of rain and silence along the narrow ways. She had the sense of being followed, of footsteps other than their own upon what, to her, were treacherous stones.

They came on the theatre, as everyone must, suddenly, entering the Campo San Fantin between the walls of the Ateneo Veneto and the church. The campo was small, and Eiko felt for a moment that she could not breathe, that someone had placed the palm of a hand upon her chest and was pushing, pushing.

There was a café across from the church and, in spite of
the weather, the doors had all been opened, exposing a
small, canopied terrace. Jun took her to one of the tables,
and ordered coffee and bottles of mineral water. Then, a few
minutes after they had been served, when he had drunk his
espresso, he said that Eiko should stay at the table while he
went across to the theatre to see about the tickets. He was so
swift and so decisive in this that Eiko found she had no time
to voice any objection, and he was gone from the table and
through the doors of the theatre, and she was alone. It was
then that she saw the small, dark man who had been with the
red-haired woman in Chioggia. He was sitting at a table just
inside the shadowed light of the café itself, and he was
staring at her.

Jun was not gone for more than a few minutes, and when
he returned it was evident from the expression on his face
that there had been some problem, that the day intended
continuing as it had begun. He did not have the tickets, and
he could not explain what had happened because he did not
understand it himself. He sat down with her again, but his
impatience was obvious and they left before she could
properly finish either of her drinks. As they walked across the
little square, Eiko risked a backward glance, but the light
inside the café was so poor now she could not see whether the
man from Chioggia was still there, whether he was still
staring at her.

They walked to the Piazza San Marco. It had not been
Jun's intention that they should visit it at all during their
stay in the city. It was, their friend had told them in London,
better read about than seen, being full of tourists, mostly
Japanese. They went because they were so close, and
because everything else they had planned for that day had
gone wrong. Eiko was glad, but she hid her feelings for she
did not wish to anger Jun again.

They walked about the square, both of them made
nervous by the constant squalls of pigeon feathers and

excrement, but did not enter the Basilica or the Palazzo Ducale, and Eiko was pleased when Jun grudgingly suggested that they go to Florian's, even though her head was already light and her heart beat like the pigeons' wings because of all the coffee she had drunk that day.

They sat inside, on the hard, narrow banquette that ran around the sides of the room. For Eiko, although, again, she did not tell her husband, it was the loveliest moment of their visit, and even the practiced surliness of the waiters, the long wait for their coffee, the non-appearance of the cakes they had asked for, could not diminish it. It was filled with Japanese, of course it was, but this only added to Eiko's happiness, particularly the groups of young girls, college students on graduation holidays, the last stolen moments before they should marry or be swallowed into the routines of offices and banks.

Eiko listened to all those girlish voices, the laughter, and she thought of songbirds let out of cages, and she thought of the cages. She looked at her husband then, and knew how lucky she had been to find him. She looked at her husband and forgave him his unaccustomed moods of that day, and the rain, and the cold, and the dark and fearful streets.

There were five girls sitting at the table closest to her. Eiko knew they were Sacred Heart girls: she knew it from their clothes, from their manner of sitting and the language, the little expressions, the phrasings, they used. She listened and she heard the name of a teacher mentioned, Sister Uchida, the woman who had acted as her mentor for the final year dissertation. She could not help but speak then, identifying herself as an alumna of the school. The response embarrassed Jun, but to Eiko it was as if she had come home, at last, after too long in foreign places, and she was, for the time she was with the girls, content.

They stayed too long and drank too much, too much coffee, too much of the sweet Italian vermouth Jun insisted on ordering for everyone. Jun offered to take the five girls to

dinner, but they declined. They were at a pensione outside of
the city and must return before it grew too late. Their leaving
saddened both Eiko and her husband, and soon they, too,
decided to go from the café, although where they should go
to they could not decide. It was as she stood with her
husband in the doorway of the café, with the light behind
her, that Eiko saw the man from Chioggia again, and this
time she knew it was him, not some other stranger whose
likeness confused her; she knew it, because he was with the
red-haired woman.

He was looking directly at her and then he spoke to the
woman, and she looked. Though she could not see the
woman's eyes behind her black-lensed glasses, Eiko read the
same signs of recognition on her face that she saw on the
man's, signs that even the most tentative of gestures with an
arm or hand would have confirmed.

She took Jun's arm then, and found comfort in the touch,
the certainty of him. Strengthened, she returned stare for
stare until her husband led her away, towards the vaporetto,
having decided they should return to their hotel.

She did not want to go out again that night, but Jun
insisted that they do so. They would walk to the trattoria
they had attempted so half-heartedly to find on their first
evening. Jun's determination to do this thing, and in doing it
exorcise the failures of the day, was apparent in his voice and
Eiko knew he would not now be dissuaded. So she obeyed
him, in spite of the ache in her feet and legs, the headache
caused by too much coffee and the necessity of changing with
her husband's changing moods; in spite of the meetings with
the man, and with the red-haired woman who hid her eyes
behind dark glasses, even in the rain. She went across the
marble space to the shower-room where she styled her hair
again, and again made up her face; she dressed in fresh
clothes, and then, when she was ready, she went out with her
husband, out into the night.

The trattoria was in the Cannaregio district. The rain fell steadily, and the air was cold enough for Eiko to see the vapour of her own breath. She wore the heavy Burberry raincoat, her new scarf, and, for the rain was as determined as her husband's mood, she carried her own umbrella. It seemed a stupidity to be out on such a night, or at least, it seemed a stupidity to be out and intent on walking to a place so far from the hotel, in an area of the city to which they had not yet been, in search of a restaurant they might never find. Jun had shown her the route they would follow on the map, and, on the map, it seemed a simple enough thing, but the rain, and the dark streets were not the map, and Jun still seemed drunk from the vermouth he had taken at Florian's.

They went over the wooden bridge which now served for those who wished to cross the Canale di Cannareggio at this point, and then took up again the path of that morning, along the Rio Terra San Leonardo, but bearing left, tonight, where the road divided, moving away from the tourist city to a new, and altogether different place, of narrow ways and sudden courts; a place where people, not paintings, held sway, where life existed, shut away behind thick walls and dirty, curtained windows.

There were few other people about; here and there some solitary souls perhaps, like moving shadows, and Eiko began to feel uneasy again. She asked Jun if they might not turn around and go back to the hotel. She was not hungry, she had no thirst even, she wanted simply to sleep. Her husband ignored her, and after the defeats of the day she knew why. He needed one victory; he needed this, at least.

They found the trattoria. It was not difficult, well, with her husband leading her, it was not difficult. The place was small, and fronting a perfectly straight canal whose bridges seemed to almost sway in the murk of rain and mist that hovered just above the still waters beneath their narrow spans. Going through the door from the street, Eiko and Jun found themselves in a single, medium-sized room, where a scattered handful of people sat at long tables covered with gingham-patterned plastic cloths.

The boy who took their order had lived in England, and his English, in fact, was rather better than Jun's. From time to time, when he came to clear away the old plates, or bring new ones, he would engage them in conversation, asking Jun where they were from, what they were doing in Venice, what was life like in Japan, did they like music, what kind of music did they like? Jun would laugh and banter with the young man, eating all the while and drinking the red wine that seemed to constantly fill the jug on their table.

When Jun said that he had tried, and failed, to obtain tickets for the opera, the young man at once offered his help in securing some. Jun explained that they would be leaving soon, but this seemed to make the offer urgent even more than enthusiastic, involving not only the young man, but other members of the restaurant's staff. A cook appeared to give advice, and then an older man, with greying hair, whom Eiko was certain was the father, or at the very least, the uncle of the waiter.

The restaurant emptied, but Eiko and Jun stayed on, Jun drinking glass after glass of the wine that was so liberally poured for him. In the end, it was almost midnight before they could get away, and then it was only because Jun had promised to meet the waiter outside the opera house the following afternoon at three, when the trattoria would be closed for the period between lunch and dinner-time. Jun was so drunk by then that he would have agreed to anything, anything at all.

Eiko had to support him on the way back because he could not otherwise have managed by himself. The rain was heavier than ever, making the water of the canals spit as if it was boiling in a pan, making the dim light of the street lamps dimmer still. She could not remember which of the bridges they had crossed to reach the trattoria, and she went too far, so that, when she did get over the canal, it was to find herself in a place where she knew she had never been before.

She told Jun that she was lost, but he could not hear her, or could not answer her, and she knew she must do this on her own, that her husband was now a dead weight she must somehow get back to the hotel.

She was in a place she knew she had never been before. It was a tight, confined space, with a building, like a prison perhaps, massive and dark before her. She had never seen a prison, of course, but she had read of them, she had imagined them. She seemed now to confront her own imaginings. There was no way forward: there was only the way back. She crossed the canal again. She started to return to the trattoria, thinking that perhaps the people there would help her, but then she saw the figures in the rain, a man and a woman, the woman taller than the man. She knew who they were, and she knew what they were doing there, waiting by a bridge in the rain so late at night. She turned, turned her husband, and struggled away from the people who waited in the rain.

When she finally got Jun into the hotel and up to their room, he vomited into the sink, as Eiko had known he would. It seemed a significant gesture to her. It was as if he vomited for her. She did not know how she had done what she had done, but somehow, after it had seemed that she would never find the way out of those terrible streets, she came to a place she knew, and from there, took up her proper path again, following her memory like a thread through the forest, until, at last, they were safe.

Somehow, for she had not had to do so before, she got her husband undressed and washed and into the bed. Then she began to clean up the mess in the sink. This too she had not done before.

Of course, Jun was filled with remorse for his actions the next day, but Eiko would listen neither to his apologies nor his explanations. They did not leave the room, even when the maid came to clean it. Jun said he was too ill. Eiko was simply disgusted and refused to answer him, preferring instead to add to his discomfort by sulking all through the morning.

A little after two o'clock Jun got out of bed and began to dress himself. When Eiko, her mood forgotten in this sudden activity, asked him why, he said only that he must keep his promise, and it was not until sometime later that she understood the urgency of her husband's desire to obtain tickets for the opera. She recalled it again when Jun told her he would go alone to keep his appointment with the people from the trattoria. There was so little time to get to the place where he was to meet them he must leave now, and by himself. He was in a hurry, he said, and she, even she, must not keep him back. Then he had his coat on, and was striding out of the room.

Eiko lay down upon the bed and tried to sleep. She felt lonely and unhappy. She had had her husband's remorse, she had wanted his gratitude as well, but it seemed as if that, and everything else, all she had accomplished and endured the night before, was forgotten because of his absurd desire that they attend the opera. They did not like opera, but they must go in order to say that they had been, letting the information out casually to friends over a drink at the bar of whatever club or restaurant Jun had decided they must go to because he had read about it in this magazine or that magazine. It was the same reason, always the same reason. They went to the bars, they went to the clubs and to the restaurants as they had come to Europe, as they had come to Venice, as they must go now to the opera, because Jun had read about it or heard about it. She was angry with her husband suddenly, angry in a way she had not been angry before and angry, at last, she fell asleep.

When she woke it was because she thought someone had come into the room. She had again the sensation that had come to her before in this place, the sense of pressure, of a hand pressing down between her breasts so that she could not breathe. She called her husband's name, softly, as a question to which she knew she would not receive an answer.

It was dark in the room; the shutters were closed, and the light beyond the narrow slats had faded. She knew she had only to reach her hand out and turn the switch of the bedside lamp and she would see, but she was afraid, more afraid of seeing now than she was of the darkness. She remembered the last night, the journey that was more like a dream than a dream itself: the sound of rain, the sound of footsteps in the rain. She remembered the figures that had waited for her by the bridge in the rain, like a sketch drawn in thickened pencil. Had the figures stepped out of the picture to follow her here at last? Were they waiting now, the man and the woman, wet still from the still-falling rain, at the foot of her bed? She remembered the night-fears she had known as a child, and like a child she stayed quite still in her own shadows, without breath, listening, only listening, for the sounds that had broken through the doors of sleep to come again.

She waited for the longest time before she reached out her hand to turn the switch of the lamp on the table, and then the room was the room in which she had gone to sleep, and the door, when she went to it, was locked, because it was she who had locked it. She felt foolish, and foolish, went to wash her hands, and rinse her face with water from the small sink in the corner. Then she began to wait.

Eiko waited and waited for Jun to return, but he did not come. She watched the turning hands of the clock: six o'clock, six-fifteen, six-twenty, six-fifty, seven. At seven o'clock she put on her raincoat and went out to look for him. She did not want to, but the desperation of her fears for her husband outdid the desperation of her fears for herself. And she did not know what else she could do. There was no one she could ask for advice because there was no one, literally no one, she could ask. Her inability to speak any language other than her own struck her dumb in this place as much as if someone had torn her tongue from her mouth.

She had thought of calling the consulate in Milan, as much for the sake of talking to someone whom she could understand and who could understand her as for any advice they might offer, or a course of action they might suggest. She even picked up the receiver of the telephone in the room, but then she heard the first babble of foreign sounds at the same time as she remembered what Jun had told her on the first day, that all calls had to be relayed through the clerk in the lobby downstairs. It was when she put the receiver back in the cradle that she decided she must go and look for her husband.

She knew she must go first to the opera house itself, in case he was still there. She knew it would be only a matter of minutes if she took the vaporetto. She knew she could not do that because she could not ask for the ticket. She turned, instead, to the long walk through the mysterious streets to the Campo San Fantin, trusting all the while to her fear and her desperation, twin needles of the compasses she carried, in her head, and in her heart.

The streets were crowded and, moving against the flow of people in the narrow squares and passage-ways as she approached the Ponte di Rialto, her progress was slow. Yet she made her way, as the salmon, as the carp, make theirs, swimming against the stream, and when she saw the bridge she knew a small moment of achievement, if not of actual triumph. She told herself that, if she could come here, then she could, in time, come to the Campo San Fantin. In that flash of clarity, she knew as well, of course, the madness of what she was doing. Jun would not be there. He would be back at the hotel, or on the vaporetto returning to the hotel. What would he do when he found that she had gone? She had not left any note because she had not thought to. She had not told anyone because she could not, because she had not even dared to try.

And if he returned and found that she was not there, what would he do? Set out in his turn, to search for her? Where would he go? Where would he look? They could wander on the circumferences of different circles all night and not meet.

And yet, and yet, she decided against returning to the room, she decided against sense. She would go on. She would go on in spite of the other thought that entered her brain in that moment, the thought of the small man and the woman with red hair. She looked to see if they were there, if they were following. She looked and she did not see them and asked herself how, amongst all those white faces, she could hope to see them; and knew, of course, how, amongst all those white faces, they, the small man and the red-haired woman, could not help but see her. She looked and wondered, and did not see the ones she most feared seeing, and decided against sense that she would go on. Looking and wondering, she did not see the ones who had seen her, and who were following her. She did not see them, but after a little while, as she strayed from the more frequented ways, she heard them.

When she passed the Ponte di Rialto Eiko decided to walk by the canal for as long as she could, thinking that, if she kept the water on her right-hand side for as long as she could, she would not need to risk the streets that, to her, were like a maze. So she followed the canal, but then she was forced away from it along a narrow street. It was here that she heard the sound of footsteps, and heard them follow her when she turned again to try to find the canal.

It was not far, but she knew she was being followed, knew the footsteps would go where she would go, would stop when she stopped. She wondered for a moment if she had somehow willed this to happen with her fears and her dreams, but it was only for a moment and then she knew that it did not matter: what mattered was that it was happening — the fears were being realized, the dreams were coming true. What mattered was to survive. As she walked she slipped from her wrist the Rollex watch her parents had given her when she had entered university, and slid it into the pocket of her raincoat.

She came to the water again and understood that she could go no further, that she must turn and confront whatever, whoever, she must confront. She stopped, and she turned. They were not the ones she had been expecting.

Two men, two boys really, even in the darkness and the rain she could see that they were young, stood at the top of the path she must go back along to get away from the water. They were looking at her. There was no pretence about them. They were looking at her and they were waiting for her. And if she stayed where she was they would come to her. Whatever would happen would happen here and it would happen quite quickly. No one would come; no one would help. It was the moment. It was now.

She stood and in the end they came towards her, and as they did she began to walk, and then as they came closer, to run. She tried to go past, but one of them caught at her arm, so that she dropped her umbrella, and then the other took her from behind and threw her up against the wall. She could smell them, a rotting, stinking smell, and she began to gag.

One held her. She could not look at him. She would not look at him. To smell him was enough. One held her. The other had her purse and shook it out onto the wet street. She could see that. She could see the fingers touching her things.

He had a knife this one. He had used it to cut through the strap of her bag and then he had cut through the bottom of the bag to get at what was inside. He did what he did very quickly, as if it was an art in which he was well-practiced. When he had finished with the bag and its contents he stood and cut both the pockets of her raincoat, disclosing the watch. He lifted the skirts of the heavy coat when he had finished with the pockets and put his hands on her, patting, feeling for anything else that she might have hidden about her, but there was nothing. He was finished with her then, and, as a sign perhaps, to tell her that it was over, he laid his knife delicately, gently, lovingly, almost, against her ear; and delicately, gently, with a movement of such speed and grace almost that, at first, she did not feel the pain, he sliced through the ear-lobe.

They left Eiko then; vanished into the rain. And Eiko stood for a long time watching the blood that fell onto the shoulder of her ruined coat in swift, wet drops.

She found Jun, in the end. He was sitting in the café across from La Fenice where she had waited for him the day before. He was with the boy from the trattoria. They were waiting for the theatre to open to see if it might be possible to obtain returns for tomorrow's matinee performance.

Of course, Jun had been shocked to see his wife, and the blood, the slashed pockets of her coat, her wet hair and empty eyes, empty of everything, even of the man from Chioggia, the red-haired woman. The boy from the trattoria summoned brandy and the police; a doctor was found. Eiko was taken to hospital and detained overnight. She was given injections, and stitches. She was examined — in spite of all that she had told the police — for signs of any other assault, particularly for sexual interference. The police were at once apologetic and defensive, saying that the robbery and assault was the work of an Italian gang who had come with the tourists from the mainland for the holy days of Easter. No Venetian would have done such a thing; it would be like a dog fouling its own bed.

Through it all, at the hospital, with the police, Eiko said only what she had to say, must say. She did not weep; she did not show anger. And when she had said what she had to say, she said nothing, because there was nothing to be said. She left Venice with her husband and she did not once look behind her at the floating city. She knew she would never look behind her again.

They flew to Frankfurt, and from there back to Japan. Her parents waited for them at Narita airport, and the next day Jun's father and mother came. They knelt before her and apologized for all that their son's reckless behaviour had brought about. Eiko said nothing. Eiko said nothing because, really, there was nothing to say.

She knew they had made a mistake, she and her husband, leaving Japan, going to Venice, but she knew as well that in that city, which had so frightened her, she had learned a great truth. It was not something she could pass on to anyone else, perhaps, not even to Jun. What she had learned was this: that the world rested on nothing so merely treacherous as a catfish, or the waters that lapped about the entirely improbable city her husband had taken her to. It rested upon the fabric of her own imaginings.

She had imagined that her life was secure with Jun. She had imagined that he was strong and brave and certain. She had imagined that he would always be with her, always guide her and guard her, always keep her from harm. She knew now that these things were not so. She knew as well the fault that these things were not so was not her husband's. She knew that the fault was her own.

She understood now what she had not understood before: that she had imagined a world, and she had imagined as well its destruction. She knew now that nothing was certain, not her dreams, not her fears; for certainty itself had no more substance than the rainbow, than the dust which falls from the wings of the butterfly in the jar, or its cousin, the gentle, flame-enchanted moth.

# HER VICTORY

As soon as Shiho entered the classroom at the British Council that winter evening and saw the lecturer who would be in charge of the course on the Metaphysical poets for which she had enrolled, she knew she would marry him. She knew as well that, if she was to realize this sudden, but nonetheless certain intention, it would require a considerable effort of will on her part.

It was not simply that the lecturer, Laurence Singleton, was such an evidently desirable man — one who was English, tall and reasonably good looking; a man whose taste in clothes suggested, even to Shiho, that he frequented the sort of small boutiques she had only ever read about in magazines; who was as well a lecturer at Tokyo University, Japan's most prestigious institution of higher education, and whose ringless fingers signalled, she hoped, the lack of any legalized entanglements of the heart.

Nor was it the fact that Shiho herself lacked the sort of beauty men most often found immediately attractive. She knew all her own faults, but she knew as well her own advantages, which lay primarily in the extremes of sexual passion that experience had proven her capable of. This side of her nature served, or had in the past, at least, as even more of a delightful surprise to the men she had allowed to undress and take her to bed, given the somewhat dowdy packaging the surprise was presented in.

No, the problem Shiho saw, the obstacle against which she knew she must marshal all her strengths and talents to overcome, was neither her own, rather unprepossessing, appearance, nor even Laurence Singleton's apparent desirability, for she had succeeded with men far more handsome already. The problem was the only other woman in the class of Shiho's age; the young woman who had seated herself at the very front of the classroom, so close to the lecturer she might as well have been sitting in his lap. This was the difficulty which Shiho saw as standing between her and the state of married bliss she was certain would follow her union with the man to whom, instinctively, she had just surrendered her heart. This young woman, Shiho knew, was her rival.

The young woman gave her name as Etsuko Wakabayashi. Shiho very quickly understood that she was indeed intent on much the same purpose in attending the class as she herself; Miss Wakabayashi was looking for a husband and, in the person of Laurence Singleton, believed she had found what she was looking for. She would prove a most formidable opponent.

To begin with, she was quite beautiful, or, at least, she had those rather cheap looks that, in Shiho's experience, suggested themselves as beautiful to foreign men when they encountered them in a Japanese girl. Miss Wakabayashi also had very good legs, unusually good for a Japanese, and, as the class progressed from week to week, she took care to display her own good fortune. She did so in her choice of clothing, which, even on those frigid February and March evenings, consisted of a flimsy silk blouse worn with a skirt so short as to touch on the very borders of decency, and tights of a sheerness that could only have been paid for in notes of a large denomination.

She calculated her position in the classroom each week

with much the same intention of effect as her wardrobe. She always took the chair Shiho had seen her occupying at the beginning of that first class, the chair at the very front of the room, and so close to Laurence he would have needed to be shortsighted to a degree verging on blindness not to have noticed the elegant pair of limbs set out before him.

If Miss Wakabayashi's lovely legs — and even Shiho had to, grudgingly, concede that Miss Wakabayashi did have lovely legs — if Miss Wakabayashi's lovely legs so invitingly displayed had not already made her intentions clear so far as her teacher was concerned, then, one evening after the class was finished, she went a little further in laying out her stall.

It had become a quickly established routine that, after the class was over, Laurence and most of the women, for they were, the students, all of them women, would walk the short distance from the Council building to a nearby coffee house. Here the discussion that had been taking place in the classroom would continue for an hour or so longer, although in a more informal atmosphere. Miss Wakabayashi was always one of those who went to the café, and she somehow always managed to insinuate herself into the seat next to Laurence's. On the occasion when she made her intentions towards him even more evident than she had already, Shiho was sitting close enough to hear every word of what he said.

Miss Wakabayashi was a translator. There was little that was unusual in this. It seemed, to Shiho at least, that most Japanese girls who had majored in English at university were translators of one sort or another. What was unusual about Miss Wakabayashi was that she actually earned a living from her translations, or said she did. Certainly, she seemed to have no other means of financial support, and yet was able to spend more on her hosiery than Shiho would willingly have given for an entire outfit.

Miss Wakabayashi had already let it be known that she lived alone, and that her parents' house was somewhere a long way from Tokyo. Perhaps, Shiho thought after it was all

over, those two pieces of information had constituted
another, and more obvious move in an opening gambit; her
long legs serving more as pawns, shapely pawns but pawns
none the less, to prepare the way for her to bring more
powerful pieces into play.

Well, on the evening in question, with Laurence Singleton
seated next to the glamorous and independent Miss Wakabayashi, Shiho, one seat further away, heard her telling him
that she, Miss Wakabayashi, that is, was encountering some
problems with the book she was presently working on, a
volume so seemingly dull, Shiho almost pitied her rival,
almost.

Laurence, the poor gull, swallowed every word, and asked
if he might see the parts of the text which were presenting the
difficulties.

Miss Wakabayashi, moistening her lips with the very tip
of her tongue, and moving her silky knees so that they were
touching Laurence's own, said that she did not have the
book with her because it was too heavy to carry around
Tokyo, but perhaps he might be able to meet her somewhere,
if he had a little free time — her apartment perhaps, because
that would be the most convenient. Perhaps one weekend
they could have a cup of tea, or she might prepare lunch for
him, something simple of course, a simple lunch, or dinner,
perhaps.

And Shiho saw that Miss Wakabayashi might, she actually might, have got him there for lunch or dinner perhaps,
but for the fact that her confidence in her own physical
charms led her into a miscalculation. She said that she had
met the author of the original work just after she had taken
the commission to do the translation; she had been in
London to do some background research and was introduced
to him at a dinner party arranged by her publisher.

Laurence was clearly impressed, and Shiho thought she
had lost him, but then Miss Wakabayashi threw in the fact

that she had seduced the elderly, celebrated writer at their second meeting, and offered the further piece of information that he was a better writer than he was a lover.

With anyone else, Shiho always felt, with anyone else, the ploy might have worked, because it was such an incontrovertible statement of sexual availability it formed the obvious copestone to all that had gone before: the flat, the distant parents, the financial independence, the legs. With anyone else, but not with Laurence Singleton. He had blushed, and his embarrassment obviously infused his knees with a sensitivity they had until now lacked as to just what lay beyond the few millimetres of green corduroy which separated them from Miss Wakabayashi's extremely expensive tights, for he shifted in his seat and a clear space was opened up between them and his temptress's most visible assets.

Relief had flooded through Shiho then, because she knew that, even if there were to be a meeting, it would not now take place in Miss Wakabayashi's apartment, but in some perfectly proper and public place, and it would be confined to that place.

But her relief was somewhat premature for Miss Wakabayashi was not one to be so easily denied, and what had happened that night was not to be her last throw.

After a concerted campaign of ever more revealing costumes, which had caused intense and almost audible disapproval among the older women in the class, came the events which followed upon the party Laurence Singleton's students gave for him in early March, at the end of the winter session.

It had been unusually cold in Tokyo that winter, and the streets outside the warm little café where the party was held were covered with a treacherous carpet of ice and frozen snow, and had been for weeks. Most people had gone home after an hour or so, but there remained the few who would not leave, who sought to stretch out the time they had with

Laurence before returning to husbands and children, or worse, to dark and cold and empty rooms and unmade, single beds.

For he was a wonderful teacher, and, if not outstandingly good looking, dressed well and was impeccably groomed; and he was sympathetic, and relatively young; and he was fit, and slim; and he was, he was, unmarried. Time, in other words, had proved him to be all that Shiho had thought him to be when first she had seen him and decided that she would have him for her husband.

Shiho, now, of course, was one of the lingering few, and so, of course, was Miss Wakabayashi. Shiho had no intention of leaving before Miss Wakabayashi did, and she imagined, for they had, in subtle but unmistakable ways, announced their rivalry for their teacher some time before, that Miss Wakabayashi's intentions were similar to her own.

In this, at least, Shiho found, she was wrong. At a few minutes before ten, when there were only three or four others of the class remaining, Miss Wakabayashi announced that she must go. She gave Laurence a small present, a book, from the shape of the parcel she handed to him, although the wrapping was of such an ostentatious and extravagant vulgarity that it might have been anything. She also gave him a card, which was clever, because it must contain a little note, to which Laurence would be bound by mere courtesy to reply, and, of course, the note would inform him of her address and telephone number.

In this, at least, Miss Wakabayashi had taken Shiho completely by surprise, but what was to follow constituted a manoeuvre aimed, not simply at defeating Shiho, but at driving her completely from the field. That it did not achieve this end was a lasting tribute to Shiho's own strength of character and tactical cunning, which, at the time, must have seemed to Laurence Singleton like nothing so much as sheer bloody-mindedness.

Miss Wakabayashi gave Laurence the gift and the card

and paused after her goodbye to him as if to invite a kiss. This kiss, Shiho thought, had it been given, she would have struck from Miss Wakabayashi's face. It was not given, and Miss Wakabayashi went from the café on heels obviously higher than any even she was accustomed to walking on, and which were, on such a night, and on such a surface as the streets outside presented, little short of foolhardy. She left the café, and within seconds there came the sound of a fall and a small, but perfectly pitched, cry of distress. Laurence was out of the coffee shop in moments, leaving a vacant chair and a space cooled by the bitter wind his going admitted through the still-open door.

When he came back, pushing his way through the small but interested throng of customers and staff that had gathered around the door, he had Miss Wakabayashi in his arms, and Miss Wakabayashi had her arms about her saviour's neck, and her head upon her saviour's breast. Her long hair, so beautifully dishevelled it spoke more of art than of nature, masked what might have been a grimace of pain, but which, Shiho felt, was more likely to be a smirk of triumph.

The spectacle the two presented was quite disgusting to Shiho. The fall had torn apart the costly tissue that ordinarily kept Miss Wakabayashi's legs covered, exposing her thighs and a part of her buttocks, as well as an extremely small article of the most intimate sort of women's underclothing. It was against this, this flesh and this silk, that the palm of Laurence Singleton's left hand was now positioned.

Shiho was on her feet at once when she saw this, and far more in possession of herself than Miss Wakabayashi, under the circumstances, could have allowed for. She at once arranged a chair where she insisted the teacher deposit his burden. This in spite of the burden's protestations that any such movement must result in the most excruciating pain. When Miss Wakabayashi was settled on the chair and giving evidence of the discomfort this had caused her through a series of little noises that fetched up somewhere between a sob and a moan, Shiho found herself forced to act again. She was forced to act again because Laurence began to display a certainty of purpose, and power of command she would not have assumed him capable of — for he seemed absolute in his knowledge of how to treat Miss Wakabayashi's injury, and absolute in his intention to put this knowledge into practice. He had, he informed all those that could understand him, been a Rover Scout. A sudden and growing sense of desperation, a sense of things slipping away from her, summoned a little scenario to shape itself in Shiho's mind.

She was not a student of English literature for nothing. She had not read the novel, *The French Lieutenant's Woman*, without its leaving a lasting effect upon her. She knew what a turned ankle had led to in that narrative, and she imagined Miss Wakabayashi was probably furnished with much the same information. Shiho went to the telephone near the door through which Laurence and Miss Wakabayashi had so recently come and called for an ambulance.

Surprisingly, the speed with which the ambulance arrived belied the reputation of the Tokyo Fire and Rescue Services, and, in spite of her protests, which became increasingly vociferous as she realized that her fall had been for nothing, Miss Wakabayashi was strapped to a stretcher and taken off, screaming now that she was perfectly all right, to hospital, one that, Shiho speculated hopefully, would be a long, long way away. She found a certain consolation for this when she remembered the grimness of the ambulance crew's countenances as they had carted Miss Wakabayashi away. These were men who took their work seriously. Shiho smiled to herself and thought that, with all the noise their patient had been making, they might even administer a sedative during the journey, just to keep her quiet.

She smiled as well because there had been one moment when Laurence seemed intent upon accompanying Miss Wakabayashi to hospital, something Miss Wakabayashi, of course, had done everything she could to encourage. That, however, was put an end to, not by Shiho, but one of the older women from the class, who had pointed out the indisputable fact that Laurence would be of little use in the casualty station of whichever hospital the ambulance ended up at because he spoke no Japanese. So Miss Wakabayashi was wheeled away, and Shiho remained: of course she was smiling.

Shiho never saw Miss Wakabayashi again, but she heard, only a few months afterwards, that she had returned to England and married the elderly, sadly deficient, author. In due course of time, following classes on the sonnets of William Shakespeare, Marlowe's *Edward II* and the selected sermons of John Donne, not to mention a weekend of extracurricular activities in which student and teacher reversed their customary roles, Shiho also married. On the day when she became Mrs Shiho Singleton, her victory was complete.

# WAKA

Waka got up early on Wednesdays. There were all the usual things to do. She had to prepare the lunch-box for Toru; she had to make sure that his school uniform was as clean now as it had been when she put it on the hanger the evening before. She had to clean his shoes. Then there were her husband's clothes to get ready; his suit to be taken out of the polythene bag it had come home from the cleaner's in, his underwear, his shirt and socks and tie to put out for him. She would clean his shoes when she did Toru's. After that there would be the breakfast to see to. It would be so much easier if Mr Matoba were content to eat eggs and toast from time to time like her friends' husbands, but he was very old-fashioned. He insisted on a proper breakfast of soup and fish, with rice, pickles, shredded cabbage. She could not even leave the rice to cook overnight because Mr Matoba said that it tasted old. Well, he was from Kyushu and so his conservatism was understandable, although at one point, what was it, two, three years ago perhaps, she had almost persuaded him to buy one of the breadmaking machines, what were they called, table-ovens, yes, she had almost persuaded Mr Matoba to buy her a table-oven so that they could enjoy fresh-baked bread in the mornings, just like the families in the television commercials. In the end, though, Mr Matoba had not been seduced by the world the television conjured up, the spacious family home, the smiling, well-scrubbed faces amidst the sunshine and the potted plants, the prints and gleaming wooden floors, the coffee cups. Mr Matoba was from Kyushu, and if she had wanted someone to share such a brave and shining world with, she should not have agreed to marry a man from Kyushu.

It was not unusual, this morning routine. It happened six days a week, and usually she could get it all done if she woke at six, but on Wednesdays Waka liked to get on with her other household tasks as well so that everything was completed by midday, because, on Wednesdays, she went to her afternoon job.

She could relax for a little while after Mr Matoba had gone. She saw him off at the door, with his mother. Mrs Matoba always knelt, but Waka would not. When he was out of sight, this being Wednesday, she carried the two sacks of garbage down from the second-floor apartment where they all lived to stack them with all the other sacks, set out in the roadway for the refuse collectors to take away. Mrs Tagawa from downstairs was there and wanted to talk, but Waka did little more than exchange a hurried greeting with her. She wanted to have the few moments of quietness she always had at this time on a Wednesday morning, because the rest of the day would be so rushed.

When Waka got back inside, Mrs Matoba was crouched on the floor reading the morning paper. The old woman knelt in the pool of sunlight that came through the window. Waka smiled, knowing that she would be alone to enjoy her tea and a slice of toast. She did not eat the breakfasts she prepared for her husband and son. She was dieting again. It seemed she had been dieting since she was seventeen, but it was worth it. No, it was more than that now, now it was necessary. If she became fat, if she became too fat, she would lose her job.

So Waka ate her slice of toast. She did not use butter, of course. She did not even use one of those special spreads that

were advertised in the magazines. Instead she peeled and
sliced a Kiwi fruit and put it on the toast. When she had
eaten, she drank her tea and she dreamed her usual dream, a
dream in which she was twenty again, single again and in
love, although she had never been in love, and independent,
although she had never been that either. And young and
single and in love and independent she lived in an apartment
just like the apartments the young and single and independent girls lived in on television. It was in New York or San
Francisco or some part of Tokyo that she had never ever
been to, and she was incredibly happy, sitting in her
underwear on a settee with a white, a pure white, sheet
draped over it, in the sunshine. And there was nothing else
and no one else in the room with her, only some paintings
stacked against the wall, and a big, white vase, and a stereo
only half out of the boxes it had arrived in, and the bicycle, a
man's bicycle, a foreign model, with curved handle-bars, just
like the one Jan-Michael Vincent used to ride around his
apartment in the advertisements a few years before, before
they had taken them off the air. There was nothing else, only
her and the sunshine and the sofa and the bicycle and the
most incredible sense of happiness.

The dream lasted for perhaps twelve minutes, and then it
was broken, as it was always broken, by the ringing of the
telephone. It was Mr Matoba, calling from the station to tell
her what he wanted to eat for his dinner that night. Waka
wrote down her husband's wishes on the pad that she kept
near the telephone and worked out the shopping she would
have to do, then she took her plate and cup to the sink where
all the other dishes were stacked and began the business of
washing them up.

After the dishes were done, she saw to the bedding. It was
a fine morning and so the mattresses could go outside. She
lugged them onto the narrow balcony that ran along the
eastern side of the apartment and put them over the rail.
When the mattresses were securely pegged down she spread

sheets of newspaper on the floor of the balcony and carried the pillows out to air, and then she went back inside to sort out the covers. After that she took the cleaner from the narrow cupboard by the front door and began to vacuum the apartment.

Waka had put some washing into the machine first thing in the morning, almost as soon as she had got up. It had been ready for a long time, but she waited until she had finished vacuuming the floors before she got it ready to put outside. Most of the other women in the apartment block where she lived had dryers but Mr Matoba would not let her have one. He said that the clothes smelt strange, mouldy, unless they were dried in the fresh air. Well, Mr Matoba called it fresh, but what was fresh about it Waka did not know. They lived down-wind of their ward's refuse incineration plant and, on days when the wind was blowing, Waka often had to do the washing twice because of the dirt that came from the plant's two chimneys. A dryer would make life much easier and she often thought that one of the things she might do with the money from her job was buy one for herself. That was just as much as a dream as the apartment in New York, of course. Even if she did buy a dryer, Mr Matoba would still complain that his underclothes smelt mouldy.

By ten o'clock the house was in order and Waka left to do her shopping. It was not far to the shops, but first she had to call in at the dry cleaners with the clothes Mr Matoba had come home in the night before. He had been very late, and that meant he had been drinking. He had not come back until after midnight, and he seemed to have fallen because the knees of his trousers were filthy. There was blood as well, on his shirt and on the collar of his jacket. When she had undressed him and got him into the bath, Waka had looked for the cut but found nothing, so that how the blood got onto his clothes remained a mystery to her. As much of a mystery was how she would explain the blood on the jacket to the dry cleaner. The shirt she had rolled up and placed with some

other things. The washing was contracted out so no one that
she knew would know about the blood on the shirt, but she
visited the dry cleaner's twice, sometimes three times, each
week. She did not like the man who owned the shop, and she
did not want to have to show him the blood on her husband's
jacket, but she must or it would still be there when she took
the clothes home again. In the end she said nothing, simply ·
pointing out the stain and saying what it was. She had every
right to do this for the shop was not yet open when she got to
it, and she had to wait for ten minutes before the owner
arrived. His lateness handed her the moral advantage, and
she accepted it enthusiastically.

Waka shopped and then she returned home again. She put
away the groceries, setting the things she would need for the
evening meal aside from the rest. She prepared the trays she
would use to serve the food on, turning the dishes upside
down to stop any dust collecting in them, and took out the
food she would prepare for Mrs Matoba's meal. Then she
went to the bathroom to get herself ready. She showered.
Waka thought of it as a shower, although it was not really a
shower, not like the showers people had on television or even
the showers they had at the place where she worked. She had
to squat on the tiles to wash herself in this shower. It was
another of the improvements she told herself she would make
to the apartment with her savings, but she knew, of course,
she would not. She had talked to Mr Matoba before about
getting a shower, a real shower, installed and he had not
even answered her.

She took more time, much more time, to apply her
make-up on Wednesdays than she usually did. Usually she
did not even bother to wear make-up at all, except on the
occasions, once or twice a year perhaps, when she would go
out with some of the women she had been at school or at
college with. She sometimes thought that if, of course it
would never happen, but if she met Mr Matoba on the train
one of these Wednesdays, he would not recognize her.

She was ready to leave the house by twelve-thirty. She had her bag, the one she kept at the back of her clothes cupboard where Mr Matoba would not look, where his mother would not look. She left Mrs Matoba asleep, having finished her lunch. She would be there when Toru came home at four o'clock. She would give him his sandwiches and see that he left on time for his evening classes at the crammer school. In three years he would sit the university entrance examinations and he had to be ready. His father wanted him to go to the University of Tokyo, but Waka was not so sure Toru was bright enough. Or, if it was not that, she wondered if he wanted it enough, if he wanted it as much as his father wanted it. Getting him into his high school had been an ordeal. Waka remembered the sleepless nights and the tears, the tears and the empty hours of darkness and the coming dawn. She knew it would be even worse the next time, and she knew she would have to deal with it on her own as she had dealt with everything to do with her son on her own. Mr Matoba would not be there when his son wept and pleaded with his mother, or if he were, he would be asleep. Still, she should be thankful for some things: her mother-in-law was kind, without the bitter tongue she knew from her friends' experience so many husbands' mothers were possessed of. And she was thankful, too, that she worked with her husband's knowledge, if not, entirely, with his approval. Of course, he knew only that she worked. He did not know where she worked or what she did; of course he did not know that.

Except for the time when Toru was a very small baby, Waka had worked. She had married Mr Matoba only three months after her graduation, when she was ridiculously young. She was not quite sure why; she had never been quite sure why. Her parents and his parents had arranged it, of course, and it was not unusual for girls at her college to marry quickly.

Half of her graduating class were engaged before the end of
the final year, but still she was the first to actually marry and
the speed with which she did marry Mr Matoba surprised
her friends and surprised her parents as well. And then she
became pregnant so quickly and her mother had been quite
angry with her, but there it was, nothing could be done. So,
Waka was only twenty-three when she gave birth to her son.
She stayed with him for that first year, but then, with her
husband's permission, she returned to her college to work as
a secretary.

Mr Matoba said yes when she asked him if she might take
up the position because they needed the money. Mr Matoba
was thirty-three when he married, and although his pros-
pects were extremely good his salary was not. With the baby
they found they could no longer manage. Waka had been
given her job by Mrs Tabata, her French teacher, the
woman who had supervised her final year dissertation on
Colette — the Claudine novels. Mrs Tabata had always been
kind to Waka: she would take her to the cinema to see
French films, and for tea afterwards at the tea-room in Wako
if they were in the Ginza. Twice she had been with Mrs
Tabata to dinner at Le Coq d'Or. The job was simply an
extension of these and other kindnesses. Waka was grateful
to her teacher.

It was not difficult, the work. She sat in the teachers' room
of the Foreign Languages and Cultures section with two
other girls, girls she had known when she was a student, but
as her seniors. She made tea and coffee for the teachers, and
she performed little tasks for them: photocopying, room
arrangements, issuing reminders about deadlines for book
orders and examination questions. It was not difficult, but it
was rewarding. She had loved that job, loved it with a
passion she had for nothing else, not even her son, and she
had wept when she knew, after three years, that she must
leave. It had only been for three days each week that she had
worked, but then Toru grew more demanding and Mrs

Matoba could not continue properly to look after him so Waka found that she must stay at home again. And they were important years for a son, years when his mother must guide him through the first real trials of his life, the pre-school and the kindergarten. She could not continue to work.

Waka often thought about her time at the Tskuki Ladies College when she cycled to the station on Wednesdays, but today she did not. Today she thought that she had not had time to wash the dishes Mrs Matoba had used for her lunch, and all because that stupid man at the dry cleaners had been late opening his shop. The minutes she had waited for him to arrive were minutes she had not been able to make up during the rest of the morning, and so one of the tasks that was always done today was left undone. It was not important, perhaps, Waka would attend to the lunch things when she got home. It was not that, it was the break with routine that irked her. A condition, the condition, of her working was that she must not neglect the home, and Waka felt that, in not completing her usual routine she was neglecting the home. Mr Matoba would never know; even should his mother notice the unwashed pots she would not report the matter to her son, she was not like that. The fact was not that Mr Matoba would not know, the fact was that Waka knew, and the knowing upset more than it annoyed her. But there was nothing to be done, she must catch the twelve-forty train to be at the club by one-thirty, and she must be at the club by one-thirty to be ready for her shift at two o'clock. She did not have time for the dishes.

Had someone suggested to her, when she was nineteen, that she would, one day, be working as a part-time hostess in a pink club on the edge of the Kabukicho district, she would have found the idea so ridiculous, so entirely improbable, impossible, she would not even have been angry; she would, simply, have laughed. It was an idea so unlikely as to be beyond the bounds of insult. When she was nineteen she sang the *Messiah* with the Tokyo Choral Society, following the tradition of her college as the principal supplier of female voices. How could she, how could anyone, have imagined that this young girl with the face of an angel, in her chorister's robes of black and white, the pristine ruff around her neck, would, in her later thirties, be spending one of her weekday afternoons sitting at a table with a man in the darkness and the smoke-filled air?

Waka wondered herself, even now. Easier to understand was why she did what she did. It was the money. There had never been anything else like the time she had spent as a secretary at her old college. When Toru was safely established in school, and she had, once again, asked her husband's permission to take a part-time job, she had found that her horizons had not simply shrunk, they had altered so much as to be entirely unrecognizable. She had bought a magazine listing vacancies for part-time work. There was plenty of it, of course there was, but the choice for her seemed to be between working as a waitress for Y500 an hour or in a convenience store for less. In the end she settled for a convenience store.

She hated it. She tore her nails on the boxes she had to open in the small warehouse across the yard at the back of the shop. In a few weeks her arms were a mess of burn scars from where the fat in the fryers spat at her. She never knew what they had in stock. She hated the boys that loitered by the magazine-racks for whole afternoons. She found herself despising the men who threw their money on the counter for her to pick up. She loathed the women who bought their family's evening meal from her, wrapped in cling-film. After three months she quit and became a waitress. It was no better. She left that after six weeks. It was a little after Toru's eleventh birthday, and it was a little after that when she made the telephone call to Mr Tanaka and went to work in the club.

Sitting on the train Waka often wondered what the people sitting opposite her, next to her, would say if they knew where she was going, and what she would do when she got there. She did not look any different from the other women on the train. Well, perhaps her make-up was a little heavy, but her clothes were as nondescript, perhaps 'proper' was a better word, as anyone else's. Yet she had a secret and the secret was simply that she would spend the time from two o'clock until five masturbating as many of the men she sat with as she could. She, this perfectly ordinary, perfectly proper housewife and mother, still so pretty and young-looking for her age, would sit with her clients and at some point in the twenty or so minutes she was supposed to be with them would reach beneath the table, unzip the fly on their trousers and put her hand inside, caressing them until they spilled their seed, which she would catch in a little towel. To do this she would be paid about Y50,000, more if it was a particularly busy afternoon, and so it was that for little more than twenty hours of her time each month, Waka earned almost half the salary her husband did.

There were disadvantages. There always are. The work was extremely boring to begin with, and physically it was sometimes difficult, for the wrist on her right hand often ached at the end of her shift and she worried about arthritis. But she had no complaints at all about how much she was paid. Mr Tanaka was a very generous man to work for, and he looked after his girls, he called all of them, all of the women, his girls, very well.

Waka had learned of the job through a flier she found in the mail-box one morning. It had seemed innocuous enough, afternoon work for married women, although she did think for one moment, it might be seeking recruits for a company that offered telephone services to men. There were often advertisements for that sort of thing, and to speak truthfully she had considered applying once or twice, knowing fully what such a service consisted of. What dissuaded her was the thought of talking into a telephone for three or four hours at a time. Besides, once, soon after she was married, her life had been made utterly miserable by some man who had stumbled across her number and persisted in calling her at all hours of the day and night, especially at night. It had taken three months for the caller to tire of his little game.

When she first spoke to Mr Tanaka he described the work as being connected with the entertainment industry, and while that was not an entirely truthful picture, it was not entirely untruthful either. She had been invited to come along for an interview and, as she walked through the streets leading to the club, she had gradually become aware of the sort of entertainment she might be expected to offer, and to whom, simply by looking around her. Still, it was not until her first afternoon at the club, a training afternoon, although she was paid her guaranteed wage of Y20,000, that she fully understood what would be required. She could have left then, as soon as the girl in charge of her training told her what she would have to do, showed her, with the aid of a cucumber, what she would have to do, she could have left but she did not, and it was not entirely the money that made her stay. Waka never quite acknowledged what that something else was, but it had to do with excitement, she knew that.

She had been with Mr Tanaka for six years now, and was one of the oldest of the girls on the staff. Well, on the afternoon staff anyway. The afternoon girls had nothing to do with the evening shifts. They saw them, of course. The club closed from four-thirty to five-thirty each afternoon, and the girls, and these really were girls, for the first evening shift arrived at about the same time that the afternoon people showered and changed to go home. They were different, the evening girls; younger and, somehow, harder. Waka imagined that they had to be. Younger, and harder. The work was different at night. The services on offer were different.

Waka knew because, sometimes, girls, older girls perhaps, girls who had been doing evening work and had left to get married and have families and who had come back to earn a bit of money, that sort of girl, would be taken on again for the afternoons. Mr Tanaka always found a space for people who had been with him before, if they were not too old, if they were not too fat.

These girls had stories to tell about the evenings, and Waka, in spite of herself, had ears to listen to them with. In the afternoons it was just talk and what the girls in the club called 'pulling the bull's tail', the regular service, mostly. But at night it was different. They had dancers then, and there were games, and the cubicles at the back of the club were in use all the time. Some of the older women said that on a Thursday or Saturday night they would be in and out of the cubicles ten or fifteen times during a six-hour shift. Of course, it was in the cubicles that the really big money was earned, but, Waka thought, it was earned. She knew she would not have been able to do that.

Waka had been into a cubicle with customers on only three or four occasions. That sort of thing wasn't asked for in the afternoons as a general rule, but if it was then the hostesses were expected to oblige. She had been frightened the first time, but then she had been frightened the first time she had put her hands under the table to unzip a man's trousers. It was something you got used to, as you got used to anything. In some ways it was better in the cubicles than at the tables, if it didn't happen too often. It was over a lot more quickly for one thing, and there were ways, little techniques the more experienced girls had taught her, to make the men finish before they'd even really begun. The club rules were quite strict over the matter; if a client went into a cubicle what happened there was entirely between him and the hostess. Whatever happened, if nothing happened even, the client would be charged the full fee, and the hostess received her full service bonus. There was never any trouble, and if there was, if one of the clients were to get out of hand, then Waka knew that Mr Tanaka's stewards would quickly stop it. She felt safer in the club than she did in her own home. Even so, fifteen times a night, it was not something she really liked to think about.

Once there had almost been a problem. Some French sailors had come in. She had known that there was a boat, a guided-missile destroyer, the newspaper said, in port at Yokohama, and she had seen some of the sailors in the Printemps store in the Ginza when she was shopping there. She had smiled to herself because they were complaining that none of the sales assistants spoke French. They had gone there to pick up girls and been disappointed. The only French they would have heard was the announcement, played over and over again, about taking care when using the escalator. Waka's major in college had been French and she wanted to speak to the men, but she could not, she dared not.

She had been astonished when three of the sailors came into the club the following Wednesday afternoon. She had not thought the boat was still in port and anyway, the club was so far on the edge of Kabukicho as really not to be a part of the district at all. Still, these three had somehow found their way there, and they would have to be entertained. Waka was not with a client at the time and so she did as she was expected to, she went over to the table where the men were sitting.

Her first surprise was that her French was not as good as she had thought. Her second was that these sailors did not behave in the way her regular customers had caused her to expect. They did not want to talk, well, perhaps that was understandable, but they did not even want to drink, not really. What they wanted was sex, and they wanted it as quickly as possible. One of the men told Waka to kiss him and she said she could not. It was a club rule, the customers could not kiss the girls at the table.

Waka took him to a cubicle and she could see the two
assistant managers watching her as she went with him. They
were getting ready to deal with any disturbance, although
they looked a little frightened because the men were foreign.
But Waka was not frightened by this man. Man? He was a
boy really; really not so very much older than Toru. His
passion was urgent, a boy's passion and she knew about a
boy's passion, she knew he would not hurt her, in spite of his
apparent strength.

He wanted to get her clothes off, but the women did not
take their clothes off in Mr Tanaka's club. It took too much
time. The sailor kept trying, and when Waka put his hands
beneath her skirt he tried to pull her underclothing from her.
Not only was that not allowed either, it was also unneces-
sary. She showed him, putting his fingers through the slit in
her panties so that they touched her skin. Then she moved to
free the man from his garments and when that was done she
tried to get herself down on the hard little sofa with which
the cubicle was provided, for they were, both of them, still
standing. She could not, the man was inside her before she
properly realized what he was doing, before she could do
anything for herself, or for him. He pushed her, hard, up
against the back wall of the cubicle, and they must have
made a noise because the curtain which screened the
entrance to the cubicle was pulled back and Waka saw the
troubled faces of the assistant managers. She tried to gesture
them away, but she could not because something was
happening to her that had only happened once before and
she could not stop it and she did not want to stop it. She let
the short and urgent passion of the man inside her carry her
along, and she did not care that the two men at the entrance
to the cubicle were watching; in fact, she was glad they were.

When she came to herself again, when the sensations of
her accomplished desire had receded and she could lift her
head from the sailor's shoulder to see again, the men were
gone. That was something else she was glad for. She was

glad as well that the young sailor left her to go back to the table alone, and was not even there when, after a few minutes, she came out of the cubicle herself. He was gone with his friends. Of course she had worried for the rest of the afternoon, through her new customers, through the tea and the chat she always had with the other women when the work was done and they had left the club, through the eighteen days that had to pass until her next time of bleeding. She bought a kit from a pharmacy close to the club that would show whether she was carrying a child. Even though the result was negative it was not until her bleeding came when it was meant to that she forgot her fears. But she did not forget the sailor, and she did not forget the moments she had known with him even though Mr Tanaka himself telephoned her at home, angry because of what she had done. It was a well-known fact that the new disease the newspapers had been so full of a few months before, the disease whose name she could not properly remember, was only passed on by foreigners. Mr Tanaka arranged for her to have her usual blood-test, all the staff had a blood-test once a month and the girls carried medical certificates to show that they were completely free of disease, the next day. She had had to invent an excuse to visit the clinic, but that result, too, when it came, was negative.

The women always had tea together after they left the club. They had their favourite place. It was quite a long way from the club, but perhaps that was why they were happy to accept the inconvenience of the walk. They did not stay long, a half-hour, forty minutes at most. They were all married, or had children at least. Waka had talked of what had happened to her that afternoon, well, not all of it, of course. She had spoken of her fears that she might be pregnant, and that her husband might find out how she was able to contribute so much to their house payments every month. One of the women, one who had been a full-time girl with Mr Tanaka, a real professional, spoke angrily to her at first, telling her that she was a fool not to have made sure she was protected, and Waka was upset, but seeing this, the other woman had softened and told her that it would be all right. If the worst came to the worst, she knew someone who would help and not ask any questions. And then she told Waka a funny story to cheer her up, though she swore that the story was true, that she had been in the club when it happened.

All the part-timers worried that their husbands might discover what it was they did, and the biggest fear was that the secret would be exposed by their husbands coming into the club. It was unlikely, in the afternoon, but it was not impossible, it was not entirely impossible. Waka knew that her own husband sometimes went to clubs like Mr Tanaka's. She had found the stains on his trousers once or twice, left by an inexperienced hand. Well, one day, so the story went, a woman on the afternoon shift was called across to a table where three men were waiting and one of them was her own husband. He was with colleagues who were his juniors and he could not lose face by showing that the woman who would service them was his wife. They were celebrating something, the woman telling the story did not recall what exactly, but some small thing, one of the little triumphs with which such men puff their feathers. The two junior men had been at the club before, and they had brought the husband with them as a treat. They ordered the full menu, and when the time came they laughed and clapped their boss into a cubicle with the woman he was married to. Again the man was trapped. He had to perform or lose face and so did his wife. Now whether it was his anger, or the strangeness of the surroundings, or even the fact that he was screwing his wife and she was getting paid for it, but the woman said afterwards that she had never known him put on a performance like the one he managed that afternoon. At first she was surprised and then she was astounded, and after that she was too excited herself to be anything she could talk about. It was a little difficult at home in the evening, of course, a little awkward, but the husband came back to the club the next time his wife was working and again they had a wonderful time. It went on like that for years. It was the perfect arrangement. The husband was happy. The wife was happy. The wife was very happy. She never had sessions with her husband at home like she did in the club. And the best part of it, the very best part of it, was that she got paid for it by her husband, and that certainly never happened at home.

Waka had laughed. It was a good story, and whether it was true or not hardly mattered. She thought of her own husband, as she always did when she remembered that time and when she remembered that story. And remembering she went back again to the dream, the dream in which she was twenty again, and single again and in love, and independent. Well, of course, she had never been in love, and certainly not with Mr Matoba. The very idea of being in love with Mr Matoba made her want to laugh out loud. But, once, once upon a time, she had thought she might have been in love with the Frenchman. Not that Frenchman, not the sailor, but the Frenchman at her college. For a little while, before he asked her to go out with him, that time they had coffee together, and for a long time afterwards, she had thought she might have been in love with him.

He was a part-time teacher, and worked only on Wednesday afternoons. She knew he liked her. She could see he liked her. It was in the rather awkward way he would approach her to do things for him that he could quite easily have done for himself; the way he would always, always, seek her out to do the things he could not so easily do for himself, instead of one of the other girls. Once, when he was to show some slides to his class, she had walked with him to the classroom, carrying the projector. He had talked to her then, asking what she did in her free time. For some ridiculous reason, perhaps because she was as nervous as he so obviously was, she said she played golf, and then found herself driven to increasing extremes of invention to answer his subsequent questions. After she had set up the projector and the screen, he came with her as far as the door of the classroom and, as she was about to go, asked if they might have coffee together some time. It was the twelfth of October. She always remembered the date. She said yes. And then, she did not know why, but somehow, for the longest time, there was never that necessary and extended moment when he could ask her again, specifically, telling her the place, the day, the time; the when and the where of — of what? Of love.

She did not know why. She knew only that his love for her, if that is what it was, continued to burn him, to redden his pale face whenever they did see one another, across rooms and tables, over the heads and shoulders of all those that seemed to come between them. At Christmas time, and at the times when he would come back to Japan from visits to his own country, he gave her gifts. It is true that he gave them to the others as well, but there was, as well, always something which separated hers from the others; a sign, unseen perhaps by all save herself, and by him, intended, surely by him. It was the unspoken word that was between them. And it must have been love, that word, she thought it must have been love. Anything else, desire merely, would have cooled in him more quickly, it was a thirst so easily, Waka knew how easily even then, slaked elsewhere. Besides, there was what came afterwards.

The time went, the hours and the days, the days, the weeks, the months, the seasons. Once, one hot August, when the department office was working restricted hours, she met him, unexpectedly, on the stairs leading to the library. Her surprise numbed her brain and, alone with him at last, she found she could make herself say nothing except an imprecise mouthful of pleasantries — was it not hot? Of course it was hot, summer sat heavily outside the door. Was he not in France? No, he was standing in front of her, so close she could see the sweat upon his nose.

He asked her what she would do during the vacation.

Waka added again to the compounding lie she had begun about playing golf. She conjured four companions and a long weekend at a club in Hakone, one with a particularly difficult course. She surprised herself with this, the sudden fecundity of her imagination. She was about to return the question when she was surprised again, but not by herself. He said that he would like to see her sometime, and, surprised as she was, she made to reply that, yes, she would like to see him, to meet, sometime, but his audacity was at once tempered. He said that he had meant, if she should, if she ever should, perhaps, come into Shibuya, or Shinjuku or the Ginza perhaps, then, if she should, perhaps, they could, perhaps, meet. If she called him. If she called him they could meet. And he was gone, down the stairs and out into the afternoon and Waka knew that she would never call him even if she did, sometime, go to Shibuya or Shinkjuku or the Ginza, sometime.

Was it the following November when he asked her again to go with him for coffee? Yes, it was. He had gained some courage, for her perhaps. She had tended his feelings for her with smiling eyes whenever they came together. She had tended his feelings and now they had bloomed, a delicate winter flower, she knew, but it had, at last and so late, bloomed. He asked her to have coffee with him that evening after the last class, after the office closed, and she said she would.

They were to meet outside a German bakery and she was late, but he was waiting for her. They went to a place of her choosing, a place where she knew they would not meet any of his students, or any of her teachers. He asked her what she would like and she said she would drink coffee, although this was as much a lie as her golf, for she never drank coffee. She lied for him, because he had asked her for coffee and she thought she should take his invitation at its word, and she lied for herself because, now that this was happening, that she was with a man in a public place who was not her

husband, it was easier to lie than it was to tell the truth even
in a thing so small as her choice of coffee or tea or anything
else that was on the menu she held before her eyes but could
not see.

He was as nervous as she. She knew he spoke some
Japanese, she had heard him with the other teachers, but the
only words he spoke in her own language this evening were
to ask if they might use French and she said yes as easily as,
moments later, she began to tell more of her lies about her
golfing friends.

The waitress came and she was glad, because for a little
while she could busy herself with the business of putting
sugar into her cup and stirring the dark liquid she did not
think she could actually drink, even for him. She looked up
from her cup — she remembered this so well — she looked
up from her cup and something had happened. His face was
pink but it did not stir her heart as it usually stirred her
heart. Something had happened and she did not know what
it was. He began to ask her questions, and when he asked her
if she lived with her parents she knew at once what it was,
what had happened. She laughed and told him she was
married and had a child, at the same time her eyes saw what
his eyes had seen, her wedding ring.

She had not considered before that he might be pursuing
her in ignorance of the fact that she was someone else's wife.
She had not considered that it was a pursuit. His attentions,
his smiles and awkward words, the little gifts and compli-
ments bestowed, were not part of anything like that. They
were tributes. They were, if they were anything, items in, not
a pursuit, but a courtship. They were . . . They were things
such as a knight might bestow upon a lady, upon his
beloved. She had read the great romances of French literature; she knew of the world of the troubadours, the jongleurs.
She had thought — but what she had thought fell in ruins as
he began to explain that he had not known, that he had
thought to ask her out properly, to the cinema, to dinner, but

now — he felt so foolish, stupid. He apologized for the
liberties he had taken. He said he hoped she would forgive
him. He said he hoped they might still be friends at school, in
the office. Then he started to ask her about her husband and
her child, and she did not have to lie anymore.

Outside, in the November darkness, they said goodbye
and when he walked away from her towards the station she
saw his head drop and she took a share of his sadness for her
own. She watched him until he was gone from her sight and
then she returned to the college car park where she had left
her car. Inside were the twigs and grasses she was to have
used that night in her flower-arrangement class. It was too
late to go now, and she knew she would have to throw them
away and prepare some story for her mother-in-law as to
why she had come home so early.

When she saw him again, and on all the other occasions
when they were together after that time, he was as kind to
her as he had always been. There was even a longing there
still, the shadow in his kindness she had known for so long.
Only it was, she thought, different now. Where once it had
been the longing of hope, now it was, she thought, the
longing of despair. That Christmas, knowing still he would
come on the last day before the holidays with gifts for all the
secretaries, knowing still that hers would be the one he truly
wished to give, she arranged with the others to give him a gift
in return. It was such a little thing, a small box of thin
chocolate lozenges. There was a card as well. Waka chose it
and inside she wrote of her gratitude for all his kindness. She
signed it, and when she signed it she did so in the English
manner, as once she had been taught, with love.

There were only two weeks of classes in January. He did
not come into the office on his first teaching day or on the
second, and when she met him in the corridor on her way to
do some errand she knew it was because she had gone, in
fact, to find him. She laughed, asking how he had passed the
short days of the holiday. He said he had stayed in Tokyo.

She wished to ask him if he had stayed in Tokyo alone but, instead, she told him how she had enjoyed that time when they had gone to the coffee shop together and how she would like to go there with him again. She added the word, 'sometime', although she did not want to. It was the sadness in his eyes that made her. He said, yes, it would be very nice to go there again, and he picked up the word his eyes had made her lay before him, 'sometime'. She knew they would never go there again. She knew it.

And a year later she resigned her position because she had to be with Toru. She heard that the Frenchman had married during the year, a Japanese woman. She heard, because he did not tell her, ever. Well, why should he? But he came to see her, to say goodbye, on her last day. It was January again and she was alone in the office. He said he had come with the marks for his classes and met one of the other secretaries. He had not known. He said he had not known that she was to leave. He wished her great happiness in whatever she chose to do in the future. For a moment, just for a moment, she thought he might embrace her, and she wondered what she should do to respond for she had never been held in that fashion before. But it was only a moment, and the moment passed.

She had never seen him again, but she thought of him often. Even now, here she was on the train going to her work and she was thinking of him. It was all such a long time ago and sometimes, when she was thinking of him, she would stop and ask herself whatever could have possessed her, whatever could she have thought she was doing. But for all the years that had passed, for all her growing qualities of sense that came with being the mother of a child, she knew that had he, had Michel Vigneau, the language assistant at her old college, asked her to go out with him that time in the coffee shop she would have said yes. She would have said yes and not thought for a moment of what she was doing. And she knew that if she had gone with him, to the cinema, to dinner, to whatever it was he had had in mind, she would have been his for as long as he had wanted her, she would have been his in whatever way he had wanted her. She would have undressed for him. She would have lain with him. She would. And she knew that, if the impossible were to happen, if she were to meet him again this afternoon or tomorrow evening, and if he asked her to go with him, she would go with him. She would. She knew it, and the thought made her tremble, for herself and also for her child.

Waka thought of Toru suddenly. She hoped he was happy at that moment, whatever he was doing. And she thought of Michel Vigneau and of the young sailor who had given her that senseless, terrifying and ecstatic moment of pleasure, and all the guilt she felt for her son could not take away the intensity of the memories of love, if it was love, and of sensation. She wondered if there were women for whom the two could be experienced together, that love and that pleasure, with the same man. She thought again of Toru, and she hoped he knew how much she loved him. She thought how it must be to be loved as strongly as she loved her son. She loved him in a way she had never loved anyone. Perhaps with Michel Vigneau, perhaps, she might have loved him in the way she loved Toru, recklessly, unreservedly. She thought perhaps that there was nothing Michel Vigneau might have asked her that she would not have done, but she could never know, not now. He was a memory, and everything that might have been with him shadows, like the shadow she once thought she saw in his smile. And she knew that these were only the shapings of her imagination, and of her desires.

She hoped that Toru loved her as much as she loved him. She hoped Toru knew how much she loved him, knew that there was nothing she would not do for him. She thought of Toru and she thought of his father. When she washed Mr Matoba's clothes it was because it was her duty as his wife to do so; when she washed Toru's it was because she loved him. When she made food for Mr Matoba, it was because it was her duty as his wife to make him food; when she got up in the grey hours of the morning to prepare Toru's lunch-box, when she put aside whatever else she was doing to make Toru his favourite snack, when she journeyed to the shops to find the best fish for Toru, the freshest vegetables for Toru, it was because she loved him. Everything she did for her husband she did because it was her duty; everything. Everything she did for Toru was an act of love. Everything.

She remembered that dreadful time of the entrance examinations for high school. It had been like a bad dream that would not end. She had sat with her child through the days and she had sat with him through the nights. She had sat with him through the times when he would not eat, and she had watched over him through the times when he could not sleep. She had watched as he wept and as he wasted, and in the few moments of the day when necessity took her away from him, Waka nursed in her heart a bitter sorrow for her son. Of course, Mr Matoba had seen none of this. He had chosen just that time to make a business trip to Osaka. No, that was unfair, and Waka reproved herself for the lack of charity in her thoughts. Her husband had not himself chosen to go. It was a directive, and one that he could not question. He had had to go. But that did not take away the weight of the burden she had been forced to carry. It did not take away the bitterness of watching her child suffer and knowing she had not the power to ease his suffering. It did not take away the bitterness of the knowledge that she herself must force her son to the tasks that so tormented him.

As the time of the examination had drawn closer, the boy's suffering had increased, and what had once been a doubt in his eyes when he looked at her became a terror. It was his terror that robbed him of his sleep. It was his terror that took the food from his stomach when, at last, he could put it to his mouth. And it was his terror that, one night, late one night when the boy could not sleep, Waka had taken away.

That day in particular had been very bad, she remembered. Her son had eaten nothing, but again and again had fled from his small table and his room to the lavatory, and the spasms of nausea which shook him. And each time Waka knelt by him, her child, held his head, held his shoulder, as he sought to empty himself of what could not be emptied.

The last time, it had been during those minutes of the night when the darkness seems to hesitate, uncertain before the sense of a coming sunrise, and the bulbs of the electric lamps appear somehow less certain of their power, that last time, she had taken her son to his bed not his table, and about to leave when she had seen him settled, as best he could be settled, he had begun to weep. He had begun to weep in that particular way a child weeps who has recognized that there is nothing to be done to ease the sorrow; who tastes, and each time it is as if for the first time, hopelessness. It is the weeping that comes from the empty heart, and shakes in sobs the empty soul. When Toru began to weep like that, Waka went to him because there was nothing else that she could do, because there was nothing else that she could have done. She went to him and she lay with him, and lying with him she took him to her. She took him to her and she began to caress him and it was as she put her hand against him, against his skin, the knowledge came that she knew a way she might give him some peace, and knowing that, she knew as well that she would give it to him.

He was a boy. He was a child. What she did took almost no time at all. And as she did it, and as it came to him, the boy, the child, found her breast and suckled as he had done when he was baby. He had slept almost at once afterwards, and Waka knew that what she had done had been a necessary thing. She had taken away his fear and she had given him what she had thought she might give him. Of course, she worried, afterwards, as she slept upon the floor by her son's mattress, with his boyish seed still wet upon her pajamas. She worried how it would be between them in the morning. But in the morning it was between them as it had always been between them, except that the fear was gone, and the sickness was gone.

That night, and every night until the time came for them to leave the house to go to the examination, Waka had gone to Toru's bed to give him again what she had given before, but it had not been necessary, for that night and each night that followed, the boy, the child, her child, had slept.

Once, perhaps two or three months afterwards, she had spoken of this to the women from the club. They were in the tea-shop where they always went before going home. Some of them were talking about their children and suddenly, in spite of herself almost, Waka found she was saying what she had not considered she could ever say.

They understood, these women. They did not laugh at her to hide their horror. They did not pretend they had not heard what she had said. If there was a silence it was one of sympathy, not disgust, and it was broken, almost too quickly it was broken, by one of the women who said that she had done herself what Waka had done, and knew of others who had done it as well. And, this woman said, she had done more than that, she had taken her son into her bed on many nights, taken him for his comfort, and in the end for her own as well. And when that had been said it all had been said and the women went on to other things before they went on to other things. And Waka had taken the words of comfort into her heart, because she knew that if ever Toru needed her again as he had needed her that time, she would give herself to him and she would give herself to him for her own comfort as well as his — when he was older, perhaps when he was older.

She would give herself to him because she knew, she had known even as she touched him and he put his face to her breast, that had his hands followed his lips, had his hands found her as her hand found him, then she would have had

again what she had had with the French sailor, and more
than that, she would have had what once she thought she
might have had with Michel Vigneau: she would have had
love. Her hands a lover's hands touching a lover's body; his
hands a lover's hands touching a lover's body.


The train stopped at Shinjuku and Waka got off, leaving her
thoughts behind her like a forgotten bag, an umbrella tossed
carelessly into the rack above the seat. Lost property that
could never be found because it was not truly lost; that
would always find its way back to its owner, to its proper
home.

It was a quiet afternoon in the club. There were just a few
customers and Waka was called to a table only once, so her
pay was a little light when she received it. Afterwards she
went with the others to drink tea and talk, and then walked
to the station and the long journey home.

The dishes were stacked in the sink, waiting for her, when
she got back to the house. Toru had been home, eaten and
gone out again. He would be in his class at the crammer
school now. Mrs Matoba was kneeling in front of the
television watching the weather forecast. Waka went to her
cupboard and put the bag containing her work clothes right
at the back. She would wash them in the morning, when Mr
Matoba had left for work and his mother was reading the
newspaper in the sunshine. She took off the dress she had
worn to go out and folded it ready to take to the dry
cleaner's. She put on a pair of jeans that were getting too
tight for her in spite of the diet, and a tee-shirt. In the kitchen
again, she washed the dishes Mrs Matoba had left, and when
they were stacked and drying in the rack, began to make the
evening meal she would serve to her son later, after he came
home. They would eat together and she would ask him about
the events of his day; she would see him settled to his
homework, prepare the bath, and in time, see him settled to

his sleep. When all of that was done, she must prepare her husband's evening meal, get his pajamas ready, and then she must wait for him.

She always waited alone. Old Mrs Matoba would be asleep and Toru, if he was not asleep, would, at least, be in his room, his bed ready on the floor for him. She always waited alone. In the quietness of the house then she would read the newspaper, or, because it was Wednesday, one of the magazines she bought for the train but never looked at until she got home. Or she would sit at the table and she would think about what she would do with all of the money she had earned, one day, one day when the apartment was paid for; one day when Toru was married, with a family of his own; one day when Mrs Matoba was gone; one day, one day when Mr Matoba did not come home, when he would never come home and then she would not be sitting in this apartment that was already falling into disrepair, that would be a slum long before it ever became their own; this apartment with its smells of old, stale food that would not leave no matter how hard she scrubbed the floors, how wide she flung open the windows and the doors. She would not be here, she would be in another apartment, the one in San Francisco or New York, and she would sit in her underwear on the bare wooden floor in the sunshine and, if she waited, if she waited, she would wait for her lover, for the one who loved her and whom she loved. But tonight Waka knew that when she waited she would not read the newspaper or the magazines, and she knew she would not dream either. She was too tired. It was always the same. It was not the work, the work had been very easy today. She was tired because it was Wednesday, but not because of the work. It was getting up so early that made her tired, too tired even to dream, and she always got up early on Wednesdays.

# A BLUE RIBBON

*T*he greatest difficulty, Nick Rossa found when he first arrived in Tokyo, was getting people to believe that he was English. He had come because of the stories, latter day travellers' tales, of the easy money to be made in Japan teaching English. He arrived without a job, on a tourist visa, after the worst flight of his life in which he had, briefly, touched down in five different countries.

He found lodgings in a foreigner's house in Nakano run by a lady who had once, as she insisted on telling every one of her new guests, done the flower arrangement for the Royal Box (somehow, whenever she said those words they presented themselves with capital letters) at the Prince of Wales theatre in London for a Royal Variety Performance attended by the Queen Mother. For Mrs Nakajima it was the high point of the year she had spent in London, and she would not let anyone lodge in her house without re-living the moment with her. Mrs Nakajima let Nick have his room but even she, with all her experience of arranging flowers for the Queen Mother, would not believe that Nick was English. Yet he was, or, at least, he was more English than anything else.

It was true that Nick Rossa's father was an Italian, and it was true that he did not arrive in England until two years after the end of World War II, when he was seventeen. He came to work in the ice-cream business his great-uncle had established in a small town in Warwickshire. He worked hard, prospered and, fifteen years after his arrival, returned to Italy to marry a girl from his home town who was almost half his age. They began what was to be their large family, three girls and four boys, almost immediately. The second child was Nick, Niccolo as he was more properly called. By chance, he was born in Italy when his mother, who had returned to her parents for a short visit, went into labour prematurely.

At first it was feared that the baby would not live, but it survived and then thrived, and when this youngest of the Rossas was taken to England, it was as a fine, healthy boy of four months. Nick spoke Italian with his parents, but English with his brothers and sisters and all of the cousins; and if he went to Italy from time to time it was only so that his grandparents might see him. In every important aspect he grew up to be an Englishman, not an Italian. Italy was a place he went to on holiday, but England was where he lived. In Italy he was a stranger, in England he was at home.

Nick Rossa arrived in Tokyo a week after he had celebrated his twenty-third birthday. He brought with him a small suitcase containing enough clothes to see him through the first few weeks of what was expected to be a two-year stay, more were to follow by sea, and his bachelor of arts degree from the University of Cambridge. It was not a particularly impressive degree, but it was a Cambridge degree. From the stories he had heard in England, Nick did not anticipate very much difficulty in finding a position as a teacher of English.

In this he was very much mistaken, for it was not only his landlady who declined to accept the evidence of his passport as to his national origins, it was each and every prospective employer that he approached as well. Even his degree did not help him. All of the English language schools stressed that they sought native speakers of English for their staffs; Nick Rossa's name ensured that his application never progressed further than the initial part of the selection process. After six weeks he accepted that he would never find work and, with his money running out, began his preparations for leaving Japan. It was then that he met with Bruno and Gina Morelli.

He was sitting on his own in the small bar he had taken to frequenting, on the north side of Nakano station. The place was run by a couple who had spent some years abroad and served a variety of the foods they had come across in their travels, all, of course, discreetly altered to appeal to the Japanese palate. Nick had found the bar by accident one evening when he had sought to alleviate his increasing sense of frustration by walking around what was his neighbour-hood, although this thought, that it was his neighbourhood, shocked him when it first occurred. He had been nervous of entering the bar to begin with, but the owners, seeing him loitering uncertainly outside, had called him in and made him welcome. Now he was a regular, and for a small outlay of cash, but a rather greater one of time, he ate reasonably well.

On that particular evening the bar was crowded with people who had come in after a concert at the hall in the Nakano Sun Plaza building. Bruno and Gina Morelli, having also been to the concert, had simply followed the crowd when it was over. Nick was sitting at the only table where there were vacant chairs when they came in, but the couple appeared to hesitate. Gina, speaking in Italian to her husband, said that she would prefer not to take the seats they had been offered, in case the man at the table started smoking. Nick answered her by saying he did not smoke, and that, anyway, he was almost ready to leave.

It is a frequent assumption of those who travel to foreign places that no one they encounter there can speak their language, particularly if the place is one as foreign as Japan is perceived to be. Within this cocoon of assumed incomprehensibility, comments are passed and conversations held in public, that, at home, would take place with caution even in private. Insults, discussions of the most intimate aspects of human life and behaviour, all and everything, are transacted and dissected in trains, on the streets, in restaurants, or, as on this evening, in bars, all with a sense of total confidence in the inability of anyone else to understand what is being said. Of course, when the cocoon cracks and this confidence is broken the effect can be truly embarrassing. Gina Morelli was embarrassed, and so was her husband. He, apologising, offered in excuse for his wife's rudeness the fact that they had not known Nick was Italian. Nick, in response, said that he was not. The Morellis sat down and a conversation, growing ever more amicable in spite of its slightly discomforting beginnings, ensued. Nick told his story. The Morellis told theirs.

They were from Turin and, like Nick, had been lured to Japan by stories of the money they could expect to earn. Unlike Nick they had not experienced any difficulty in finding employment. In the beginning, Gina had worked in a hostess bar in Akasaka, one which prided itself on the international nature of its girls. Bruno, although he lacked both training and experience, was able to secure a place as a waiter at a restaurant called 'La Granata'. The management felt that a real Italian would complement the expensively authentic decor their interior designers had provided them with.

Of course, neither Bruno nor Gina had the correct visas for their work, and they worried constantly about being caught and deported. But, as Bruno explained, everyone has the luck they deserve, and their luck was that one of Gina's customers at the hostess bar turned out to be involved in educational television. He was quite taken with Gina, his admiration unshaken even by the knowledge, which came to him at last, that she was married and that her husband was with her in Japan. He said that his station's Italian programme, 'Itariago Ciao!', needed replacement personnel, as two of the regular native speakers were leaving. He arranged for Gina and Bruno to take over their places.

Nick Rossa's luck was that he had met the Morellis. They had saved a great deal of money in the time they had been on television. It was not so much that the station paid them unusually high wages, but that they, more particularly Gina, had become stars — talents to be exploited by a variety of quiz and chat shows. From the fame generated by their presence on these programmes had come the real money, for personal appearances at college festivals, product endorsements and so on. In addition, Gina's admirer had moved on from educational broadcasting to higher things, his admiration increasing in direct proportion to the growth of his own power and Gina's public glory.

This man had recently settled a very large sum of cash on Gina in the hope that it would induce her to buy an apartment where he might see her on her own from time to time. Gina, for her part, had decided enough was enough. She had accepted the money and did, indeed, intend to purchase some property with it, but in Turin rather than Tokyo. She and Bruno were to leave Japan at the end of the month. They would set up their own language school in Turin, teaching Italian to Japanese. Their fame and contacts were such that there was already a waiting list for enrollment, although the school was not yet even established. Nick's luck, Bruno told him, was that 'Itariago Ciao!' was still short of a native speaker and the producers were growing increasingly desperate to find one. It was this desperation, allied to the power of the Morellis, that would secure the post for their new-found friend, smoothing over any problems that Nick's British passport might cause.

And it was as Bruno said. True, there a minor difficulty when it was discovered that Niccolo Rossa was not quite as Italian as his name and abilities in the Italian language had led others to assume, but Gina prevailed upon her admirer to help, and he did. Nick was hired and then given an excusion ticket to Seoul so that his visa could be properly processed from outside the country.

The afternoon before he was due to leave for South Korea, Gina continued her ministrations on his behalf by taking him to bed while her husband was away on a short business trip to Osaka. Afterwards she told Nick, for whom this was his first complete sexual encounter, that she was still embarrassed over her behaviour on that first night at the bar in Nakano. She said she had wanted to make it up to him. The Morellis had left Japan by the time Nick returned from Seoul and he never saw either of them again.

And so Nick Rossa, in his turn, became a star. He was young and good looking, and he was foreign. Naturally, he very quickly attracted a following, of mainly very young girls, some of whom would be waiting at the entrance to the television studios for him whenever he entered or left. They would scream when they saw him, in a very peculiar way, somewhere at the top of the pentatonic scale perhaps, but were always quiet and exceedingly polite when he came up to sign their autograph books, or pose with them for photographs. The screaming would begin again only when he left them, the sound following him along the street or down the corridor as he made his way to the studio for another rehearsal and taping.

He also began to make appearances on other shows, and, as his command of Japanese increased, so did his curiosity value to the television people. He quickly passed from being the cute foreigner that the other Japanese performers made fun of, to the cute foreigner who was quite able to make fun of himself. He found a slot in the public's awareness of foreign personalities into which he could fit himself, and once this was done his success was assured. Yet, for all this, Nick Rossa did not lose sight of who and what he really was. He continued to live modestly, keeping on his room in the foreigner's house in Nakano, and it was for this reason that he met Kiku Miyashita.

There was a party in one of the rooms downstairs. The girl who lived there, Monica, was leaving. Monica was from London, from south of the river. She had been in Japan for three years, all the while on a student visa although she had not seen the inside of a class-room for a long time. She worked as a hostess, just as Gina Morelli had and, just like Gina Morelli, Monica had also found her pot of gold at the end of the rainbow: one of her clients had offered to set her up in an apartment. Monica had been to see what was on offer, liked it, and so she was moving out. It was Monica who was giving the party, although 'giving' was not quite what Nick Rossa thought of as the right word when he came down and Monica asked him for a Y7000 'entrance fee'.

The room seemed as if a week of parties had been held there: there was a table filled with opened bottles of beer, and pints of Johnny Walker with the caps undone. There was cigarette smoke, blue and swirling in the lamp-light. There was noise as well, and yet, the small space Monica had occupied for so long did not seem crowded because the guests were all seated in a circle on the floor.

Despite the fact that it was meant to be Monica's party, Monica was not very much in evidence. After making sure that everyone who came in paid, she had gone off to finish her packing, which seemed, from what Nick could see, to consist of filling a succession of black polythene rubbish sacks with shoes, all of them silver and all of them with high, spiked heels.

Nick was seated by a man he did not know, next to a girl he did not know, and he at once began to think that he had made a mistake in coming. He did not even like Monica. Her face was as hard as the heels of her shoes, and it did not belie her character. In the beginning, when he found out how she made her living, Nick had felt sorry for her, constructing a hypothesis as to how she could have come to such a pass.

In fact Monica had not come to anything she had not intended to come to, but Nick Rossa who was, at heart, a romantic, could not understand that; not, at least, in the beginning. In the beginning he had even been a little in love with her, or, rather, he had been a little in love with his idea of her. Unable to believe that any girl could be happy being a hostess, that any girl could have come all the way to Tokyo from south London with the express intention of becoming a hostess, Nick determined that she was trapped in a life she had not chosen, and he would be the means of setting her free. However, the cloak of his own imaginings in which he wrapped her was quickly unravelled, snagged on the thorns of Monica's own personality, and their brief liaison, such as it was, soon ended.

In any case, it, their liaison, had consisted mainly of a series of loans Nick made to the girl and which she never repaid. It was the return of the sum involved in the latest of these loans that Nick had actually come to the party to talk to her about, but he had missed his chance when he had given her the money at the door. It was his last chance as well, for Monica, having counted the evening's takings, left without a single goodbye to any of her guests, chauffered away into the night with her shoes on the front seat of her boyfriend's BMW.

After fifteen minutes of increasing unease Nick Rossa thought about leaving himself, but then one of the bottles of beer began to make the journey around the circle and he found himself being served by the girl at his side. He started to introduce himself, but she knew who he was. She had seen him several times on television. In halting Italian she told him her name. She said she had been trying to study the language, and then, and she laughed, that her lack of success was evident. They continued the conversation in Japanese.

She called him Mister Niccolo, until he told her he preferred the diminutive. Then she called him Mister Nicco, all the while using the English title without any awareness of the irony of her actions. She was twenty-eight, she said, a painter working with a small group of other artists that had formed around a more well-known figure of the Nihonga school. As she spoke, Nick, who knew nothing about painting, particularly Japanese painting, found himself wishing that he did.

They talked and talked in the thickening air and, when she said that she must leave, Nick went with her to the station. After he had said goodbye to the girl he knew that the feeling within him as he walked back to his room was regret.

She had told him she was going to Europe the next week, to London first, and then Italy, to Florence, although she used the Italian name of the city and Nick, for a moment, was lost. She would study the technique of *tempera* in Florence, the use of raw pigment and water, which she felt would complement her own style and practices. Again, Nick was lost. He thought she was going to Italy to study a style of Japanese cooking and could not understand why.

As he walked back along the narrow street towards the house where the talk and the smoke and the drinking continued, Nick thought of Kiku Miyashita and the ribbon she had worn in her hair. It was blue.

The following January, Nick moved to an apartment in a new block close to Fujimigaoka station on the Inokashira line. The house in Nakano had changed; when Monica left, it seemed as if her going dislodged something in the minds of all the other tenants, and Nick soon found himself living with strangers. He decided to look for somewhere else.

The people at the television studios laughed when he told them his new address. They had imagined he would take a place in Azabu or down near the Sumida river, where everyone was talking of going. Kugayama, in fact almost anywhere along the Inokashira line, was almost in the country.

Nick smiled at the smiles and set about buying some

furniture, although in this he was not particularly successful. After three months he had managed to acquire a very large refrigerator, two thin, beautiful, expensive, and extremely uncomfortable chairs, a floor lamp, a narrow bed, two breakfast cups, a soup bowl, a dinner plate, a complete set of cutlery, a lavatory brush, several towels, two kitchen knives, a frying pan, a medium-sized saucepan and three blankets. The flat remained without curtains, carpets or ceiling lights, so that, at night, Nick would sit on one of his chairs with a blanket draped around his shoulders, trying to read by the atmospheric glow of the floor lamp. As he also had no form of heating, and snow lay, frozen, on the streets of the city for much of that winter, it was not often that he spent his evenings at home.

And why should he, for, within the small orbit that is, still, the world of Tokyo, Nick, Niccolo, Rossa was a star, a celebrity. There were places to go, people to go with, and there was money to be made. It took only two or three hours a week for Nick to write his material and then record each programme of 'Itariago Ciao!', but being a star took up almost all of every day that was left. His face and his name were constantly in the media: television chat shows, the Friday scandal sheets, although, it must be said, never in connection with scandal, and even the society pages of *The Tokyo Weekender*. He had ventured into business early, under the guidance of his management, opening a menswear boutique called NiCo and investing in a restaurant in Shibaura, an Italian restaurant of course, although he had not liked the food on the only occasion he had eaten there. The food in his restaurant was not the only thing about his new life Nick Rossa did not like: he did not like the clothes in his shop, he did not like the friends he went to parties with or the shows on which he appeared. He did not like the crowds of schoolgirls who, increasingly, followed him from the studios now. But more than anything, Nick Rossa did not like himself.

When he had some free time, an evening early in the week
perhaps, or a Saturday afternoon, he would go back to
Nakano and the little bar on the north side of the station
where he had first met Bruno and Gina. He was not a star
there, he was only a customer. It was that, perhaps, which
made the food taste better than it had done in the old days; it
was what made him always ready to return.

Five months after Nick moved house he received a post
card from Kiku Miyashita. She was in London again, and
would stay there until July to attend a language school and
visit the galleries and exhibitions. She said she wanted to
come and see him in his new apartment when she got back to
Japan. The card was written in an uneasy mixture of English
and Japanese *kana*, but at the end, just before her name, she
wrote, in Italian, 'I love you'.

Of course, Nick knew that it did not mean 'I love you' in
the literal sense, and he knew that the girl must understand
this also, or she would not have written it. But for a lot of the
Saturday afternoons and evenings early in the week when he
sat in the bar on the north side of Nakano station, he did
wonder.

She telephoned late on a Sunday evening just as Nick was
getting ready to go out. There was a private party at the
Lexington Queen and he had an invitation. His management
insisted that he attend. He knew who was calling as soon as
she spoke, and he went out into the hot August night happier
than he could really account for. Why this girl, someone he
had met only once before, should mean so much to him he
did not know, but she did. They were to meet the following
weekend when she would come to see him. In the train on
the way to Shibuya, and then in the taxi from the station, he
thought about her, he thought about the ribbon she had
worn in her hair, and the way she had ended her post card
with the words of love.

He was to meet her at Fujimigaoka station at three o'clock, but at three-forty, when she still had not come, he went home. At six the telephone rang and answering it he heard her voice. She had mistaken the station, getting off at Kugayama, one stop further down the line. It was an understandable mistake, one that others had made. He bit on his disappointment and when she said she would come the following weekend, found that he could not even taste its bitterness anymore.

That next time there was no mistaking of stations, and she was neither early nor late. When she came past the ticket-collector and he saw her, Nick felt as if a flower had opened in his heart.

She was thinner than he remembered, and her hair was longer. The ribbon had been replaced by a large, black velvet bow. She wore a long, full-skirted sundress of narrow grey stripes and her neck and shoulders were bare. When she came up to him, she offered her hand, and he was surprised at its coolness, and the length of the fingers that he held so briefly in his own.

Her face was long, and the jaw sat slightly out of line when she smiled, when she laughed. It was not the face Nick Rossa remembered. It was not the face he had called before him in the time she had been away. It was an old face, the face of the women in the book of prints someone had given him as a house-warming present. She had smiled when she met him. She had laughed when he took her into the apartment. She was smiling now, and telling him she would help him buy some furniture.

They went from the flat to Omotesando and walked down the long, broad avenue with all the other couples who went there on Sundays and pretended, dreamed perhaps, that they were in Paris. Kiku talked about Paris as they walked along, she had spent her twenty-ninth birthday there, on her way back to London from Florence. It had rained, she said, and laughed again. Nick wanted to ask if she had spent her birthday in the rain alone, but he could not and so he took her into a sidewalk café and ordered two cups of espresso, looking through her smiles and her words as if they were windows opened to the spring.

They shopped. Kiku knew the best stores, and she knew what to buy. At the end of one long Saturday, the apartment was furnished, and the following week, when everything had been delivered, Nick placed the things that Kiku had chosen exactly as Kiku directed. When it was all done, she cooked for him and they ate what she had made at the new marble-topped table. Even the thin chairs that were of Nick's own choosing seemed a little less uncomfortable then.

She kissed him when she left that night, lightly, once on each cheek, and she kissed him again when she left him the next day after they had been to see the Modigliani exhibition at the museum in Takebashi. Then he did not see her again for a long time, and he knew what sadness was.

They were to have gone to the cinema together. Nick waited at the exit to the Tokyo line in Shibuya station, as they had arranged, but she did not come. He waited for half-an-hour and, thinking perhaps he might have made a mistake, walked to the other exit inside the station. She was not there either. He spent an hour moving between one exit and the other, and then he called her at home. Her mother answered. He asked to speak to the girl but she was not in. He asked when she would be coming back, but her mother could not tell him. She knew who he was, she called him Mister Nicco just as her daughter did, and she said she would get Kiku to call him as soon as she came back. Nick took the train back to Kugayama and waited by the telephone until after midnight, but she did not call and the house that she had furnished seemed to him as empty and bare as if not a table or a chair, lamp or book, were in it.

She did not call, and she did not return Nick's calls and so, at last, he made up his mind that he would not see her again. When he had just begun to get over her, when he had just begun to feel that there had been nothing to get over, his doorbell rang and when he answered, she was standing there.

She took him to meet her parents, driving him to her home with a speed and skill he would not have thought her capable of. The Miyashita house was in Jyugaoka, large and impressive behind its grey walls and screen of garden trees. Kiku's mother met them at the door; she had been a beauty once, Nick could see that, but now she had gone to fat and fussing. Like the house, she seemed to have closed herself off from the world at some point.

Kiku took him upstairs to see her room, in spite of her mother's protests that it was too untidy. It was painted in powder blue, although the colour of the walls was not what first caught Nick's attention. Her things were everywhere: drawing pads, opened boxes of pastels, paintbrushes and pencils. Mrs Miyashita, who had followed them on their progress through her house, pushed her daughter to one side and hurriedly picked up an item of what Nick thought might be Kiku's soiled underlinen from the carpet. He was more than a little taken aback by the mess the room was in, but what stayed in his mind after everything else had faded was the bed: it was covered in teddy bears, fifty, sixty, a hundred even, of all shapes and colours and sizes. It was a sea of fur and sightless, unblinking eyes.

He was taken into the sitting room, which was large but so filled with furniture that access to the ponderous sofa could be had only with extreme care, and Nick followed Kiku as if she were a jungle guide. When he was seated, she went out to the kitchen with her mother, the two women returning with trays of tea and peeled fruits so quickly that they must have been prepared ready for his coming. Drinking tea and eating fruit, Nick was engaged in a curious conversation in which Kiku acted as intermediary, carrying her mother's questions and small talk to him, and then returning his answers and other responses as if she were an interpreter, although everything that passed was in Japanese. Nick was a little uncomfortable with what was happening, but it was not an ordeal and as the minutes passed things grew easier.

At about seven-thirty Kiku's father came home. Nick had looked and looked for a trace of Kiku in her mother's features, but found none. As soon as Mr Miyashita entered the room, however, it was impossible not to know who his daughter was. He had that same long, square jaw, the same mouth set so firmly in it. What was missing in his face was the slight and curious twist in the jawline; what was missing in his daughter's was the deep and livid scar that gauged his forehead from one side to the other.

Nick stood up to be introduced. Mr Miyashita's breath said that he had been drinking. When the introductions were over, and the men were seated, Kiku took her father a glass of whiskey and water from the tray her mother had brought from the kitchen, knelt by the side of his chair while he drank it, and then brought him another. He sipped this, and his daughter stayed where she was, kneeling by his chair. Nick, alone now on the large expanse of sofa, felt exposed and isolated.

There was a long period of silence, and then Mr Miyashita said the word 'Englishman'. Nick was startled, and so slow in his response to what he assumed was a question that Kiku replied before him. She told her father that Nick was Italian, not English, and then she explained about 'Itariago Ciao!', and how she had met Nick and the kind advice he had given her about Florence, where he had been born, and the institute of fine art she had attended there, which Nick had also attended. She went on to say that Nick had agreed to give her private lessons in Italian, which was why he was there this evening because he had insisted that he meet both her parents before beginning the lessons. From the sofa Nick listened with a mouth that was metaphorically, if not actually, open.

Kiku's father seemed not to be listening, but he obviously

heard everything his daughter said because he then began to talk about the Italians and how they had been allies of the Japanese in the war, although, he added, they made poor soldiers. He started to tell a long and intricate story that, at one point, Nick understood was a joke about the first ambassador from the new German Federal Republic coming to Tokyo after the war and explaining to the Japanese foreign minister at a diplomatic party that 'the next time' they would both be better off without the Italians. Nick laughed because he felt he was expected to.

Then Mr Miyashita began to talk about opera. He liked opera, but not Italian opera. He liked German opera. He did not, he said, emphatically, like Puccini, who had traduced the honour of Japanese women. During the dinner that followed, Mr Miyashita kept referring to Nick as Signor Puccini.

Kiku sought to explain her father's behaviour as she drove Nick back to Kugayama through the dark and narrow streets. She wanted Nick to understand that her father had not been drunk, he was always like that. She and her mother took no notice of him when he was at home, and he was not at home all that often. Tonight had been a special occasion. She had made him come back to the house early in order that he might meet Nick. He was the head of a small paper manufacturing company and so was always busy in the evenings entertaining his clients or being entertained by the directors of the large company group with which his own firm was associated. At weekends he played golf.

Nick did not really care about Mr Miyashita; what he wanted to do was talk about the lies Kiku had told, but he did not know where to begin. Eventually, just as the girl had parked the car in front of his building, he found a way. He told her he was not Italian, he was English.

'I know', she said, and it was as if she had spoken to him for the first time; as if all their other conversations had been conducted under water; as if, when he heard her voice, it was a voice he had never heard before. He looked at the ribbon in her hair, tied in a bow like a little girl would wear, and he understood that it was a disguise.

She knew he was English, and that was by no means the whole extent of her knowledge. She had gone to the party in Nakano with a friend who was a friend of one of the boys that lived in the house. She had gone because she had been told she might meet Nick there. Nick was shocked. He asked her about the things, the lies, she had told her father. She answered that she had been forced to lie because if she had not, if she had told the truth about Nick's being English, her father would never have permitted her to take lessons with him, never allowed her to see him again, and she wanted to see him. She would like to learn Italian, she said, but the lessons were just an excuse so that she could see him at least twice a week.

On Friday evenings Kiku took a life class with her painting group. They hired a room and a model, and then, afterwards, went off to eat and drink together. Before she left him, she invited Nick to come and meet her friends the next Friday.

The class was held in a room in Ogikubo, a few minutes walk from the station. He was supposed to meet Kiku at the station, and she would take him there. Nick was early, and the girl was late, so he decided to use the map she had given him, just in case, to find the place for himself. It was not difficult and soon he was climbing the stairs up to the third floor.

The door to the room was slightly ajar, and he could hear music playing from inside. Thinking that the class must be over he left his shoes with all the others in the corridor outside and walked in. He regretted his action as soon as it was complete.

Immediately he was inside the room Nick found himself the object of intense and sudden interest from ten or fifteen people, all of whom seemed to be glaring at him, but none so coldly as the girl who had been the centre of their attention until Nick's rude entry. She was naked, of course, and still held her pose, but her eyes were angry, and there was even the faintest blush of colour in her cheek. Nick saw that, saw her eyes and reddening cheeks, saw as well the paler forms of her breasts, like little moons, and the shocking, to him, beard of black hair that covered the mound below the pudding shape of her belly. He saw because he looked. He looked because, for all that his own face was flush with blood, he could not make his eyes go anywhere else until he heard Kiku laughing, laughing and saying to the others that it was all right, that this was Mr Nicco, her friend, the one she had told them all about, her friend who was on television. The tension in the room ebbed, the eyes of the artists went back to pads and pencils, to the girl in the middle of the room, the girl who, alone, still stared angrily at Nick.

Kiku took him outside, although whether it was to spare him his own embarrassment, or the model's evident annoyance, or even her own giggles which she could not contain once they were on their own by the stairwell, Nick could not say. He simply kept apologizing and saying that he would just go home, but Kiku was so nearly choking on her own laughter she could not reply. She probably could not even hear him. Nick could hear. He heard someone clap their hands once and then a girlish but still authoritative voice, he imagined it was the model, announced the end of the session. Soon there were others with them out on the stairs, and Nick found himself being introduced to this one and that one. The model was the last to come out. Dressed, she was not quite as formidable as she had seemed in her anger and her nakedness. Kiku pulled her over to meet Nick. Her name was Fumiha Suzuki and close up she was just another Japanese girl with short hair and black clothes, and just a little too much make-up, especially around the eyes. She was the sort of girl Nick had met a thousand times in Tokyo, who pulled together the corners of a living by working part-time in the shops of Minami-Aoyama, or helping out in a recording studio, or on a photographic shoot. Nick had met the type so many times before at parties, at openings; he had just never met one without any clothes on before, and it was for this reason perhaps that he could not look this girl in the eye when Kiku introduced her to him, and why, as well, he compounded his difficulties by delivering his apology to her chest.

He did not stay long in the bar where they went afterwards because he did not feel altogether at ease. There was only one other girl among the members of Kiku's group present that evening. She sat with Nick and Kiku, and the model, in a tight little group at one end of the long counter. Nick tried, unsuccessfully, to start a conversation with one of the men sitting on the other side of Kiku but it came to nothing. After half-an-hour or so he said he would have to go. The girl had her mother's car for the evening and offered to drive him but Nick refused.

She came with him to the station, at least, and when they parted she kissed him, not as she had kissed him before, but full upon the lips. Her action excited him, and he kept his excitement like a magic pebble at the bottom of a jar through the journey home and through the depression he fell into on the train. He kept it too when he went to his bed. He had never seen a Japanese woman naked before, and, when he first closed his eyes in preparation for sleep that night, there came again to him the vision of the model in the room in Ogikubo; but now, although her body was the body he had so briefly glimpsed, the sketch his mind held etched in by his imagination, her face was the face of Kiku Miyashita.

The lessons began. It had to be a flexible arrangement because of the nature of Nick's work. Sometimes they would meet in the afternoon, sometimes in the evening, sometimes, even, in the morning. The time did not matter to Kiku, who did not work and had very few pegs around which to knot the strings of her days; she had the life classes, and she attended a tea ceremony school once each week, but that was all. Her parents had apparently agreed to her learning Italian with Nick in order to have her do something that they considered worthwhile. Evidently they did not have a very high opinion of her painting although she was, in her way, successful, having won a place in the national exhibition of the Nihonga school for three years in succession. Their first lesson was on a Tuesday evening.

Kiku was to come at seven o'clock and she had asked Nick to cook something. He had called his mother in England for help with recipes, and when the girl arrived the apartment was rich with the smells of tomatoes and garlic and wine. She would not drink because, again, she had her mother's car, but she ate, and she ate an amount that surprised Nick. The food was wonderful, that was another surprise for him, but by the time they had finished eating it was nine-thirty and time for the girl to leave. They had not used Italian at all, beyond Nick's description of the dishes he had prepared. Kiku did not seem to mind. She did not, actually, seem to care. When she kissed him her breath was ripe with the food she had eaten, and she surprised him again, parting his lips with her tongue and then slipping it deep into his mouth. Like an Italian girl, she said afterwards.

That was the way of things at the beginning. She would come to his apartment; they would eat, they would talk, and then they would kiss; and each time, Nick would be left wondering if, the next time, they would, he would, dare to take things further. In the beginning they, he, did not. And then, one afternoon when Kiku came to see him, finally, they undressed and went to bed together.

She had come straight from a matinee performance at the Kabuki-za. It was an outing organized by the woman who was her teacher in the rituals of the tea ceremony, and she and all of her fellow pupils had gone to the theatre together.

Kiku was wearing a kimono, and for once, was not driving her mother's car because of the constricting nature of her costume. She arrived at Nick's place in a taxi, for which Nick paid because the girl had only two Y10,000 notes tucked into the purse she carried with her, and the driver claimed he could not give her change.

She was hungry, but Nick had nothing prepared because he had not long returned home himself from a recording session of the quiz show on which he was a regular guest. The girl looked through the telephone directory to find a nearby noodle shop from which they could order lunch. In less than fifteen minutes the trays of food had been delivered, and Nick and Kiku began to eat.

They were sitting on the floor in the small living area, on one of the pink and beige cotton durees Kiku had chosen because they pulled down the colours from two of her own paintings that she had given to Nick and which hung now on the wall of his room, although the truth was that Nick did not altogether care for the subjects, a vase of pink hydrangea, and a pot of pink geraniums, both painted on a lacquer table against a gaudy screen. The food was gone, and they were drinking tea and looking at an album of photographs the girl had brought with her, photographs from her year in Europe, but which she had only just had developed and printed.

Some of the photographs had been taken at a beach resort where Kiku had stayed and showed her, tanned and wind-blown on the sand, in only her bikini bottom. She laughed when she turned the page to let Nick see these because he blushed and she told him that, really, there was nothing to blush for, because she had nothing for him to see. And she was right, there was nothing for him to see: but for the long hair blown back by a summer breeze, she might have been a boy, a famished boy she was so thin, but the blush came to his cheeks nonetheless. He blushed, perhaps, for the contrast that was there between the naked figure in the sunlit photographs and the tightly bound form she presented in his sitting room, everything wrapped so tightly, from the white glove-like socks buttoned onto her feet to her coiled hair, everything so tight, so tight, but for the exposed softness of her throat, and the unrouged pallor of her face.

And Kiku put aside the photographs and turned to see to the trays of dishes she had earlier pushed behind her. And turning on her knees, she presented her buttocks to Nick, the silk of her kimono stretched across her haunches. Nick reached out his hand like a child in a toy shop and his fingers brushed the taught and gaudy patterns of the material, felt the vague contours of the flesh beneath.

She stopped what she was doing when she felt his touch, and it seemed for Nick as if he was caught with her in a living photograph, the moment held forever, his arm held out, his fingers reaching, numb. He could hear his breath and the ticking of a clock from the next room, but he could not hear anything else. At last she turned to him again, half-turned, and spoke the words of love that once she had written.

They went together to the bed and sitting on it shyly kissed, like children perhaps. For a long time that kiss was all there was between them, but then the girl took his hand, the hand that had first touched her, and placed it inside the small vee left by her clothing at the neck and the hand became a bird warming to the nest. Nick moved his fingers slowly, gently, seeking her breast but then Kiku began to laugh and said it was just like she had told him, there was nothing there. But there was something; he found it, small and warm, the softest, smallest bud, too small to cup even, but there, like a whisper of the flesh, like a child's promise.

Still laughing, and with Nick's hand still inside her clothing, the girl began to untie the cord that held the stiff brocade of her belt in place. He watched then in wonder as the yards of material were uncoiled, only to reveal other strings, yards more of silk, of cotton. Undressing herself, Kiku revealed more than, perhaps, Nick might have wanted to see: the cushions and towels that were used to round out her figure and, finally, his hands together again in his lap, she stood and her opened garments let Nick see what she wore beneath all this finery: a pair of quite undistinguished girl's panties. She saw him looking, and said that she had bought them in London, from Marks and Spencer's. She seemed to understand his disappointment more than he did himself and was quiet when she got into his bed.

She was so thin. But she delighted him. Her hair, unpinned, lay across his pillows like the waves on a painted ocean. He could not keep his hands from her: from her arms which he could close his fingers about, from her waist which he could circle with his arm, the skin of her back with its down of fine hair about the spine, the small slope of her buttocks, the nubbled areolae that, as she lay on her back, seemed fixed like badges of brown seaweed to her chest, arbitrary, mysterious. And then the sudden touch of the pubic hair that tufted at the apex of her thin thighs.

Did Kiku Miyashita know in him a similar joy to that which he found in her? Nick wondered and hoped, but he could not really tell. He could not tell, in part, because he was not greatly experienced in these things. The afternoon when he had been taken to bed by Gina Morelli had been his sole sexual experience, except for one or two desperate and, finally, unfulfilling moments with a girl he had been seeing when he was at Cambridge.

He could not even say he had actually enjoyed what had happened with Gina Morelli. It had been shocking, at first, and then frightening, for some of the time painful even, and if there had been, as well, excitement, it had been too much mixed with those other emotions to make the experience enjoyable while it was taking place. And then, afterwards, had come regret and sadness, a little fear, even.

Gina had kissed him and it was the strength of her, of her desire, that put the fear into him. When he looked at her after the kiss, when he saw her face turned stupid with desire, when he saw the thick rouge of her lips smeared across her face so that her mouth seemed turned spastic like some drunk's, he had wanted to leave, to get away, but he could not because she was stronger than he was and he knew she would not, willingly, let him go. She had pulled the clothes from him and buried his face between her heavy breasts and arms, while he gagged, caught between the urge to release the desire she had summoned into being between his legs, and the smell, like raw onions, that came from her unshaven armpits.

He was called back to himself, to his own bed, to the girl he held tightly in his arms. He was called back by the girl. She asked him if he had something. Stupidly, he asked what. She did not speak, but circled the thumb and index finger of her right hand and threaded the loop over the stiffened forefinger of the left. Only then did he understand. he went from the bed, from the girl, and found his clothes.

He knew where the contraceptives were kept at the supermarket that was only a little way from his apartment, but all the same he half-filled the basket he took from the stack by the door with stuff he neither wanted or had need of before going to confront them. The boxes were stacked in between the toilet paper and women's sanitary supplies, in a row, each successive box more grandly wrapped than the one preceeding it, like progressively more expensive assortments of chocolates. There was no Japanese at all on any of the boxes, and the English that was there made no sense to him. He stood, undecided, until the approach of a woman with a small child made him take one of the most expensive and bury it amongst his other shopping. Of course, when he got to the check-out he was confronted by a young girl who could not make the automatic register scan the bar code on the box, and who did not, herself, know the price of what he had bought. When it had been held up for everyone in the store to see, when the question of price had been shouted and, shouted, answered, the girl then wrapped it, for modesty's sake, in a brown paper bag.

If desire had left him as he stood stupid amidst the shelves of the supermarket, it returned when Kiku Miyashita pulled him down beside her in his bed again. She kissed him and touched him, held herself against him and, when it was time, she placed one of the sheaths upon him. They she lay back and as Nick pushed himself up on his arms above her, she raised her knees. But she was a virgin, and this was not what he had expected.

That first time was difficult for them. Nick was a gentle boy and afraid he would hurt Kiku, as she was afraid of being hurt. But for her, at least, the desire to complete this thing they had begun was greater than her fear of doing it and, in the end, because of her desire, they succeeded.

What they experienced then was not what either of them had anticipated perhaps, but when it was done they were not unhappy with each other, and Nick knew that, whatever else, they were confirmed in what mattered between them, their love.

And it was five o'clock. The afternoon seemed to have lasted for ever. The afternoon seemed never to have begun. Kiku telephoned a nearby beauty parlour to ask them to dress her, and then borrowed clothes from Nick so that she might go to the shop. She left quickly and would not let him accompany her. As she walked from his door to the stairway, Nick watched her, ludicrous in his jeans and sweater, her bare feet in the ornate slippers she had come in. He watched her, and his heart ached with the love that it held for her.

It was this love which made him go, the next day, to Kamiyacho and the medical centre to which he had been directed once by his agent. There, he explained to an American doctor, a woman, that he wished to be tested for the presence in his blood of the Human Immune Virus. When she had heard his sexual history the doctor attempted to counsel him against having the test, explaining the extreme unlikelihood of infection for a man from a single, unprotected encounter with a woman who was no longer menstruating; but Nick loved Kiku Miyashita and he knew what he must do and why. His test result, when it came back, was negative.

Their passion, after the drawn-out comedy of their first coming together, surprised and then pleased Nick and Kiku. Where before they had unravelled the silks of Kiku's kimono now they pulled upon a cloth entirely other, a cloth, an ever-unfolding cloth, of delight. There was no pretence at all now between them, they met as lovers and when they parted, parted as they had met, as lovers. What began with the shedding of Kiku's coat in the hallway of Nick's apartment ended moments later in his bedroom as the girl shook the last garment from her nakedness. Between her coming and her going they went unclothed, for they were lovers, and their skin was all the covering their bodies required or their hearts had desire for.

They made love. They made love in his bedroom, his kitchen, the bathroom. They made love once in his hallway after Kiku had called from a phone-booth outside the all-night grocery store just a few minutes' walk away from the apartment. She told him to undress and be ready for her when she arrived. Inside the apartment she stood before him in a fur coat that belonged to her mother, but she was as naked underneath it as he was. She said afterwards that she had gone into a lavatory at the station and undressed, putting her clothes into a bag she had brought out with her.

And, once, they made love in her room, in her father's house, rolling among the teddy bears, with her mother downstairs in the kitchen cooking their supper. That time Nick had laid his hand across Kiku's mouth in case the sounds she made in her pleasure should betray them, flying down the staircase and into her mother's ears like spiteful little birds. Kiku had sulked afterwards, saying, finally, that even had her mother heard she would not have known what the noises were.

Kiku had her pleasure in him. His question was answered.

It was not what it had been like with Gina Morelli. That had frightened him, her bellowing and her rolling, bulbous eyes. Kiku cooed, quietly, softly, the soft throatings of pigeons in a green summer wood, quietly, softly, more, and again, more.

Nick's pleasure in her was that he loved her, and he knew that she loved him. He wrote to his mother, telling her of Kiku, of the love that was between them and of his certainty that he would marry this Japanese girl, that she would be the mother of his children. The reply to that letter was a long time in coming, but when it came contained his parents' blessing. They asked him to send them photographs of the girl; they asked to meet her; they asked that he please his mother and his father and marry her in Italy, in the church where they had married.

Until he wrote to his mother, Nick Rossa had told no one of his love for Kiku. After he received his parents' reply there was no one that he did not tell, no one, that is, except Kiku. He did not tell her because there was no need to tell her. She knew, as he did, what was between them and what its consequences were.

They had talked for some time of holding a party in his apartment. At the end of January they decided it would be a Valentine's party. They drew up a guest list, organized a menu, and bought all that they thought was necessary. Nick made an additional purchase. He went, alone, on the morning of the party, to the Wako store in Ginza and purchased a ring for Kiku, a single diamond set in a slim platinum band. It would be her engagement ring and he would give it to her at the end of the party in the moments of quietness and tired caresses that there would be after the other people had gone, before she too must leave. Nick had the ring in his pocket when the first guests began to arrive. His anticipation of the time when he would offer it to Kiku burned inside him, as if he had somehow swallowed a bright, piercing star.

The girl was late coming to the party. She had been at the apartment for most of the afternoon, but had gone home at five o'clock to change, saying she would be back before eight. But it was almost nine o'clock when he opened the door to her and then he hardly knew her. The dress she wore was in some stiff, satin-like material, patterned with Regency stripes, as if the cloth had been purchased for curtains and then thought better of. The hem reached almost to her ankles, the neck was high and the sleeves, augmented by some fussy lace at the wrist, all but hid her hands. It was only the ribbon in her hair that told him who she was.

She did not stay, and when she left she would not tell him why she must go so soon. After she was gone the ring was still in his pocket, but the star of his anticipation was only a little dimmed when he walked back through the darkness to the party, for he knew he would see her tomorrow. He would give her the ring then. Tomorrow and its pleasures were so much in his mind when he got back inside the apartment that he did not understand when some of her friends began to laugh about how there would be no more late nights for Kiku, and it was Fumiha Suzuki, the model he had angered that night at the life class, who told him that Kiku was engaged to be married to a man with a promising career before him in the insurance business. The couple's families had settled the last of the business between them with the matchmaker that morning in one of the lounges of the Okura Hotel, while Nick had been busy buying his ring.

He called her, of course he did. He called her that night, and the next morning, and again after that, and then again after that, and again. She was never at home. He left messages for her to call him. It was as if he spoke into the empty air. After two weeks he stopped calling, and the place inside him where the bright little flame had burned was cold and empty, and in his mouth was the taste of ashes where once there had been the taste of love.

She came back, as she had done before. One day at the end of August he went to answer the door and she was standing there. He looked at her, and then turned away because he was ashamed for her to see his face as it collapsed into sorrow. She stood with him like that, one white gloved hand upon his shoulder. That was the last time she ever came to his apartment, but it was not the last time he saw her.

She was to be married at the end of November, to a man she had known, slightly, since she was a schoolgirl. He was three years older than she. They had spoken, once, when they were children, and he had always remembered her and thought of her a suitable person to be his wife. Kiku had known before she went to Europe that she must prepare for marriage when she returned. It had been an agreement she had made with her father in order to make the trip. He would allow her to have this European year for herself, and then, when she came home, she would at last accept the duties of a daughter and allow herself to be given in marriage to a man her father deemed suitable. She had been to three meetings with prospective bridegrooms in the time she had been Nick Rossa's lover. The man she had agreed to marry was the man she had been introduced to at the third meeting. She thought a marriage with him might be possible because of the thing they shared, their school, and the fact that, although she had not recognized his face when they met again, they were not complete strangers. Nick asked her about love, about happiness. She said that these things were not necessarily required for a marriage to be successful.

They began to see each other again, whenever they could. When they were together they went to film shows and concerts, sometimes to a gallery to see an exhibition by one of the members of her painting circle. There was not a lot of time for them to talk, and what time there was Nick wasted. He wasted it because he did not say to Kiku what he wanted to say: that he loved her, that he wanted to marry her, that he had in his pocket the ring he had bought for her, for her.

He said none of this. He asked, again and again, only if she thought she would be happy married to a man she did not love. In the end, Kiku stopped replying to the question.

The autumn came, and on a warm October evening they went together to see a film, an Italian film. Afterwards he took her to the Borsalino restaurant in Roppongi. He was known there. They had the best table reserved for him. This time Nick did not ask Kiku if she was happy, instead he told her that she did not have to marry the man she was engaged to. He told her that if she wanted, he would give her a ticket to Europe and enough money to live on for a year.

She touched his hand. It was only a touch, a whisper from the past, but he had not touched her for such a very long time, such a very long time. She touched his hand and she said she could not run away from the life she had to live. Nick told her that she could, that she only had to want to do it. She shook her head.

Two days passed, and he found a card from her in his post-box. She wrote, 'My dearest, I think you are the kindest person I have ever known. Thank you for the gift you offered that I could not accept. Last night was one of the happiest nights of my life. Take care and try to be as happy as you make me.' She did not sign the card, instead she had drawn upon it a parody of her own face, with a ribbon, coloured blue, on the crown of her head.

Nick went to her wedding. It was expected, she said, because he had been her teacher of Italian, because he had been a guest in her father's house. Her father expected him to be there, and he expected him to make a speech.

He was seated at the table closest to her, because he was a celebrity. On his right was the head of the Tokyo office of the Yasuda insurance company, on his left the wife of the managing director of a large department store. Nick looked neither to his right nor his left, he looked at Kiku, although he could scarcely recognize her beneath the mask of heavy make-up that had been applied to her face, and with her hair piled up to accommodate the cap of white feathers that gathered her veil. There were no ribbons, not even white ones.

He did not eat. The waiters carried away his plates untouched as one course followed another. He did not drink. He made his speech and when, afterwards, he left the room and did not return, it was assumed by the others at his table that he was ill. He was. His heart was breaking.

He did not go to the second, more informal party, but he waited in the hotel bar for some of the people from Kiku's painting circle who had attended the wedding. It was a subdued gathering, and after one drink it broke up.

Nick walked back to the subway with Fumiha Suzuki and, on the way, she asked him if he wanted her to stay with him that night. The abruptness of what she said shocked him as much as the words themselves, so that, for a moment, he could not answer, but when he did it was to decline. The girl did not say anything else until it became time for her to leave him to get to her train, then she told him that he might as well have her because he would never see Kiku again, ever.

But Fumiha Suzuki was wrong. Nick did see Kiku again. She and her husband went to Australia for their honeymoon. Six weeks or so after their return to Tokyo, Kiku telephoned Nick's apartment. He was out when she called, but she left a message on his answering machine asking if they could meet. She said she would be in the café in Shibuya they had sometimes gone to after a film. She would wait for him there on the following afternoon between three and four. She said she hoped he would come.

She was so changed Nick almost did not recognize her. It was only when she got up from her seat and came over to where he stood by the door, uncertainly, that he knew who she was. He thought she stumbled as she approached him, but her arms were reaching out in an embrace, that was all. He held her, and he held her for too long so that, when they separated and walked to the table where she had left her coat and purse, there was an awkwardness between them.

She had cut her hair, and what was left hung lifeless about her ears and neck. Her face, always thin, was gaunt now, and her skin seemed utterly bleached of colour. She told him she was pregnant and having a difficult time because she was nauseous for most of the hours that she was awake. She thought she must have conceived on her wedding night. Her mother was furious at what she had allowed to happen to herself. Her husband's mother was delighted, however. She had already decided that the child would be a boy.

Nick listened to her and thought only that he could not now ever reach across the space that separated them, although its distance was no more than the breadth of a café table. The child she carried bound her in her marriage as nothing else could. She was as lost to him now as if some wicked magician from a pantomime story had conjured her away to the farthest star. He could only watch her; he had watched her as she became a wife, and he must watch her as she became a mother. And he knew he could not bear it.

He saw her once more after that meeting, when her thin belly had begun to show that she was carrying a child. She kissed his lips when they met, and she kissed his lips when they parted. She kissed him, perhaps, because she had determined on what he already knew, that they would not meet again. When he lost sight of her that last time as she walked away from him, it was as if the door of her life closed behind her. She walked away and she did not once look back.

A little while afterwards, when he had tidied his commercial affairs by breaking almost every contract to which he was a party, Nick Rossa returned to England. Unsure of what to do with himself, he went to work in the family business. After a year he was recruited by a large multi-national food corporation which employed him in its foreign licensing section. He did well, much to his own surprise, and was quite quickly rewarded with promotions and increasing responsibilities. At a food fair in Milan he met a Japanese woman named Eiko Ohira, who was a freelance translator attached to the delegation from a Sapporo brewery interested in producing under license some of the British beers controlled by Nick's company. Miss Ohira confessed that she had been a great fan of 'Itariago Ciao!' when she was first introduced to Nick, and he was flattered that anyone should remember him from his days as a star in Tokyo.

After the second time that they had a business meeting together, Nick took Miss Ohira out to dinner, and at the end of the evening, she went with him back to his hotel room where they became lovers. She was the first woman he had been with since Kiku Miyashita. Six months later, when Nick had introduced her to his family, and gone to Japan to meet her parents, they married.

The marriage was happy. Eiko gave birth to a daughter a little after their third wedding anniversary. They named her Sayuri Lucia. She was born in Switzerland because Nick had been transferred to the corporation's head office in Berne when Eiko was three months pregnant. Eiko's mother came to be with her daughter for the birth and the weeks that followed it.

The marriage was happy. Another child, a boy, Toshiyuki Alfredo, was born. Nick rejoiced in the children he had made with Eiko, and he rejoiced in his wife, treating her with care and gentleness and great affection, but he did not love her. He did not love his wife because he could not, for he still loved Kiku Miyashita. Eiko knew that Nick did not love her. She did not think it was important. There were other things, respect, reliability, things more durable, more trustworthy than love. She looked to her children, and her happiness, to justify her feelings. Of course, she did not know about Kiku Miyashita. She did not know, because it was the one thing her husband had never confided to her about his past.

There was a drawer in the desk at his office which Nick Rossa always kept locked. Sometimes, not often, but sometimes, if he was working late and alone, he would open the drawer and take out the single post card it contained. 'My dearest, I think you are the kindest person I have ever known. Thank you for the gift you offered that I could not accept. Last night was one of the happiest nights of my life. Take care and try to be as happy as you make me.' He had read the card so often he no longer looked at the words she had written such a long time ago. He did not really even see the card anymore when he held it in his hand. What he saw was a blue ribbon, all tied up in a girlish bow.

# HOUSEWORK
## or
# THE IDEAL HUSBAND

The talk started as soon as the foreigner moved into the apartment building with a Japanese woman, and it increased when the two names went up outside the door and on the front of the mail box, suggesting to most people that they weren't even married, although there was a clause in the lease which specifically prohibited co-habitation. Of course, Mrs Okuda said that they might be engaged and intending to get married later on, but then she would, wouldn't she? It was well known that Mrs Okuda was a rather simple soul, a bit on the soft side really, and always too ready to see good in others where there was probably none at all. Separate names up in public like that for all the world to see was practically throwing it in people's faces. Of course there was going to be talk.

There was a lot more, however, when Mrs Tanaka met the foreigner that morning leaving the rubbish down for the bin men. Well, that was unheard of, for a man to take the rubbish down. It was unheard of, and more than that, it just wasn't done. Bachelors, yes, but married men had wives to do work of that order, and so what if he wasn't married, there was still a woman in the house. For Mrs Tanaka ethics always took precedence over morality.

When the foreigner was seen leaving the rubbish down again, on the second collection day, and again on the third, and when he met Mrs Hiraishi on the stairs as she was bringing down the hard garbage and offered to carry it down for her because it looked so heavy; when he insisted, in spite of her protests that she could manage quite well, thank you very much, and took the sacks from her — pulled them out of her hands was the way Mrs Hiraishi expressed it — well, it was clear that things could only go from bad to worse after that.

He didn't seem to work. None of the women in the building had ever seen him going off to the station in the morning, properly turned out and presentable, like the other men, like their husbands. In fact, it was she who went off to the station all la-di-da in her suits and black stockings and heels so high that, as Mrs Matsuoka pointed out, 'if they'd been any higher she wouldn't have been able to walk at all.' He used to see her off at the door. Mrs Tanaka said she had even seen him kissing her one day, kissing her on the mouth, in public. It wasn't right.

He didn't seem to do anything at all. He went shopping sometimes, and he kept on taking the rubbish out; he cleaned the windows. Mrs Horiguchi, who lived next door to them, said she heard the vacuum cleaner every morning after the woman had gone off to wherever it was the woman went off to, and the bedding was always out on fine days, so he must have done that as well, but he didn't, as you might say, work. Well, not men's work anyway, and there was another slap in the face for convention, if you like.

Mrs Okuda said that there were a lot of foreign men like that, who stayed at home all day and did the cleaning and the shopping, even looked after the children some of them, if there were any children, while the wife held a job in business. Nobody said anything, they just let her run on. It was another of her daft ideas, of course, of course it was. Nobody said anything when she said that, anyway, he did work — not housework — but real work. She wasn't sure, she couldn't be certain, and they were all waiting for her to get on with it and tell them whatever it was she had to tell them even though they knew they would not be able to believe it, she wasn't sure but she thought he might be a writer.

Well, of course, this was just another of Mrs Okuda's little fancies, but everyone was very good, nobody laughed. Nobody laughed even when she said she thought he was a writer because she'd walked along the corridor and seen him working. The window had been open, apparently, and Mrs Okuda had seen him sitting in front of a computer screen — writing. At least she thought that was what he was doing, but of course, she couldn't be sure. She hadn't wanted to stop and stare into the room; it would have been rude and, besides, he might have seen her.

Not that Mrs Okuda would have been any the wiser if she'd have stuck her head through the window and asked him to move over so that she could get a better view of the screen. He could have been playing Nintendo, and she wouldn't have known the difference. She was soft, you see, and a bit silly as well, but it was sad really because everybody knew that Okuda knocked her about a lot. He drank. He drank a lot, and when he drank he knocked her about. It wasn't something people talked about, well, not in front of her, but they knew what went on. You could see the bruises. There were other women as well, apparently. Mrs Nakajima had seen him in Shinjuku once with some painted little trollop who didn't look old enough to have left school, never mind doing the sort of job she looked like she was doing. Mrs Okuda was a simple soul and life hadn't treated her right, so, if she wanted to have these daft ideas no one was going to stop her. It wouldn't have been right. Mind you, it was one of her stupid ideas that took her to the foreigner's apartment one evening to introduce herself, wasn't it, and look what came of that.

She really had no business going to see those people like that, that was Mrs Tanaka's view of the matter once what had happened came out. They'd done what was necessary when they moved in, you couldn't say that they hadn't. They might not have been married, they might have announced the fact to the world by putting their names up over the door and on the mailbox, but they did at least take a little present to each of their neighbours when they moved in, or at least the woman did. The man would not have known about any of that sort of thing. They did what they were supposed to do and that was that. If they didn't want to get married, then they didn't want to get married, and that was that. Never mind about the conditions in the lease. There weren't supposed to be any pianos in the building, but there were. There weren't supposed to be any dogs or cats either, but there were. If that's how they wanted to live, well, let them live like that, that was Mrs Matsuoka's view of the matter. Live and let live. There was certainly no need for Mrs Okuda to go and introduce herself, and there was no need for her to have gone into the apartment when the woman asked her to, but she did.

She went in and she was there for nearly an hour, and wasn't she just full of it when she saw people the next day. She couldn't stop talking about it, Rie and Philip this, and Rie and Philip that, until Mrs Horiguchi all but told her to shut up, that nobody was interested in what she had seen, and nobody was interested in what she had to say. The trouble was, they were.

Of course, coming from Mrs Okuda it was all a jumble. She kept jumping from one thing to another with no sense at all, so it was very difficult to follow what she was saying most of the time, but when she'd finished, and when she'd gone home because she had to get Okuda's dinner ready for him in case he came back that night in a state fit enough to eat anything, there was a lot of talk about what she'd said. Mind you, whether you believed any of it, well, that was another matter entirely.

First of all, according to Mrs Okuda, they were married, but the man, Philip, didn't believe in the woman having to take his name. Well, as Mrs Tanaka said, there was nothing unusual about that. In Japan a lot of men took their wife's name when they got married and went into the woman's family. Mrs Okuda got very agitated about that because it wasn't what she had tried to say. No, this foreigner didn't see why anyone should change their name just because they got married; he thought marriage ought to be a contract between two equal partners, and you could only show this if you kept your own name. So then Mrs Nakajima said, well, what is his name, although it was up outside the door and on the mail-box and had been for nearly a month by that time, but she swore she didn't know. Mrs Okuda told her it was Stevens, but when she called him that, when she called him Mr Stevens, he told her to call him Philip.

It was the same with the woman. Her name was Okada, but she said that, after living in Australia, she'd just got used to being called Rie, and, if Mrs Okuda didn't mind, would she call her Rie, and, if Mrs Okuda didn't mind, could she call her by Mrs Okuda's given name as well. Mrs Okuda, the soft thing, said, of course she didn't mind, and then told them her name, which is Yuka.

Well, the fact that the woman had lived abroad for a long time explained a lot, everyone agreed with that, but it didn't explain why the man took the rubbish out all the time, and did the housework and the shopping, and didn't have a proper job. It did nothing to explain any of that, and neither did Mrs Okuda. All she could do was go on about the apartment and how different it was and how clean everything was.

The apartment, at least according to Mrs Okuda, was like something out of a film. There was hardly any furniture, just a chair and a sofa, both leather, like in an office, and they'd put wood down on the floor over the linoleum instead of a proper carpet like ordinary people. They had a stereo, but there was no television. The woman said that television was a waste of time, and there were much better things to do in the evening than sit staring at a lot of idiots on a screen. Even Mrs Okuda was able to understand what she meant by that, and by the way she looked at her husband, if that's what he was. Mrs Okuda thought it was all very 'romantic', but then she would, wouldn't she?

The apartment was kept spotless, even in the kitchen. Mrs Okuda said you could see your face in the stainless steel around the gas-table, and, when she asked how they kept it so clean, the man said it was because he polished it every day with metal polish. And everywhere was the same — the room where they slept, the bathroom, the toilet. The only things they had out on the balconies were pots of plants and even they were perfect, watered properly and kept just so. When Mrs Okuda asked how everything stayed so nice the woman had laughed and said it was nothing to do with her.

The woman, according to Mrs Okuda, worked in the fashion industry. She wasn't clear what she did exactly, but it was something to do with fashion. Whatever it was, it certainly kept her busy. You used to see her going off in the morning at about eight, and then she was almost never home before nine. That evening Mrs Okuda had called was unusual; she'd come back at six. So that was what she did with herself all day. As for him, well, it turned out that Mrs Okuda was right after all, he was a writer. Of course, she didn't know, or if she knew, she didn't say, what he wrote, it could have been anything, all that mattered for Mrs Okuda was that he was a writer, in other words, an artist. That was all she needed to know, and really, as Mrs Tanaka said afterwards, you would really rather she had not known because, once she did, that was all she could talk about, that, and what a kind man he was, what a wonderful man and what a wonderful husband. An ideal husband, she said, ideal.

She met him one day when she was on her way back from the supermarket. He was just on his way to do some shopping himself, he said, but when he saw the two big bags she was carrying, well, it was just like the time with Mrs Hiraishi and the rubbish. He insisted that he'd carry them back to the apartments for her, and he did. Well, she couldn't get over that. She just couldn't get over it. She kept going on and on about what a kind man he was, what a kind man.

She was always over there after that. She'd hang about in the corridors, or down by the mail boxes, waiting for one or the other to come along and bump into her, and invite her back for a cup of tea. Mrs Tanaka saw her one evening, standing about in the cold downstairs with just a cardigan on. Eight o'clock it was, and when Mrs Tanaka asked her if everything was all right, because she thought, you see, that Okuda might have come back early for once and shut her out of the house again, because that had happened more than once before. Well, the girl looked at her as if she didn't know what to say, and the truth was, of course, that she didn't know what to say. In the end she said she was waiting for the postman to come. The postman! It was eight o'clock at night and she was waiting for the postman. The daft trollop actually stood there and watched Mrs Tanaka emptying her mailbox, and then says she's waiting for the postman!

Well, she was waiting for someone, but it wasn't any postman. It was the woman. Mrs Tanaka stood at the top of the stairs and watched her. She waited and then she heard the click-clack of those heels coming along, and she saw the woman come into the building and go to the mailboxes, and then round the corner, as if she was just coming to check the post herself, comes Mrs Okuda and gives an impression of surprise so well done, Mrs Tanaka said, it would have taken her in if she hadn't met Mrs Okuda herself only five minutes before and seen her shivering with the cold and her face and hands all frozen.

Well, the next thing is, the woman takes Mrs Okuda up the stairs with her and into her apartment, and Mrs Okuda goes with her just as nice as you please, just like a little dog that's been waiting for its master to come back.

If she wasn't in with the two of them, then she was outside with one or the other. It soon became a regular thing to see her walking back with the man, him carrying her shopping as well as his own, and once, once, they were even seen together in the park, nowhere near a shop, and without a bag of groceries between them. Someone should have put a stop to it then really, but no one did.

She had too much time on her hands, Mrs Okuda did. There were no children to keep her busy, and Okuda was never in the house unless he was too drunk or too sick from the drink to go out. She was on her own too much with nothing to do, and then, as well, she was such a poor, sad little thing, that none of the other women ever took her seriously. That was the only way people could put up with her, you see, her and her daft ideas about things. They did take her seriously though, the foreigner and the woman, they must have done or why else would she have hung about them so much? It was probably the first time in her life anyone had, and all that attention must have gone to her head. Well, it must have done something, because soon she was there with the man in the afternoons as well as with the two of them at night, and it was obvious what was going on. Anyway, Mrs Horiguchi next door could hear the racket they made when they were doing it.

It was bound to happen really, bound to. It probably started that time after Okuda knocked her about so badly. Well, Mrs Hiraishi saw her the next day and even she was shocked. She said she told her she should go to see a doctor. She didn't of course. She went to see him, the foreign man, Philip or whatever it was she called him. You can imagine it,

can't you, and understand it as well, really. She'd have gone
to him with her face all broken and the bruising on her arms
where Okuda had got hold of her. She'd have wept and wept
and he'd have touched her, the way foreigners do, and she'd
have lifted up her face to his and spoken his name and, well,
that would have been that. That was that, really, wasn't it?

It was Mrs Tanaka who tackled her about what was going
on. Well, it was a disgrace really, and you couldn't allow that
sort of thing in such a small building. It would get out.
Bound to really, and then the whole neighbourhood would
be talking and Okuda would hear of it and she'd be covered
in bruises again. Worse than that, probably. No, Mrs
Tanaka, was only doing what was best, or what she thought
was best. It had to be stopped. Well, it did really, it had to be
stopped, but by that time it was too late to stop it because
there was more than Mrs Okuda involved, by that time, at
any rate. There was Mrs Horiguchi for one.

It all came out when Mrs Tanaka got hold of Mrs Okuda
that day after the grocery van made its delivery. Everyone
was there and perhaps that was the reason Mrs Okuda let
slip about Mrs Horiguchi. Well, it was more by way of an
announcement, in fact. Mrs Tanaka was really giving it to
her, to Mrs Okuda that is, telling her what a silly girl she
was, how it could come to no good, no good at all. Mrs
Okuda wasn't having any of this, and was giving back as
good as she was getting. Well, this was a surprise in itself,
you see. Little Mrs Okuda? Daft little, soft little Mrs Okuda
standing up to Mrs Tanaka? No one could believe it, really
they couldn't.

Mrs Tanaka tried to shame her into tears. She said as
how, if Mrs Okuda wasn't worried for herself, she might at
least show some concern for the man's wife, and Mrs Okuda
came right back at her with the fact that Rie, as she called
her, knew all about what was going on and didn't mind a bit.
She'd told Mrs Okuda that they didn't see why being
married should stop the giving and taking of love with other

people. She said, Mrs Okuda did, that Rie didn't mind at all about what she and Philip gave to each other, and she didn't mind about what Philip and Mrs Horiguchi gave to each other either and neither did she, Mrs Okuda. She'd been a bit jealous at first, Mrs Okuda had been, but then Philip had explained how the only way to change the world was by giving love to people who needed love and wanted to give it in return.

Well, when she'd finished that little speech there was complete silence and poor Mrs Horiguchi was as white as a sheet. Everyone just picked up their boxes of vegetables and went in, leaving Mrs Okuda down in the car park on her own. Not that she was there for long. As soon as she thought she wouldn't be seen, she went straight up to the second floor. Well, for once, she was a little bit too late because Mrs Horiguchi was there before her, shaking like a leaf. Mrs Okuda went in anyway, and the three of them must have come to some arrangement because afterwards Mrs Okuda and Mrs Horiguchi were as thick as thieves, in and out of each other's apartments, shopping together, and whenever they got the chance, over at the foreigner's.

It ought to have ended there, but it couldn't. It was infectious, the thought of what was going on, all of that loving, it was as if the idea was like the flu: sooner or later · everybody would go down with it. And they did.

Mrs Matsuoka was the next. Mrs Tanaka saw her at the foreigner's door about half-past eight one Thursday morning. She must have waited for his wife to go to work and then gone round with some excuse. She went inside and it was nearly twelve before she came out again. Mrs Tanaka knew that for a fact because she stood and watched the door all morning and it never opened once from the minute Mrs Matsuoka went in until the minute when Mrs Matsuoka came out again, smoothing her apron and looking pleased with herself.

Mrs Matsuoka! You could understand it with the other

two perhaps, but not Mrs Matsuoka! At least Mrs Okuda and Mrs Horiguchi were young, and Mrs Okuda was actually pretty when she took the time and trouble to see to herself, comb her hair and put a bit of make-up on, but Mrs Matsuoka was old. She was fifty-five if she was a day, and had two grandchildren! It was disgusting, so it was.

It had to stop. It had to, but it didn't. After Mrs Matsuoka there was Mrs Nakajima, running about in short dresses and ankle socks as soon as she'd seen her children off to school, behaving like a schoolgirl herself; and then not long after Mrs Matsuoka there was Mrs Hiraishi. Well, if Matsuoka sneezed Hiraishi would have to take the cold, that's how it was with those two and always had been ever since the pair of them had moved into the building, so it was no surprise really. No, the surprise was Mrs Tanaka.

Mrs Tanaka couldn't stand it. She just couldn't stand it. The other women in the building were behaving like mares with a stallion. She'd come to understand that they'd even organized a rota: who was to visit when, and for how long. And it wasn't just for that they had a timetable. There was a work schedule as well. They were worried, you see, that Philip, well that's what they all called him now, Philip would get behind with his writing, and then Rie was so fussy about how the place was kept, so they came to an arrangement and shared the housework in the same way they shared the man. Fussy about how the place was kept! Fussy about the place! When Mrs Tanaka heard about that — they told her, you see, well, it was all they ever talked about once they were all in on it — when Mrs Tanaka heard about that she decided enough was enough. She made up her mind to stop it. She did, she made up her mind to go and see the couple, the Stevenses, and if that didn't work then she would go and see the landlord and put a stop to it that way.

She went across one evening, after she had seen the woman coming home. Her own husband was out, of course. She didn't want him involved in any of this. She went across and the woman came to the door. She didn't invite Mrs Tanaka in, but Mrs Tanaka was not in any mood to wait for an invitation. She more or less pushed the woman aside and went in. She was so worked up about things she only remembered to take her shoes off after she'd put her foot on the wood they'd got down over what had been perfectly good linoleum.

Perhaps it was that little slip that undid her, or perhaps it was the strangeness of the apartment, all that space, and those plants and the leather chairs. Or perhaps it was the drinks they gave her, accepting the first one of those was tantamount to an admission of defeat before she'd even begun to speak her piece. Well, whatever it was when she left she had tears in her eyes, and it wasn't because she was unhappy.

It was, it was because it had been such a long, long time since she'd had feelings like that, if she'd ever had feelings like that. It had been such a long, long time she couldn't properly remember even. All she could remember was that he'd said late on Thursday mornings would be a good time for her to come round, and the woman, Rie, had kissed her just before she went out and told her that she was always welcome in the evenings at any time, no need to ring first, just come round.

And that was that, you see. They all had their regular times: Mrs Okuda was Monday in the afternoon, and Mrs Horiguchi came on Tuesdays. Wednesdays it was Mrs Matsuoka, and Thursday mornings was Mrs Nakajima, who went in about eight and had to be out before ten because she still went to the tennis lessons her husband had paid for to keep her mind occupied. Mrs Tanaka was right after Mrs Nakajima and always stayed until one. Well, she was the senior resident in the building, so that was only right. On Fridays, in the morning, it was Mrs Hiraishi. It wasn't a strict schedule of course, Philip and Rie were both very accommodating, and when any of the women were over there getting on with the housework, well, from time to time, Philip would put aside his writing for an hour or so.

Everyone was happy with the way things were arranged. Everyone was very happy. It was funny how things changed. There was none of the nastiness that there used to be: none of the quarrels and the moods, people not speaking and that sort of thing. Mrs Okuda positively blossomed, blossom she did, you wouldn't have known her really. Even Okuda saw the difference in her — he didn't care about it, but he did notice. No one ever thought her daft or soft anymore.

They all changed, all of them. Even Mrs Tanaka. She took to weeping a good deal, but like that first time, she didn't weep because she was unhappy. No, it was quite the opposite, quite the opposite. Mrs Tanaka didn't properly understand why she seemed ready to burst into tears at a moment's notice, she just knew that that was how she felt. She was so happy, so happy it made her want to cry all the time. She knew as well that Thursday mornings had never been the same since, since that time when she'd — well, when she'd done what she'd done, and she hoped, wiping another tear away, that they never would be again.

# THE SEA, THE BEAUTIFUL SEA

It was the same every year. You'd go into Wilson's for a 'Tarzan' comic and a Bounty Bar, and you'd just be on your way out of the shop when old Mr Wilson would remember that Mam's copy of *Dalton's Weekly* had come in. It was a weekly, but Mam only ever put in the one order, the second week of February, every year. When you got home she'd take the paper off of you and put it underneath the cushion on the chair where she sat at night and she wouldn't say anything except that you'd to go back to Wilson's with the money because she didn't want people talking about her owing anybody anything. There were just the two chairs then, Mam's and Dad's, one on either side of the fire. The rest of us sat where we could, on the hearthrug, at the table — under the table in my case so I could play with my toy soldiers and not have them trodden on.

After we'd had our tea, our Sally and Noreen would do the dishes, and then me and Noreen would be sent round to Cooper's for Mam and Dad's beer. Usually it was two pints of mixed, but on Saturdays Dad drank stout and Mam would have a bottle of pale ale. We got Vimto and a packet of crisps on Saturdays, although our Sally, if she was in that night, which she wasn't very often, would get a Babycham or else a miniature bottle of egg flip she'd mix up with the lemonade that came from the Corona man every week.

When we got back the radio would be on, and we'd settle down for the evening to listen to Radio Luxemburg if it was the weekend. Dad would open the beer and pour out a glass for Mam and then one for himself. I liked it if he had stout because he used to make a face in the froth on the top of the glass. He used to say that when you drank the beer, one of the eyes would wink at you but I don't remember that it ever did.

About eight o'clock Mam always went out into the kitchen again to cut up some sandwiches. On Sunday nights they'd be cold beef and dripping, but the rest of the week it was either cheese and onion, or else egg and onion. I liked putting crisps inside the bread if it was cheese and onion, though I used to get a clip off of Mam if she saw me doing it. The big plate of sandwiches was always set on the hearth, and if there was a fire, which there usually was, the edges of the bread would start to curl up because of the heat. I remember our Noreen saying once that the sandwiches were probably the warmest thing in the house, but that was a long time afterwards, when Mam and Dad were gone, and the house was gone, and we were all grown and married with our own families. It was only ever when the big plate was empty that Mam would fetch the paper out from under her cushion. Most nights it was the *Mercury*, but every year, one night in February, it would be *Dalton's Weekly*, and Mam would start reading it, looking for somewhere we could go for a fortnight in the summer.

She'd sit there with a pencil, putting a mark against something that sounded all right. Sometimes she'd ask Dad what he thought about this place or that place. Dad never said much, usually. We said nothing at all, because we were never asked. The fact that we were all going away for the August fortnight wasn't something that was open to question for any of us, including Dad. It was understood. It was also understood that Mam was responsible for deciding about wherever it was we would end up going away to, even though in the past she'd landed us in some right holes.

We usually went to the East Coast, to places like Mablethorpe, or Ingoldmells or Clacton. We never went to Skeggy, well, not for holidays anyway, although we did sometimes go for daytrips. Our Sally reckoned she got headaches in Skegness. I didn't like Skeggy because the sea was such a long way out.


I think about it now, when I take my family to Italy, the States, Morocco we went to two years ago, and Mam's little excursions seem like nothing. At the time, though, they were very serious undertakings. When I was small, going to the Evington Park was a journey to another country to me. Getting everything ready for the big holiday: getting all our clothes washed and ironed and packed, and the house closed up; stopping the papers and the milk, the laundry and the delivery from the Corona man; cancelling the order for the meat at the butcher's; me and Dad getting our haircuts on a Friday night instead of a Saturday afternoon; our Sally sulking because she had to come with us; our Noreen sulking because our Sally had to come with us; then getting to the bus station and making sure we were on the right bus and our luggage was on the right bus and we hadn't put the thermos and the sandwiches Mam had cut up the night before in the bag that had gone in the back of the bus with the cases — well, that all seemed like going to another world.

Nobody slept much the night before, because of fights or worry or excitement; and then you were got up early and there was just a cup of tea and a bit of toast to eat; and there were fights again with our Sally and Noreen about who could get to the sink in the kitchen to have a wash first; and there were fights with our Sally and Noreen about Dad sitting out in the lavatory smoking; and fights about who had whose nylons; and then there was Mr Bodicoate from the next street at the door with his car. I remember it all. I remember feeling cold and hungry and tired, and I remember how the new clothes Mam had bought me for going away were itchy and smelt the way that new clothes used to smell then. Somehow though we'd get on the bus, all of us, and the bus would pull away, out of the garage, out of the town, and we'd always be just coming into the country with the fields and the trees and the smell of manure and Mam would say to Dad, 'Oh bleeding hell, Pat, I've left the address on the table.' Dad would say, 'What address do you mean?' and then Mam would say, 'The address of the bleeding digs, what bleeding address do you think I mean?' We were off on our holidays.

The bus ride seemed to last for ever then. I'd sit there, next to Mam, and I'd start to get hot in my new clothes, and I'd want to stretch. If I moved at all though, I got a clip from Mam for fidgeting, so I watched the fields to one side, or I watched Mam emptying her bag out on the other, looking for the address of the place where we were supposed to be staying.

At some point the bus would pull up at a transport café and everyone got out for a stretch, a pee, a cup of coffee or tea at this strange building in the middle of nowhere, with a couple of petrol pumps, and a few apple trees, and garage and café smells, you know, petrol and oil and coffee and bacon frying in a pan. Mam usually made us come straight back to the bus after we'd been to the lavatory, because she couldn't see the sense in spending money on food and drink when she'd gone to the trouble of bringing sandwiches and flasks of hot tea. I didn't mind. I liked the way the tea tasted out of the flask, and I liked the little bottle Mam used for the milk, with a bit of greaseproof paper stuck in the top with the cork so the milk didn't leak. I liked the sugar, in a twist of blue paper from the sugar packet at home. I always thought it looked like a giant version of the salt in a packet of crisps.

Our Sally and Noreen weren't keen though. I suppose it was because they were that much older than me. Sally was old enough not to want to be on holiday with the rest of us in the first place, and Noreen was old enough not to want to be sat out in the bus eating egg and onion sandwiches, when everybody else was inside having a proper meal.

Just once, I remember, we didn't stay on the bus. That was the year we found Uncle Francis and Auntie Eileen and their Molly and Peter already on the bus when we got to the garage. Well, Mam never had much time for Uncle Francis or Auntie Eileen, and as for their Molly, who was a student at the art college when she could have been at work and earning good money, well, Mam was beyond words. We had to sit near them, of course, otherwise it wouldn't have looked polite, and then, when we stopped and they trooped off with everybody else to go into the café, well, we couldn't help but follow, or, at least, that's what Mam said afterwards when she was talking to Dad.

I was glad that Uncle Francis and Auntie Eileen were there because I liked them, and I liked going into the café instead of sitting in the bus, and I liked eating the big bacon sandwich Dad had to cut in half for me because the taste of the hot bacon and the melted butter mixed itself up in a nice way with the milky coffee I had for a change instead of Vimto or Tizer. Most of all I liked watching my cousin Molly, with her long black hair and her big red sweater and the funny black trousers she had on that didn't come much past her knees. She put some money into a juke-box and a record called 'Freight Train' started to play, and Molly danced in front of the juke-box all alone. I thought she was beautiful, and I fell in love for the first time, just looking at her.

Mam usually found the address of where we were going to stay just when the collection for the driver came round. She used to have money ready, and she would make me put it in the hat. It was always a sixpence on the top, and then coppers underneath, so that it sounded like a lot when you put it in, but wasn't really. Mam always said the driver got enough for driving the bus, that we'd paid before we got on the bus, so she couldn't see why we had to pay again before we got off. It was a bus, she said, it wasn't a church.

Mam liked to tidy herself up a bit before we arrived, and in my memory all the journeys I took sitting next to her end in the same way. The fields beyond the glass begin to change: caravans appear, and then buildings. The road seems streaked with sand, and then the town is all around me again but not the way the town where I live is all around. This town is different. I don't know why it is different, but it is. Perhaps the difference has to do with the sand in the streets. Perhaps it has to do with where the sand comes from, blown by the wind. Perhaps it has to do with that, but more, perhaps it has to do with what is still beyond my senses to see or hear or smell, but which I know is there, somewhere, lending this town, these streets and buildings, their difference: the sea. Then I think that I can smell it, smell that sea smell, but I turn and it's the little towels moistened with cologne Mam is using. She keeps them in her handbag with the bottle of sal volatile she has in case somebody has a funny turn on the bus, and her powder compact, and the chalky white medicine she gets from the doctor for her stomach. I look at Mam, but the sea is all I can think of.

The sea is all I can think of, but Mam has the address for where we're going to stay, and suddenly the journey ends. We're here. We get out and stand about, and we're strangers, smelling the smells we've smelt before, petrol and oil, the hot engine of the bus, but that smell different now. The cases come out of the back of the bus. Ours are always the last. Mam gets hold of them and we all follow her out of the garage, Dad and our Sally and Noreen and me, and there are boys with pushcarts waiting for us. Mam chooses one, puts the cases in his cart, shows him the address, and then we set off again, a line of us, explorers in Africa, following our guide.

There's a photograph. I don't know who took it, perhaps it was one of those men that used to walk up and down the sea front with a camera, taking pictures and then more or less forcing you to buy the one he'd taken of you, plus an enlargement. Whoever it was took this picture, it wasn't one of us. It couldn't have been because we're all in it, Mam and Dad, me, our Sally and Noreen. We're walking along a road, Mam's holding my hand, then comes our Noreen, looking miserable, then Dad, struggling along with his sticks. He looks miserable as well. Our Sally is lagging so far behind you wouldn't think she was with the rest of us, and, from the photograph, you wouldn't even know it was our Sally, because you can't see her face. I imagine though, that she looks as miserable as the rest of them, Mam, Dad, Noreen, do. Mind you, you'd think we were all out for a walk in mid-December rather than the start of the August Bank Holiday fortnight. We've all got our heavy raincoats on, scarves, umbrellas. Perhaps we were just cold. The only way you'd know we were on holiday is the boy with the pushcart right at the front of the photograph. He's just in his khaki shorts and sandals, and short-sleeved shirt, but he looks as happy as Larry. I hated those boys.

I hated those boys because they made me feel uncomfortable. They irritated me, like my new clothes. They weren't any older than me for a start, and yet, there they were, running these little businesses and earning more money than I thought I'd ever see as long as I lived. Then, they had these funny ways of talking, and it made them seem older than me, and better than me. They were cheeky as well, cheeky to Mam. I mean, if I'd have talked to Mam the way those boys did, I'd have ended up sitting in the gutter with my head spinning. Looking at that picture again, I think I look miserable as well.

I don't know where or when that photograph was taken. Our Noreen reckons it was one year when we went a bit further than usual. We went to a place called Littlehampton.

I remember going there, but whether or not that's where the photograph was taken, I don't know. Our Noreen swears it was. Our Sally swears it wasn't. Still, I do remember going to Littlehampton. I remember because it was when Mam and Dad had a row. The row was about where we were staying.

I remember it all looked wrong when the boy who was carrying the cases took us along this sort of canal. I thought there were snakes in the water, but it was just a funny sort of seaweed. We finally fetched up in front of one of those gates that factories and garages used to have, you know, there's a big gate, with a little door in it so you can go in and out and not have to open the big gate all the time. I remember Mam asking the boy if he was sure he had the right place, and, when he'd gone, I remember Dad telling Mam that she'd really picked a beauty this time. Our Noreen started to cry and our Sally said she wasn't stopping. Mam fetched our Noreen one across the back of her head so as she'd have something to cry about, and she told our Sally to shut up as well or else she'd get something to think about herself.

We went in through the little gate and we were in a sort of yard, with cobblestones. If you looked up at the sky, all you could see were the gas-works. The lady that owned the house where we were to stay was called Mrs Cottrell. She was very old, and she was dirty as well.

Usually, when you arrived at your digs, the lady took you into the front room, but Mrs Cottrell took us straight into the kitchen. There was a funny smell in there and at the time I didn't know what it was because we didn't have a cat. Mam couldn't abide cats in a house. There were a lot of cats in this house. They were all over the place: on the chairs, on the window-ledge, at the side of the sink. There were three big ones on the kitchen table where Mrs Cottrell was getting somebody's tea ready, in fact it was our tea, and there was another watching a saucepan boil on the cooker.

I don't remember much more about that holiday except

the row Mam and Dad had on the first night in their
bedroom. I had to sleep in a little bed next to theirs so I
heard what was said, even though they were whispering. The
bedrooms weren't in the house where Mrs Cottrell lived,
they were across the yard and you had to climb what she
called the steps but what was really more like a ladder than
steps, and of course Dad could hardly manage it because of
his sticks and his big boots. Dad had been a boy soldier in
the Great War and he'd been wounded very badly and
crippled. I think it was having to get up and down that
ladder that made him have the row with Mam. They didn't
have a lot of rows, mainly because Dad was a very patient
man. This time, because I had to lie in bed and listen to
them, I got really frightened. That night I had a dream
about falling into the canal with the snakes, and when I woke
up I found that I'd wet the bed. Mam said she was going to
give me a hiding, but Dad said she wasn't and they had
another row about that.

That wasn't the only time I wet the bed when we were on
holiday. I did it on the very last holiday we all had together.
I'd remember that holiday anyway, because it was the last
one we all of us went on together, wetting the bed again just
makes it that bit easier to remember. It was a disaster from
start to finish, that holiday was. The thing is, I can't
remember where we actually went to. I think it might have
been Cromer. I remember the name of the lady where we
stayed, Mrs Lake. I remember her name because it seems to
fit with everything else that happened that year.

Mrs Lake was what Mam used to call very good living. What
Mam meant by that was that she went to church and she
didn't hold with drinking, smoking, swearing or gambling.
In her front room there were some very old pictures showing
what happened to people who did any of the things that she
didn't hold with. There was also a picture of a sailor, and it
had a black ribbon tied around it that our Sally said was

morbid, but Mam told her to shut up again or she'd clip her one, big as she was.

Mrs Lake had a lot of rules about what you mustn't do if you stayed in her house. It wasn't just that you mustn't drink, smoke, swear or gamble. You couldn't do any of those things, of course, in the house; in fact, you couldn't do them outside either really, because she said that she didn't want people coming in with the smell of alcohol or tobacco on them, and she didn't want people bringing in things that they might have won on games of chance at the fun-fair near the beach. I remember she called that fun-fair 'the Devil's playground'.

There were lots of other things you had to remember not to do as well. For a start, Mrs Lake didn't want lights on in the house after ten at night. Then, there was no washing of clothes allowed. In fact, there wasn't a lot of washing of any sort allowed. There was a bathroom upstairs, but it wasn't for guests. Guests had a jug and bowl provided, and the gentleman, she meant Dad, would find a kettle of water for him to shave with outside the door at six-thirty. The lavatory was in the bathroom, and as it was the only one in the house, we were told we could use it, but that was all. Mam had to promise we wouldn't use the water in the bathroom under any circumstances, and she had to promise to take me when I wanted to go, in case I had an accident and wet the seat.

Mam and Dad smoked. Well, I mean, everybody did then. Our Sally did. Dad smoked a lot, in fact, you seldom saw him without a cigarette going. He used to smoke at night as well, when everyone else was asleep. He used to wake up all the time; I suppose it was the pain he was always in, or else dreams about the war. Well, he used to smoke, sitting on the edge of the bed in the dark.

Both Mam and Dad had to have a cigarette when they got up to the room, but Mam opened the window as soon as we got in and they both more or less stood leaning out so that the smell wouldn't stay in the room. I suppose Dad remembered that. In the night he must have got up to have a smoke and lit the cigarette by the open window. The trouble was he didn't think to move the net curtain, so when he went to put his head out of the window the tip of his fag went straight through the net; then he dropped it, and by the time he'd got the thing put out, he'd woken Mam up and he'd woken me up and there were three or four burn holes in the curtain.

Mam took the net down and put it up back-to-front so that the heavy curtain more or less hid the damage, and then she had to go out and buy another pair to put up instead. The trouble was the new ones were that white it was obvious they shouldn't have been there. They had to go up though, even if they didn't look right, because Mam couldn't think of anything else she could do. Then, that night, Dad had another accident.

At home we just had a lavatory out in the yard, so there was a chamber pot under each of the beds for the night. Mam and Dad had one each. Dad used to use his a lot. You always knew his when it was out on the stairs with Mam's, waiting to be emptied, because it had cigarette-ends floating in it. Mam's didn't. Well, that night, Dad must have reached under the bed from sheer force of habit and found what he thought was the jerry. In fact it was one of his boots. He didn't realize what he'd done until the next morning when he'd got dressed and he went to put his boots on. Then he found that one was wet. He even found a couple of soggy fag-ends inside it.

The worst thing, of course, was that the carpet was sodden because the pee hadn't stayed in the boot. So, Mam had to try and dry it out. She had to use her spare underwear because she daren't use Mrs Lake's towels, and then she had to bundle what she'd used up ready to take out of the house with her when we left after breakfast. She said she'd have to take them to a laundry. Even then, after she'd tried to dry the carpet with her vest and knickers, it was still wet, so she moved the bed and turned the carpet back and put sheets of newspaper she fetched out of the drawers underneath. Then she sprinkled Yardley's lavender water everywhere in case there was a smell. She shouldn't have bothered. That night there was another accident and she had it all to do again.

It wasn't Dad's fault this time. It was Mam's. Mam used to go a bit funny when we went on holiday. Usually, she was very careful about money. Well, she had to be because there were five of us, and only Dad's wages coming into the house. Our Sally worked of course, but she only paid her board and she couldn't afford very much of that. Still, Mam used to go a bit daft with money on holidays. She had this weakness for new things. One year she got Dad Brylcream in a tube. Usually, he just bought a little jar of it from Stan Bonsor's when we went for our haircuts the Friday night before we went on holiday. Mam said the tube was better.

Dad didn't argue with her, he almost never did, and he was more or less coming round to the idea of having his Brylcream in a tube when he got mixed up one morning and he cleaned his teeth with it instead of the toothpaste. He threw it straight out of the window after that, and he wouldn't leave the house until our Noreen had been sent out to get him a jar like he was used to from the chemists.

The new thing that year, the year we were staying at Mrs Lake's, was beer in tins. It was called Long Life, and again, Dad wasn't very keen on the idea; it was Mam.

They both of them liked a drink in the evening, but they only ever went to pubs on holidays. Even then, they wouldn't actually go into the pub, they'd find one with a children's room so that we could all go in, or else, if the weather wasn't too bad, we'd sit out in the yard if there were tables there. I liked it. I had Vimto to drink every night, and crisps every night, and sometimes I'd have a saucer of hot peas or a cheese cob as well. Mam and Dad would have eels, or a bag of boiled shrimps, or a plate of cockles or whelks.

The year we stayed with Mrs Lake though, they daren't go into a pub even to sit in the children's room or in the yard.

Mrs Lake was very choosey about who she let have a front-door key, or so she said to Mam the day we arrived when Mam went down to ask for one. Mrs Lake only reckoned to give out keys to regular guests, people who came from one year to the next. She didn't actually say Mam couldn't have a key, she just pointed out that this was the first time we'd made a booking with her. After that Mam just came back up the stairs.

What this meant was that when we got back at night we had to knock for Mrs Lake to let us in the house. Well, even if they'd done what Dad wanted and sucked on a mouthful of violet cashous to hide the smell of the drink, Mrs Lake would still have smelt the cigarettes. Mam and Dad had tried to cut right down, but sitting in a room in a pub, everyone else would have been smoking and the smell would have been there on our clothes. This was why Mam bought the tins of Long Life. She said that they would go in her bag better than bottles of beer, and they wouldn't clink the way bottles did. She showed Dad and he had to agree she was right, about that, anyway.

The man in the off-licence had given Mam a special opener for the tins, but she couldn't find it sitting in the dark. It was usually late when we came back, and Mrs Lake made quite a to-do about turning off the lights in the hallway and on the stairs and the landing when the clock she had downstairs chimed for ten. The first night Mam and Dad had put their light off, but our Sally and Noreen kept theirs on, and Mrs Lake stood out on the landing clearing her throat until Mam went and turned the light off in the girls' room herself. Mam had bought a little torch from Woolworth's, but it wasn't much use really. In the end, they just used to sit in the dark, talking about what a miserable place they'd come to.

When Mam couldn't find the opener for the tins of beer she made Dad give her his penknife, and she used it to punch a hole in the first tin. I can still remember exactly what

happened next even though it was all over, well the first bit
was all over, in a few seconds. I can still remember because
even though it happened so fast, when I remember everything it happens very, very slowly, like in a film or in a dream
when you try to run and you can't make your legs go. What
happened was that the beer sprayed out of the tin; it sprayed
out of the tin with such force Mam dropped the tin. The tin
went onto the floor then, and started spinning round and
round, like a firework, spraying beer all over the place, all
over the carpet, all over the walls, all over the beds, over
Mam, and Dad and me.

It was dark of course, just the light from the little torch
we'd got from Woolies was all we had to see by. It was dark,
but in my memory it isn't dark at all. There's a sort of golden
light coming from that tin, and it's as if it's this golden light
that is spraying round the room, not beer. It's like a firework,
like a Catherine wheel on Guy Fawkes' night, except that it
isn't sparks that are lighting everything up, it's this mysterious golden liquid spreading itself all over the room, all over
everything.

It couldn't have lasted much more than a minute, but the
place was soaking again. Mam was down on her hands and
knees trying to get the worst of it up before it went into the
carpet. Dad was trying as best he could to get the blankets off
the beds so he could sponge them a bit with what water there
was left in the jug. Our Sally and Noreen came in because
they'd heard the noise when the tin went off, and then they'd
heard Mam and Dad carrying on. Our Sally put the light on.
Then, of course, Mrs Lake was at the door, wanting to know
what was going on, and our Sally said, 'It's all right. It's all
right. It's only me little brother. He has fits. He'll be all
right, only we've got to keep the light on for a bit.' I could
only have been seven or eight, but I could have killed our
Sally for saying that.

The room smelt really badly of beer the next morning.
Even we could smell it, and we'd been in there all night long.

Mam had had the windows open all night, and she'd put sheets and blankets and pillows out on the window ledge to try and get them a bit dry. It had been really cold that night and we'd had to sleep in our coats on the bare mattresses. I remember Mam saying to Dad that she didn't know what to do, and she didn't. In the end it was our Sally that did something. She went down to Mrs Lake and said that she was terribly sorry, but that her brother had been poorly on the carpet and she'd have to ask for a bucket of hot water and some strong disinfectant and a bit of newspaper.

Well, Mrs Lake didn't come up to see what it was I was supposed to have done because she could imagine it, and when we went down to breakfast that morning, after our Sally and Mam had finished, the room smelt like the inside of a bottle of Jeyes' Fluid. Mam was ever so pleased with our Sally, and perhaps it was this that gave our Sally the courage to tell Mam that she was going home that afternoon.

She said it was because of her headaches. It was the air pressure that was doing it, she said, just like at Skeggy. She'd been moping about the place ever since we arrived, fighting with our Noreen, fighting with Mam. It was Dad who said she could go. I think he'd just had about all he could stand. He said she could go the next morning, and she did. Of course, after she went our Noreen started playing up.

Dad always used to say that if our Sally had one thing, then our Noreen would want two of the same. He was right. They're still like that. Then though, Noreen just kept going on and on about our Sally being let do whatever she wanted, and nothing said. When Dad asked what she meant, our Noreen said about the dances.

She meant the dances on the pier. There was a dance-hall there, and the second night our Sally had said she was going and Mam had said she was if she was going with Noreen. There was a row about that. Afterwards Noreen wanted to go again, but Mam said she couldn't go on her own, she'd have to ask Sally. Sally wouldn't go. She said it was because the place was no good, but now I suppose it was just to spite our Noreen. Well, with Sally gone, Noreen went on and on about being let go to the dances. Mam said no, but again, Dad, in the end, said yes, just to put a stop to the rows. Mam said that our Noreen was only sixteen and that was why she couldn't go, but Dad said that sixteen was old enough if she was in by a quarter-to-ten, and she was.

One of the funny things about that last holiday was that we hardly saw the sea. The weather was bad. It was cold. It was raining. The second day that we were there, these very strong winds started blowing. It wasn't that you didn't want to sit on the beach, you couldn't. We dragged around the town most of the time. For a bit of a change we started going to this hotel where they had a palm court, with a little orchestra, and you could have morning coffee. After we found it, we went there nearly every day.

We'd tried sitting in one of the shelters on the front, and Mam had fetched jugs of tea and coffee, but in the end the weather got so bad the stall selling refreshments shut and so we started going to the hotel. None of us liked it. It was expensive for a start, and you had to put on quite decent clothes or else the waiter who took you to your table gave you a nasty look, or so Mam said. I hated the place. I had to sit still all the time, and the chairs used to hurt my legs. I wasn't even allowed to eat the biscuits you got the way I wanted. They had a picture of a coffee cup on them, those biscuits did, and I used to like to eat them by biting round the shape of the coffee cup. Mam made me stop because she said people were looking.

The only good thing about the weather on that holiday was that I got bought lots of toys. I always got things, toys, I mean, when we went on holiday, but that year I got more than I'd ever had. Well, we were in and out of the shops all the time, especially the toy shops. I got soldiers, and a gun, and a cowboy suit. I was supposed to go and have my picture

taken in that cowboy suit, but when we got to the shop I
wouldn't go in.

I remember our Noreen saying that I was a spoilt little sod
because of all the things I'd been bought on that holiday,
and Mam clipped her one right there and then. We were in
the restaurant where we went to have our dinner everyday.
We went there because they did very nice fish and chips,
with as much bread and butter and as many pots of tea as
you wanted, all for the one price. There's another photograph, taken just after we'd come out of that restaurant.
We're walking through an amusement arcade, me and Mam,
and our Noreen, and Dad. Mam's got hold of my hand and
her face looks like thunder. Our Noreen's face looks like
thunder as well, but that was because she's just had Mam's
hand across it. Dad looks like he always does in holiday
photographs, fed up. I suppose it was one of those men from
the sea-front who took the picture again. I suppose he'd been
driven inside by the bad weather just like we had.

Still the sun did shine, in the end. It was the day before we
were to go home. I remember waking up and thinking
something was different. It was something about the way the
room smelt, and it was something about the way the room
looked. It was the sun, is what it was. The room looked
different because the sun was shining into it, and was
lighting everything up, the wallpaper and the wardrobes and
the chest of drawers and the picture of 'The Gleaners' over
Mam and Dad's bed. It was the sun, and it was the sea.

We still kept the windows open, even though it rained all
the time; we kept them open because Mam swore she could
smell the beer coming up through the Jeyes' Fluid, and Dad
swore he could smell something else — he meant what he'd
done in his boot — coming up through the Jeyes' Fluid and
the beer. This morning I could smell something else again: I

could smell the sea. I could smell the sea, but the funny thing was, I couldn't hear it.

We went down on the beach first thing. The sand was so clean. It looked like somebody had got up early and washed it. The sun was hot. There was no wind. The sea — the sea was flat and still and bluer than any sea I'd seen before, and the sunlight that came off it was golden, just as if it had come straight from the sun itself, so that you had to squint wherever you looked.

It was wonderful that day. We had cheese cobs for our dinner instead of fish and chips, and we didn't even think about going to that hotel for a cup of coffee. In fact, Mam fetched a big jug of coffee at half-past ten, and when she came back with it, she had some little packets of those biscuits with the coffee cup on them with her. She gave me a packet for myself, and with every one I bit out the coffee cup and Mam never said anything. Then the Salvation Army came round collecting, and I remember that I was lying on my tummy and the lady tickled my foot and when I squealed, she said that showed I'd been born at home. Mam was so impressed by this, because I had been born at home, she put two shillings in the collecting tin.

It was the best day of the holiday, and when it was time to go I went down to the sea because we were going home early in the morning the next day and I shouldn't see it again. I went down to the sea, and I stood right at the edge. It was so calm, so still, the water almost didn't break against the sand even, and I could stay there and not get my feet wet. I stood there, I remember, I stood there and I thought I had never seen anything as beautiful as this, not even my cousin Molly, when she'd danced by herself to that record in the café all that time before. Until then, I'd thought Molly was the most beautiful thing in the world, but I knew now she wasn't beautiful the way this sea was beautiful.

We had to go back to Mrs Lake's that night because Mam had to put my swimming trunks out to dry so she could pack them for the morning. She had to put some calamine lotion on me as well but I was so happy I didn't mind, and I didn't mind when it was dry and we went out again and I had that funny shivering feeling you get when you've had calamine lotion put on and then you go out with your best clothes on at night.

I think we were all happy, Mam, Dad, even our Noreen. She didn't go dancing that last night. She came with us to play bingo. Mam and Dad had stayed away from the pubs, but they'd had to do something in the evenings and so they'd taken to playing bingo at the fair, what Mrs Lake called 'the Devil's playground'.

Mam had been quite lucky, and had usually managed to get at least one win most nights, but she hadn't taken a prize yet because on this stall you got points for every win and you could save up these points towards one of the big prizes they had on display in the middle of the stall, where the man stood when he called out the numbers. Mam wanted the canteen of cutlery. She only needed one more win and she could get it, but that night it was our Noreen that won, not Mam.

When Noreen shouted 'House!' Mam got her coupons out ready to ask for the canteen of cutlery, but she wasn't quick enough because Noreen got hold of them and she said to the man, 'We'll have the teddy bear, the big one,' and even though Mam clipped her again, that's what we got. Of course, to make things worse, that night I had a dream that I was swimming in the sea, all calm and flat. The next morning I found I'd wet the bed again. This time there was no hiding things from Mrs Lake, and Mam had to go down and apologize and get the sheets and blankets washed. We nearly missed the bus back home.

Coming back from holiday was always the same. There was this feeling of relief that you were back home, and yet the house always seemed different. It was as if it wasn't your house, as if you'd come back to one that was like your house,

very like it, but this house hadn't just been empty for a
fortnight, it had been empty for years. I used to like to go
straight out into the yard when we got back, while Mam was
getting the cases unpacked and Dad or Noreen or Sally was
off round to the fish and chip shop to get our supper. I used
to like to go out and walk in the grass and look at the plants
and the trees. We had a couple of apple trees in the backyard
and the fruit was always so much bigger on them than it had
been before we went away. It was the same with the grass, it
was always so long.

In the backyard, even more than in the house itself, you
could imagine that you were the first person to stand where
you were standing for years and years and years. The time
we came back from Mrs Lake's, it was a bit different because
Sally had been in the house, so there wasn't that cold smell
that houses get when they're left empty, even for a little
while, but she hadn't touched the garden and I went out and
stood there, the way I always did. That night, when I went
up to bed, a Jacky Longlegs ran across my pillow and I
wouldn't lie down. I slept with Mam and Dad again, just like
I'd done all through the holiday.


It wasn't just all the things that happened on that holiday
that make me remember it so well; in fact, I sometimes
wonder if all those things did happen on that one holiday or
if perhaps I'm remembering things that happened at different times and in different places and I'm mixing them all up.
It's like the sea being so calm that day. I mean, I don't really
see how it could have been, not so soon after all the bad
weather we had, but, then again, it was. I suppose anything's possible really, and they do say as how the mind can
play tricks on you. Still, I don't think I am mixing things up,
and I know that I'm not when it comes to what happened
afterwards because what happened afterwards changed

everything, and, as I said, we never went on holiday together again.

I was too young to understand what did happen, to understand it properly, I mean. I know now, of course, but then, well, I was just a little boy. What I remember are the rows that started around the Christmas time. I remember one, it was actually on Christmas Day, and I remember Mam shouting at our Sally. She shouted 'Done nothing? Done nothing? Who do you think you are, the bleeding Virgin Mary?'

Well, of course, what had happened was that our Sally had been seeing this fellow on the quiet, and she'd come back to be with him, and having the house to herself, she'd had him in to stay, of course, and, well, she was going to have a baby. She did have a baby. It was born just after she came back from honeymoon, because, in those days, you had to get married, if you could; it was either that or the baby was adopted. That's what happened to our Noreen's baby. She was pregnant as well, you see. It was some man in the band that had played for the dances on the pier. Mam went back and found him, but he was married, so there was nothing for it but to give the baby up for adoption.

You can understand it, well, I can. In those days, like I say, you got married if you could, and if you couldn't, well, you couldn't keep the baby, not in the sort of neighbourhood where we lived, not being the sort of people we were. Noreen never understood though. She came back home one Friday and said she wanted to go into the WRNS. She had her medical, got her forms, everything, in a week. It was Dad who signed her forms. When she went away she told Mam she wouldn't ever come back and, apart from Dad's funeral, she never did. She didn't come back when Mam died and we buried her, and she didn't come back when me and our Sally cleared out the house afterwards.

I remember that night, the night when we'd more or less done it all, all the packing. It was in August and for me it was just like the nights when we'd be getting ready to go away. Well, that's what we were doing, except this time I knew we would never be coming back. I went out into the yard on my own because I wanted to be there on my own for this last time. Mam had been gone for about a month then and, of course, nobody had looked after the garden. We'd been too busy. The grass was long, and the apple trees were there with all the fruit on them, and as I stood there it seemed as if two things were coming together at the same time, as if I was back from a holiday I hadn't been on yet.

I was out there for a long time. I watched the sun set and still I stood there. Our Sally came out in the end and asked me what I was doing. I told her. I said I was remembering. Well, that more or less shut Sally up because she doesn't like talking about the past. I can understand it really. I remember though. I remember a lot. Sometimes I think I remember so much because my two sisters don't, or won't or can't. That night, the last night I ever stood in Mam and Dad's house, the last night I ever went out into their backyard, that night I remembered a lot. I remembered a lot, and that night it really did start to get all mixed up, but what stood clear of everything else was the fortnight at Mrs Lake's.

I stood there in the dark and I thought about Dad peeing in his boot, and me peeing in the bed, and the beer spraying round the room, and the curtains burning and then that day when the weather turned so hot and the sunlight came off the sea and how beautiful it made the sea and everything else look.

I remembered as well that Mam took me to see our Noreen in the hospital, just like she'd taken me to see our Sally. She never told me our Noreen had had a baby as well, of course. I thought she was just ill. Our Noreen had the big pink teddy bear she'd won with Mam's points on the bingo in the hospital with her. I thought about that when I stood out in the back yard all on my own. I thought about that, and I thought about how everything had flowed that summer. Everything, pee and beer and disinfectant and water and, even though I'd been too young to know it, the seed of the men that had been with our Sally and our Noreen. That had flowed as well. It had burst and sprayed and flowed inside my sisters just like that beer had inside Mam and Dad's room. Long Life that beer was called.

The one thing that was still the day I saw it was the sea. They do say all life comes from the sea, don't they? Perhaps that day the sea knew what we didn't, me and Mam and Dad, even our Sally and Noreen, because they couldn't have known either. Just the sea, it knew and because of that it knew something else as well: the sea knew that there'd been enough flowing and so, that day, it could be still, it could be almost still.

# TELLING STORIES

The birth of a son to Mrs Florence MacNamara, was, depending upon how you viewed the matter, either a miracle or a disgrace. Certainly news of the birth divided the little community of immigrant Irish in which Mrs MacNamara lived, as it divided the workforce of the Empire Thread and Yarns factory on the Rollestone Road where many of them were employed, including, as it happened, Mrs MacNamara's husband and eldest daughter, inclining people to the one side or the other.

The reason for these extremes of opinion lay not so much in the fact that Mrs MacNamara had given birth, but that, at the time when she was delivered of her child, Florence MacNamara was fifty-one years old; as old as the century itself.

From Mr and Mrs MacNamara, Mrs MacNamara's condition, as they referred to the pregnancy between themselves, had elicited rather more restrained responses; even from the moment when Mrs MacNamara, having gone into the surgery of her doctor, Dr Costello, 'young Dr Costello', as he was called so as not to confuse him with old Dr Costello, his father, in order to seek his advice over her slow but now steady weight-gain, had come out, not with the diet sheet she had been expecting, but with the knowledge that she was more than six-months gone with child. Mrs MacNamara had taken herself home and got the tea on the table for three of her four daughters, and then, when the younger girls had been fed and dismissed from the table, and were settled with their various tasks — doing the dishes, getting in the washing or a bucket of coal for the evening fire, homework — she had gone to the kitchen again and set to with her frying pan so as to have something hot for her husband and the eldest child when they came in from their work.

In the evening the family listened to the radio together, and then, each in their order, the girls went upstairs. It was only at eleven, after May Louise, the eldest of the girls, had gone up the stairs, and Mr and Mrs MacNamara sat alone on either side of the dying fire with the last of the brown ale they habitually shared of an evening in their glasses, it was only then that Mrs MacNamara said to her husband that she had a surprise for him.

To judge from his reaction to the news of his wife's pregnancy it was more of a shock than a surprise for Mr MacNamara, but in the course of the next few days he got over it, and came to accept the reality of the condition his wife now found herself in, perhaps largely because there was nothing that either he or Mrs MacNamara could do about it. It was not that Mr MacNamara was entirely sure that there was nothing that could be done about it, he simply assumed that were there some other recourse open to them, his wife would have told him so. As it was, she said nothing.

Mrs MacNamara had, in fact, popped in to see Mrs Egan, who lived at the top of the street, on her way back from the doctor's. It was well known among the women in the street that Mrs Egan, who had been a nurse, had directed one or two of the younger, unmarried girls who had found them-selves in difficulties to a sympathetic, former medical gentle-man living not too far away in one of the big houses at the top of the hill by the park. Mrs Egan though, on hearing the news, said that, given Mrs MacNamara's age, and the advanced nature of her pregnancy, there was no possibility of 'her friend', as she called the abortionist, agreeing to see her.

After that Mrs MacNamara had gone home and made up a plate of potted beef sandwiches for the girls' tea, with mashed banana and evaporated milk to follow, as she always did on Wednesdays. She was, you see, a creature of habit, if she was nothing else.

It was habit that had been indirectly responsible for the state Mrs MacNamara now found herself to be in. Every Sunday afternoon, after the Sunday lunch had been eaten and all the dishes cleared away, when the younger girls were on their way to Sunday school and the older ones had settled down with the papers or a book, Mr and Mrs MacNamara would go up to their bedroom for what was known in the family as their Sunday afternoon rest. Of course, what they did during this period together, although it was, of necessity, almost furtively quiet and gentle, perhaps a little too gentle at times — but only at times — for Mrs MacNamara's proper enjoyment, was certainly not restful, in the true sense of that word. It was pleasurable, however, for Mr MacNamara and more often than not, for Mrs MacNamara as well, though they were not the sort who would ever have talked about their own feelings and responses in such matters to each other.

In over thirty years of marriage Mr MacNamara had not once seen his wife entirely naked, nor she him, for that matter. The only men who had ever had Mrs MacNamara before them without her clothes were her doctors, the Costellos, father and son; and even then it was in the sense of a composite rather than a full picture, for, during those medical procedures which had required her to be undressed, she had usually managed to keep some article of apparel about her, for the sake of warmth as much as modesty. The Costellos were notoriously parsimonious when it came to heating their surgery.

So, because of who they were, and the circumstances in

which they came together each Sunday afternoon, with the two girls down in the living room positioned directly below their parents' double bed, the MacNamara's acts of copulation were necessarily quiet, somewhat timid affairs. Yet they were enjoyable, they were; and the enjoyment each achieved was deepened after that difficult period which Mrs MacNamara thought of as 'the change'. This had come to her rather late, according to Dr Costello, old Dr Costello, that is. It would have been perhaps eighteen months after it was all over, eighteen months, perhaps, when she fell pregnant again, and two years before she knew that she had fallen pregnant again.

In spite of Mrs MacNamara's rather advanced age, in gynaecological and obstetric terms, her confinement went quite without incident. It was a Monday morning when she thought she felt the first, mild contractions begin, and she was still able to strip the beds and see to the laundry man, to whose care she always entrusted the family's sheets and Mr MacNamara's shirts; the shirts, not the collars: they went to the Chinese laundry next to the paper shop on the Park Hill Road. Mr MacNamara was very particular about his collars and insisted on a clean one every day, even though he took it off as soon as he got into work.

She stripped the beds, she saw the sheets and her husband's shirts safely off in the Co-Op van. She turned to her own washing and soon had a line full of clothes out in the uncertain sunshine. She was still standing over the big dolly tub, agitating the clothes inside it with the dolly peg, when Carmel, the youngest child, came back from school for her dinner, and then Rita. Nell, the next girl, was at the big school and did not come home.

May Louise would be back at the same time as her father, for they worked in the same place, well the place where everyone round there worked, the Thread and Yarns, only May Louise was in the General Office, not on the factory floor. Mrs MacNamara put the last of the washing through the mangle, and then out on the line, while Carmel and Rita set the table. Just when Mrs MacNamara was getting the food out on the plates, her husband and eldest daughter came in, and as they were washing their hands at the sink, she felt a sudden sensation of wetness about herself, and her waters showed.

'For God's sake, Mammy,' May Louise said, 'are you after wetting yourself or what?'

Mrs MacNamara said nothing, other than that perhaps May Louise might like to go and fetch Mrs Egan from the top of the street, and then she got on with putting the potatoes and the cabbage and the lamb chops that had gone down to nothing in the pan, onto the plates. She took the food through to the table, and saw her daughters sit down, and her husband sat down, and then she said that she'd come over a little strangely and would go up to bed for a bit. Carmel and Rita, who had heard their eldest sister's remark from the kitchen, and who could see the darker stains that had spread now on the dark grey of their mother's skirt at the back, were grey themselves, touched as all children are, aren't they, by such sudden announcements of their parents', particularly their mother's, mortality, and all that it might mean for them.

Mrs MacNamara told them not to mind, she was just a little tired was all, and when she came back down from her rest, maybe before, she'd have a surprise for them. The surprise, although the MacNamara girls were not shown it at once, of course, came at a quarter-to-six in the evening. Mr and Mrs MacNamara had chosen names for the child as part of the other surreptitious preparations they had made for its arrival; in the case of a boy they were to be Stephen Desmond. To his sisters, however, he was, from the first moments that they were aware of his existence, Stevie.

Just exactly when the MacNamara girls became aware of Stevie's existence was always a bone of contention among them. In fact, many years later of course, in the evening of the day when the MacNamara children had buried their mother, there had been a bit of a row about it, during which Stevie, a man now, already married and divorced, something which his mother had never quite managed to get over — the marriage, I mean, not the divorce, she had said she would die happy after that, and presumably she did — Stevie had sat and listened to the unfolding disputes with much amusement.

May Louise claimed, with some apparent justification, that she had known all along. That she had sent her mother to the doctor's because of the belly and hips she was getting on her, wondering all the while was it just the food her mother had started putting away over the last few weeks or was it something else. Her sister Nell, who had not herself ever married and lived a somewhat mysterious life in Sydney, called May Louise a bloody liar, and asked how would she have known her mother was pregnant when she'd not had even the faintest idea what it was Poggy Arthurs was doing to her, leant up against the garden wall with the front of her dress all up round her hips and her knickers round her knees, and how, if she hadn't have come along when she did and frightened him clear out of her sister, there'd have been more than a funny stain on her petticoats to explain the next Monday morning to their mother, there'd have been another like Stevie, only eighteen months younger.

Well, after that, all rational discourse was impossible, but then Nell and May Louise hadn't been able to speak for years without flying at one another's faces, and Rita and Carmel were just as bad with one another. Perhaps it had to do with sharing bedrooms when they were young, and stockings and petticoats, and boyfriends, sometimes, as well, when they were older.

The truth was though, that if the girls knew anything at all about their mother's pregnancy with Stevie, it had nothing to do with anything they were told, because they were told nothing.

Mrs MacNamara found most things to do with the more intimate parts and functions of the human body difficult to talk about. She had dreaded the time when her daughters would come to their first courses, and when it happened with May Louise she'd sent the girl up to see Mrs Egan, who sorted things out. When the time came for Nell to start, Mrs MacNamara dealt with the situation more directly, at least to her way of thinking: she left a box of Dr White's on the coverlet of the bed Nell shared with her elder sister and hoped that the two girls would deal with things between themselves.

Apparently they did, for Mrs MacNamara heard no more from Nell, or from May Louise either, for that matter.

Given this degree of timidity then, how could Mrs Mac-Namara have announced to her girls that she was expecting again, especially at the age she was herself, and with May Louise old enough for marriage and motherhood? The answer was that she could not, and so, Mrs MacNamara began to wrap her steadily enlarging figure in a tissue of silence and lies. For the most part she said nothing, but when any of the girls commented on her size, or on the amount she was eating, or the fact that she had changed her drink in the evenings from brown ale to stout, she told some story or other. The problem with telling stories though, is that, in the end, the one who tells them is inevitably found out. Which is how it was with Mrs MacNamara when she at last produced Stevie.

It was Mr MacNamara who officially announced Stevie's presence, though, what with the sudden summoning of Mrs Egan and then the arrival of old Dr Costello, and the first cries of the child that came to the ears of the girls as they waited downstairs, surely it was obvious what was happening.

Mr MacNamara had given much thought to how he should make his announcement, and he had more or less settled on proclaiming the event as an unlooked for, and so unexpected, gift from God. In the end, however, he simply said to the girls that their mother had had a baby and that it was a little boy. When they were allowed upstairs to see their mother and the baby, they saw as well the changes that had been made to their parents' bedroom: the cot, the small cupboard bulging with the various paraphernalia peculiar to babies, and they understood then why they had been forbidden access to this room for the past few days, even Carmel, who had a tendency to wake in the night and want to sleep with her mother.

And Stevie, the mysterious, miraculous child? In spite of his secret origins he was loved by his sisters; cossetted and caressed by them. They took him for walks in the pram that was bought for him second-hand from an advert in the paper. They nursed him when he would not sleep, and kept him up, playing with him, when he would. They were, in other words, like four mothers to him, changing before his myopic stare in size and complexion and smell, but all functioning in the way that he best desired for the greater comfort of Stevie.

Mrs MacNamara adored the child, her unexpected, long awaited son. After four girls the MacNamaras had decided that enough was enough, and they began to exercise what Mr MacNamara always referred to as 'restraint', because to his ear, if to no one else's, the word 'precautions', which was what he really meant, sounded too much like a transgression. Well, he brought his restraints, if that is what they were, home with him on Saturday afternoons after his usual visit to the barber. 'Something for the weekend, sir?' became a familiar phrase to Mr MacNamara, until the Sunday after-noon when his wife told him they need not have all the bother of that sort of thing anymore, so Mr MacNamara slipped the little packet back into his wallet, and never thought of such matters again.

Stevie's mother loved her child, her boy child, her last child. She fed him herself until he was almost three years old, in spite of May Louise's evident disgust, and Nell's comment that the child would end up with the marks of the playground railings on his cheeks if his mother didn't wean him before he was old enough to go to school. Stevie was weaned, suddenly and without warning, after he almost bit through his mother's nipple one morning when she was feeding him just before she had to get ready to go shopping.

That incident marked a distinct alteration in Stevie's relationship with his mother. It seemed as if, in almost severing the flesh that had nurtured him for so long, he had severed as well an invisible tie that held him to his mother's body and to her heart. He was, in a sense, cast off from her, and when he turned to his sisters for comfort instead, for Stevie had discerned at a very early age that all women of a certain size had what he wanted hidden just within their blouses and whatever it was that they had on underneath their blouses, well, he found that they had cast him off as well. On his own, suddenly, Stevie turned inwards, away from his mother and his sisters, away from all the big people who seemed to populate the world. He turned to himself and he turned to his imagination.

Stevie found a friend, another little boy. He knew him, for no reason that Stevie was aware of, as Frank. This little boy lived somewhere at the top of the garden, Stevie was not quite certain where, but he could always find him playing there in the mornings, usually in front of the kennel Mr MacNamara had made for the dog that had died before Stevie was born. Stevie thought Frank might actually live in the dog kennel, and he worried about his comfort, especially on cold or rainy nights.

Stevie's was a lonely existence, except for Frank. The neighbourhood where the MacNamaras lived was changing. When the young people May Louise had grown up with married, they moved away, to a nice house with a bathroom on one of the new council estates that had been built on the edge of the city, sometimes even to private estates. Those who stayed were the ageing and the old. There were no children of his own age for Stevie to play with, except sometimes on a Saturday, when married daughters would come back to the little streets where their parents lived to leave their children for the afternoon while they went shopping in the town. Had it not been for the mysterious boy who slept in the old dog-kennel, Stevie would almost always have played alone.

Mrs MacNamara had seen Stevie out in the back garden talking to himself, and had wondered, even then, if he was all right. However, Frank's existence was not properly known of until the afternoon when May Louise and her fiancé, a young man from the next street who had worked with May Louise in the General office at the Empire Thread and Yarns and was now home on leave from the Royal Air Force, offered to take Stevie with them to the flower show at the Abbey Park.

Stevie liked May Louise's young man, particularly when he wore his Air Force uniform, and so he was happy that he would be going with them. So happy was Stevie, in fact, he invited Frank along as well.

They were just settling into their seats on the bus to town, and the driver had begun to ease out into the traffic along the Horton Lea Road, when Stevie realized that Frank was still standing at the stop. He jumped up from his seat at once and began shouting. The clippie, acting out of instinct, rang the bell twice and the driver, also instinctively, applied his brakes.

As May Louise said afterwards, it was a wonder no one was killed, and it was. The traffic behind the bus came to a halt suddenly, of course, and afterwards there was that smell of rubber in the air and a great deal of cursing from the drivers; some of the passengers on the bus itself were thrown about a bit, but the only person to suffer actual hurt was

Stevie when May Louise slapped his face, once for stopping
the bus, and twice for insisting that his friend was still
waiting at the stop.

May Louise, along with her fiancé and Stevie, got off the
bus at once. Well, as May Louise said to her mother when
they got back to the house, they could hardly have done
otherwise. As it was, she knew she'd never be able to get on
the same bus as that clippie again and it was all because of
her lying little brother. So Stevie got another smack across
his ears, from his mother this time, and May Louise and her
fiancé went off to the show on their own.

As it happened, this was the last time May Louise was to
see her fiancé. The young man had been so shocked by May
Louise's outburst against her little brother, he found the
thought of spending the rest of his life with her, as she was
now revealed to him, more than he could bear. That night he
got a train back to camp, telling his mother and father he
had had a telegram saying all leave was cancelled. The next
morning he put in for a transfer overseas.

The young man's transfer request was granted, although
the only sea he crossed was the Irish Sea. He was sent to a
camp just outside Belfast and within six months was married
to a farmer's daughter from County Down.

May Louise never forgave her fiancé for abandoning her,
and for the longest time she talked openly about suing him
for breach of promise, although she never did. May Louise
also never forgave her little brother. When she was forced to
acknowledge his existence in some way, she would always
refer to him as 'that little liar'.

Stevie did tell lies, and the older he got the more he told
them. Yet, the funny thing is, he hadn't lied that day about
Frank having missed the bus. He had. He'd been about to
get on when the clippie had rung for the driver to start, and
he had been left behind. Stevie tried to settle things with his
friend afterwards, but Frank was obviously very hurt about
what had happened. He started playing with Stevie less and

less, and then, one day, he just wasn't there anymore; and the bottom of the garden, the bit by the dog kennel, was as empty for Stevie as it was for everybody else. It was after that, after Frank left, that Stevie really started telling lies, telling stories.

What did Stevie lie about? Oh, all sorts of things, his mother for a start. Stevie loved his mother, he did, but she embarrassed him because of the way she looked. She didn't look like the other mothers Stevie saw in the park when he was taken there, and she didn't look like the mothers of the children he sometimes played with in the street on Saturdays. Those mothers looked like May Louise. His mother looked old. His mother looked like his granny.

A lot of the people who saw Stevie's mother must have thought that too, because often, if they had to ask Stevie about her, they'd call her his granny, not his mother. It was like when the new laundry man started coming. One week he came a bit early, and Stevie's mother was still upstairs, stripping the beds. Stevie's father and Stevie's sisters were all gone, to work, to school, and Stevie was on his own in the living room, eating a bit of cold toast and playing with his toy soldiers. Stevie heard someone go down the entry, and then he saw the new laundry man open the back gate. The laundry man knocked at the door and Stevie went to open it. When he did the man said, 'Is your granny in, son?'

This happened a lot — not with the new laundry man, but with other people. To begin with Stevie had said that it wasn't his granny, it was his mother, but, in the end, he stopped saying anything at all. He did more than that even, he started telling people, people and other children if he was far enough away from his mother for her not to hear him, that she was his granny, not his mother. He told people that May Louise was his mother. Quite soon a lot of the people around where Stevie lived believed that May Louise was his mother, and when May Louise heard about it and came home with the story from the Empire Thread and Yarns one

tea-time — because a woman in the yarn room had called
her a little trollop and a shame to her mother and her father
— there was a big row in Stevie's house and nobody actually
had any tea that night.

Mrs MacNamara said it was a devil that had got into
Stevie, a lying devil, and she'd knock it out of him once and
for all. She was having a good go at this when Stevie's dad
came in from work and put a stop to it, but Stevie was sent
up to bed on his own anyway. His legs were sore from where
his mother had hit him with the stick she kept for stirring the
washing when it was in the copper, but the beating didn't do
him any good. By this time Stevie was a confirmed liar.

Stevie told lots of lies, and he told them for lots of reasons.
Sometimes it was to get people into trouble; sometimes it was
to get himself out of trouble. Sometimes, like the story he told
about May Louise being his mother, and his mother being
his granny, it was to make himself more like other children.
Most of all though, Stevie told lies because the lie made
things seem better than the truth did, and things went on
seeming better until the truth came out, when they got a lot
worse again. This deterioration was usually of a sudden and,
often, a violent nature as well. It didn't stop him from telling
lies though, any more than his mother hauling him off to see
Dr Costello, just young Dr Costello it was now, did.

'The child's bleeding lairy,' Stevie's mother would scream
at his father as she got her hat and coat on to go out to the
doctor's again.

'He's just got a vivid imagination,' his father would reply,
despairingly.

'He should be sent up to the Towers,' his mother would
say to Dr Costello.

'I'm sure it's just his imagination, you know, Mrs MacNamara. Is it possible that the child is simply a very lonely little
boy?' Dr Costello would reason in reply.

These visits to the doctor were not infrequent, and usually
finished with Mrs MacNamara marching out of the surgery

and into the street with a prescription for a tonic for her son. The tonic, which was a bitter liquid, greenish in colour a bit like Stevie's mother's best coat, was simply a mixture of vitamins and minerals in a syrup base. It did the child no harm, and probably much good from a nutritional point of view, but, of course, despite its bitter taste, the evident effects of which Mrs MacNamara thoroughly approved, it did not lessen Stevie's proclivity for telling stories a whit.

Young Dr Costello's diagnosis was more accurate than his supposed remedy was proficient. Stevie was lonely. He had no friends. His sisters had outgrown him just as he had outgrown what had been his initial attraction for them, his babyhood. Now he was simply a nuisance, dragging after them all the while, spying on them, carrying tales to his mother about this and that, and lying most of the time.

Stevie was lonely. He spent much of each day on his own. He played on his own. It was in his loneliness that he turned to companions he could summon at will, those of his own imagining. These companions were not like Frank; they were not, to begin with, constant, as Frank had been, but changed according to the game Stevie required them to join him in. If Stevie played at cowboys and indians, then his companions were cowboys, or seasoned cavalry troopers. If he were playing at war, then it was honest English tommies who materialised about him, or unshaven GIs, with their helmets tilted at a rakish angle, and stubble on their chins and cigarettes dangling, half-smoked, from the corners of their mouths. It is true that many of these men bore the same name, it was usually Bill, but this had more to do with the limits of Stevie's vocabulary than anything else.

So there was this, and then there was something else as well. Frank had been real. Stevie knew that. These others were not. Stevie knew that. They were summoned to play with him from his own imaginings. Stevie knew that. His mother didn't. That is why, when she looked out of the window and saw her son tying himself to the line-post and then calling out for aid to someone she could not see, she became more and more convinced that this child of her middle age was wrong. Because the doctor would do nothing to help her, she began to wish away the time until Stevie should go to school. Perhaps there he might be saved.

Stevie went to school when he was four and a half years old. It was because of his birthdate. He could either go a half-year too soon, or a half-year too late. Mrs MacNamara made strenuous efforts to see that it was the former, even though the only place she could secure for him at that age was in a Church of England school. Stevie began attending what was called the nursery, his story-telling got worse and worse and Mrs MacNamara saw it as a sign of God's displeasure because she had put her son into an institution in which his immortal soul could only be injured, to weaken and perhaps even die over the coming years.

She went to see the sister in charge at the Sacred Heart school to which all the girls had gone. It was not a happy visit. The sister more or less told Mrs MacNamara she had brought all her sorrows upon her own head, and she did not refer simply to the matter of Stevie's education and its effect on his lying. She made several references to Mrs MacNamara's age at the time when she had given birth to Stevie, and mentioned the Church's teaching on continence and sobriety in daily life. Mrs MacNamara came away determined never to set foot in a Catholic church again as long as she might live. She even, when the time came round, gave permission for Stevie to take part in his school's nativity play.

Stevie's lies were getting out of hand. At school he told stories of uncles he did not have, of boyfriends his sisters did not have: strong, determined men who explored jungles and crossed deserts; who worked as rodeo riders in America, or cattle ranchers in Australia. At home he talked about his very best friend, a Chinese girl whose father was a magician.

So persistent were these stories that, first, Mrs MacNamara went to see old Tom Wong, who did her husband's collars every week, to see if one of his relatives had come from Hong Kong with a girl of Stevie's age called Margery. When this did not provide an answer, Mrs MacNamara went to the school, on the first of what were to be many visits. Of course, there was no Chinese girl, but there had been a child, a girl called Penny, with whom Stevie had made friends, but she had been removed from the school because her father had changed his job and the family had followed him to Sheffield. Perhaps, the teacher said, Stevie missed his little friend and so had invented one that could never be taken away from him. When she got back from the school with Stevie, Mrs MacNamara gave him another thrashing.

If Stevie never mentioned the Chinese girl and her wonderful family at home again, it had less to do with the punishment he had been given than the coming of the school nativity play, in which his mother had said he might take part. He announced at the dinner table one Sunday in late November that he was to play the part of a king, and that he would be made to look like a black man, and wear a long robe of gold cloth, a white shirt like the top bit of May Louise's nightdress, and baggy trousers made of red velvet, and shoes with toes that curled up, and a sword and a turban made of gold cloth like the cloak, with a big red feather in it.

There was more. He would ride a horse, he said, a large, black horse, with a golden saddle and silver stirrups, and the reins and harness would be jewelled, and two other children would run before him with flaming torches. The other principal characters in the drama were, according to Stevie, to be costumed in just as lavish a manner, and there was to be a great deal of livestock used, other horses, of course, for the remaining kings and their servants, sheep for the shepherds to drive before them, an ox, an ass, chickens, ducks, geese.

Mr MacNamara asked Stevie if all of this was really to

take place inside St Barnabas Church Hall, and Stevie assured him that it was. Mrs MacNamara said nothing. She blamed herself. This was God's revenge. The next morning she left the beds unchanged and went to see Father Gilfillan. Carmel took Stevie to school, with a note for her own teacher explaining why she was late.

Mrs MacNamara carried with her to the priest a fear in her heart, a fear that her son was not insane, as she had always thought, but was actually wicked and one day would be called to a reckoning for his wickedness. Father Gilfillan did his best to soothe the troubled soul that came before him, but it was only when Mrs MacNamara got Stevie home after his performance in the nativity play a few days after her visit to the priest that she knew peace again. Stevie had sung in the choir, as an angel, in white, with wings of cardboard, and a cardboard halo held above his head by a bit of bent wire. He'd kept the halo on all the way home and it, at least, had soared heavenwards momentarily, when the first clout Mrs MacNamara had given her son as he went in through the back door sent first his head and then his halo spinning.

It was only when Stevie went up from the nursery into Mrs Martin's class that he stopped telling so many lies. The reason was quite simple: Stevie had fallen in love and his beloved was so far beyond all his previous conceptions of the wonderful that now the mere truth astonished him. He was in love with Mrs Martin.

It was easy to understand why. She was young, just like May Louise was young. She was young enough to be his mother. She had long, wavy brown hair. She had green eyes. Her lips were very red. She wore lovely clothes, which always smelled of lavender. For some reason, which had nothing to do with the Yardley toilet water she wore, when Stevie thought of Mrs Martin he thought of flowers growing in a garden on a hot summer's afternoon, and bees buzzing loudly in the air, and the soft thwock thwock of racquet and ball coming through the trees like the call of the cuckoo from all that leafy greenness. Stevie would have done anything for Mrs Martin. He would have died for her, and in his games, his imagined worlds, he very often did.

In Mrs Martin's class they were learning to read. Some children, like Joanne Spencer and Philip Bagshaw, already could read. Stevie couldn't, yet. He was still having difficulties with his alphabet, and he couldn't remember all the different sounds the letters were supposed to make. He wished he could remember his alphabet, because those who stood up in the class and sang the alphabet song were sent by Mrs Martin to Miss Foster, the head teacher, who let them choose a boiled sweet from the big tin she kept in her cupboard next to the strap.

He wished as well that he could remember at least some of the sounds the letters were meant to make because, if someone was asked what sound this letter made, and gave the right answer, then Mrs Martin would smile her lovely smile at them, her lips so red and her teeth so white.

Most of all, though, Stevie wished he could read, because then, if he could read, on Friday afternoons he could be one of those who brought a book to school and told Mrs Martin which story they wanted to read and then were allowed to read it to the whole class, sitting in Mrs Martin's high chair with everyone looking at them and everyone listening to them and, afterwards, Mrs Martin would give him, Stevie, a hug and a kiss which would leave the pattern of her lips on his cheek, and not somebody else's. That was what Stevie wanted. He wanted that attention. Most of all he wanted that kiss, and the red mark on his face as a testament to the world of what he had done and what he had become, Mrs Martin's favourite.

Stevie's father worried sometimes because his son was a little slow with his reading. The girls had all read early, but then they'd talked early as well. Perhaps it had something to do with them being girls. Stevie had plenty of things to read, books and comics and the like, but he was a bit slow catching on with the reading itself. When he was a little boy his mother had read to him, her in her chair by the fire and Stevie sat on the arm, his own arms around his mother's neck, looking at the pictures while she read the words to him.

She didn't do that now. Well, there wasn't the time. She'd used to read to him after the lunch, while the girls did the washing-up. Stevie had to be back at school now for two o'clock. It was more than just the time though, Mr MacNamara knew that. His wife seemed to have taken against the child. It was because of the lying. She called it lying, anyhow, though he didn't think it was lying himself. It was more that the boy was very imaginative, very imaginative.

Mr MacNamara wished he could read more to Stevie himself, but the only time he had was on Saturdays. He'd come out of work and go to the barber's for a haircut and a shave, and then go and get the fish and chips for the Saturday lunch. In the afternoons Mrs MacNamara would go into the town for the shopping, and Carmel and Rita would go with her. Nell and May Louise would be off out by themselves, in the town probably, but he wasn't really sure. At any rate, it was always just himself and the boy at home.

Mr MacNamara did the washing-up on Saturdays, not that there was much of it from fish and chips. Then, when it was done, he'd take Stevie over to the newsagent's and get him some sweets and a comic. At home again, Mr MacNamara always used to make tea for himself in his own cup, the one he kept hidden at the back of the cupboard so that his wife couldn't see it. He made his tea in the cup, very strong, with a lot of sugar, and when it was ready he always winked at Stevie and said as how it was their secret. Then he'd settle down with the boy, and he'd read to him. Stevie loved the comics, but his favourite thing was a book, *TV Comic Annual*.

The MacNamaras didn't have a television. If there was something special on they might be invited two doors up, because they had one, but for the most part, the characters from the stories Mr MacNamara read to his son had no existence for either him or the child beyond the pages of the book in which they appeared. Stevie really didn't know who Sooty was, or Bill and Ben, and he didn't much care. Their stories were all right to listen to, but the one he loved, the one he hungered for each Saturday, was not about them, or Andy Pandy or Ragg, Tagg and Bobtail, or the Woodentops, it was about a doll called Zena.

The story took place at Christmas, in the garden of the house where Zena lived with a teddy bear and a gollywog. Zena was a beautiful doll with a china face, and china hands and feet. She was so beautiful that the teddy bear and the gollywog knew there was nothing they would not do for her if she asked. In the story, what Zena asked was to be taken outside, into the snow and the cold air, and carried to an island where she could have a picnic. In spite of all the difficulties and all the dangers, the teddy bear and the gollywog did as Zena wanted them to; they took her to her island. They made her dream come true.

Stevie loved that story. He loved it because he thought that Mrs Martin looked like the doll Zena, and because he had decided that her name, Mrs Martin's name, was also Zena; and he loved it because he knew that, like the teddy bear and the gollywog, there was nothing he would not do for Mrs Martin, his Zena, if she asked. Except, except that what Mrs Martin asked, he could not do. Mrs Martin asked who would like to read from the big chair on the next Friday afternoon, and Stevie could not read. That is, he could not really read, but he could give a pretty convincing imitation of reading.

Some of the stories in the books he had, Stevie knew so well he could recite by heart. He knew 'An Island for Zena' by heart. He knew as well what people looked like when they read; how the finger should be moved across the page, how the eyes should follow the finger. He knew what the children who read from the big chair for Mrs Martin looked like when they were reading, and what they did. He knew the stumbles, the retracing of sentences, the intimations of doubt and the sudden descent from the chair to ask Mrs Martin for help with this word or that word. He knew he could do that, or, at least, he could give the impression he was doing that, and he knew that he would, soon.

So, the next time Mrs Martin asked for someone to read from a favourite book, Stevie put his hand up and perhaps because he was so blinded by his own and coming glory, or because by that point in his deception he had deceived himself, he did not see the expression of doubt in his loved one's face. The following Friday Stevie came back to school in the afternoon with his *TV Comic Annual* and when it was time he announced that he would read 'An Island for Zena.' He looked very hard at Mrs Martin when he said this.

It was a brilliant performance. He was a little nervous at first, but then, what great actor isn't? As he went on, though, Stevie gathered his powers. He had his place in the high chair. He had the upturned, wondering faces. He had his story. He read, as he had seen others read; he stumbled, here and there, not too much, not too little, but just enough to convince the sceptics in the class. He could see them, Joanne Spencer, Philip Bagshaw, Jimmy Eyres. He could see them. He could see the doubts begin to cloud as his performance and the story powered on. He was so taken with what he had achieved, the control he had, he almost forgot to slip from the stool from time to time for help from Mrs Martin, Zena, as she would always be to him now.

At the end there was utter silence in the class, instead of the usual applause. It was, in part, due to the power of the story, but more than this, the silence came from astonishment. Was this really Stevie, who did not know his alphabet even, who did not know the sound of 'b' in 'ball'? Stevie MacNamara who, just last week, had cried and kicked so as not to have to go with his reading group into Miss Forster's room to undergo again the ordeal of *Janet and John*? It was.

The silence, when it ended, was ended by Mrs Martin.

She congratulated Stevie. She praised him. Stevie went to get down from the big chair for his reward, the closeness of her flowery embrace, the bright red streaks upon his face. He made as if to get down from the big chair, but Mrs Martin stopped him. She came to him. She took the book from him. She turned the pages as if looking for something. She stopped and then she said, 'Well, children, that was a wonderful story, wasn't it? Would you like to hear another? Stevie, you read that one so well for us, please read again, read this one.'

She gave Stevie his book again. It was a story about Sooty, and the little dog he played with, sometimes. Stevie didn't like Sooty. He would stop his father reading the stories if he started one. He didn't know the name of the little dog. He didn't know what happened in this story, although, because there were a lot of pictures, he could make a guess. He looked at Mrs Martin. There was no sign that she knew. He looked at the faces gazing up at him. He looked at Joanne Spencer's face, and Philip Bagshaw's and Jimmy Eyres'. He started to 'read'.

It was another bravura performance. The gestures, the intonations, the pauses, everything was in place, just as before. The problem was that, this time, there was something lacking: the actor had no script. Stevie tried, he tried as hard as he could, constructing the story as he went along according to what was happening in the pictures. Somehow though, it lacked the polished quality of his first rendition. The attention of the audience began to wander. When he got off the chair to ask Mrs Martin the meaning of a word that looked as if it was one he might really not know the meaning of, which, of course, it was, he saw at last that he had been found out.

Mrs Martin kept him behind that day when the others had gone. She spoke harshly to him and never once smiled her lovely smile upon him. When she was finished she took him by the hand and led him into Miss Forster's room. She explained their presence there, and Miss Forster reached into her cupboard to bring out, not the tin of boiled sweets, but the strap. Stevie got it twice, once on each hand. He felt his throat thicken and there was a burning in his eyes, but it was not the pain in his hands made him feel like this, it was the pain in his heart.

Of course he was late getting out of the school. His mother was waiting for him at the school gate, worried sick as to why he had not come with the others. It was her worry made her get hold of Stevie by the shoulders and shake him, asking him where had he been, what had he been doing now. Mrs MacNamara shook him so hard he dropped his book. It fell open on the ground and when he retrieved it the pages were all soiled from the wet pavement. His mother asked him again what had he been doing to be kept so late. Stevie thought, and he knew that if he told her the truth she would only beat him, a beating for the beating he'd had already. In the end he did what he always did in these situations, he told her a story.